Bless your Heart

Bless your Heart

≈

SUSANN CAMUS

Also by this author:
See Me: A Jeannie Johal Thriller

Suggested questions for book clubs appear
at the end of this book.

Thank you for purchasing this book and for your support of this author.

First printed edition: May 2025
First Kindle edition: May 2025

ISBN: 979-8-218-99627-7 (Kindle)
ISBN: 979-8-218-99628-4 (Paperback)
FIC022000 FICTION / Mystery & Detective / General
FIC031040 FICTION / Thrillers / Medical
FIC044000 FICTION/ Women

Cover design by Marilyn Pettitt.

Check out the author's website at www.susanncamus.com

Acknowlegments

Bless Your Heart is a work of fiction inspired by living in Greenville, North Carolina, and volunteering as an Extension Master Gardener at the Pitt County Arboretum. Any errors – typographical or descriptive – are unintended and attributable to the author.

I'd like to thank Matt Stevens, Pitt County Extension Director and Horticulture Agent, for an informative interview. I'd like to thank Matt and the many wonderful Extension Master Gardeners who enthusiastically shared their knowledge of gardening and continue to volunteer their time and expertise to maintain and enhance the Pitt County Arboretum and its serene gardens.

I have used some real settings. For example, the Pitt County Arboretum is a wonder-filled setting where people enjoy strolling through gardens brimming with beautiful plants. Mother Earth Brewing in Kinston is among the best craft beer companies anywhere, and The Rickhouse in Greenville is known for its wide selection of bourbon and whiskey. Thank you to the people of Pitt County who helped me appreciate their deep love for and attachment to the area, especially Kathryn and Norman, whose names I adapted for inclusion in the novel. Thanks to the dedicated public health, emergency medical technicians, and law enforcement professionals who make our communities safer. Thanks for sharing your stories.

To my Beta readers: Thank you to Cindy C. of Winterville, NC, and Anne C. of Burnaby, Canada, for reading early drafts. I am very appreciative of the energy and expertise offered by Denise C. of Ottawa, Canada, and Dawn A. of Nepean, Canada, particularly as it relates to the many hours wrangling stray timelines and identifying pesky but important points that needed clarifying. Thanks to Susan C., my writing buddy in North Vancouver, for keeping me grounded. Thanks to Frank Jones, my Greenville-based marketing guru, for dragging me into the 21st century to help promote my first book using social media. A big thanks to Marilyn Pettitt, the Canadian graphic artist, for designing my book covers. We worked together in the publishing industry in the mid-1980s, and the depth of her artistry continues to astonish me.

Finally, thanks to my readers for spending a few hours immersed in the adventures of Jeannie Johal.

Table of Contents

Dedication

*To my husband, for his wholehearted support
in writing and in life*

Prologue

Jeannie and Rani sat across from each other in the doctors' lounge, unaware that one was about to lose her life while the other would begin a new life. Rani was sipping an iced chai after performing surgery to close a hole in the roof of a toddler's mouth when the explosion catapulted her off her chair, launching her across the room. A big boom sounded, followed by an eerie, still silence.

Regaining consciousness, Rani found herself propped next to a sofa. She was missing a running shoe. Although her scrubs were soaked with cold, aromatic coffee, she was hot. She heard a sizzle and a snap. Her olfactory bulbs were in overdrive. She was not sensing the acrid, unforgettable scent of a woman's face etched with acid, a smell all too familiar because of her work as a plastic surgeon in a non-profit maternal and children's health clinic in Mumbai. No, it was something else, a different kind of charring. It was overwhelming, and she tried not to inhale.

The white T-shirt under her scrubs was turning crimson and the scent of fresh blood was overwhelming. Part of her wondered where the red was coming from. But Rani was not alert enough to pinpoint the source. Her head seemed spongy and thick. Her thoughts felt as if they were crystals in a pool of slow-churning molasses.

Rani's sense of smell was unusually acute. Jeannie used to joke that, in another incarnation, Rani could get a job as the canary in a mine. Neither surgeon was joking now.

There was a hum in the air, accompanied by terrifying thuds and plaster raining down from the damaged ceiling onto both Rani and Jeannie.

Rani sniffed the odor of singed electrical cords. Not the thick black cables that take ages to heat up, but thin, plastic-coated wires that gave off a one-two punch, a sweet scent as the plastic burned, and a sharply bitter smell when the wire began to melt.

Rani remembered when she was a little girl and tried to help her mother with the ironing pile. As hard as she tried, the hot iron was too heavy to lift. She knocked the iron over and it burnt a hole into the clean sheet. There was no supper for Rani that night. From the bedroom she shared with her brother, Rani could hear her mother cry. Many years later, she learned that the burnt sheet cost her mother a week's worth of wages and a stern tongue-lashing from the matron whose sheets she carted home to launder and iron.

Rani was overheating. She needed to cool down. She tried to get up. But she couldn't. She wasn't even able to sit upright because she was trapped. She moved forward on her stomach and freed herself, her arms quivering from the effort. When she attempted to stand up, she fell, striking her head against the wooden arm.

She had only one thought. She needed to find Jeannie. She staggered to the other side of the room, lurching forward and stumbling every second step. It hurt to open her eyes. Her ears were ringing from the blast. The linoleum floor was covered with gray ashes and vinyl remnants. They felt rough on her bare foot. Most of the ceiling had collapsed. The air was smoky. She tried not to cough. Drawing on the self-discipline that made her a successful surgeon, she redirected all of her energy and called out to her friend. The only answer she heard came from a set of sizzling wires.

She lay on the floor, as if doing a front crawl on land, but still couldn't find her friend. Her lungs felt as if they were about to burst. Panic began to well up in her throat. There was an image in her mind of The Hanging Gardens of Mumbai in Malabar Hill and she clung to the picture. The shrubs surrounding the terraces were cut in the shapes of animals. From out of the shrubs, the animals took the form of young women wearing ornate fascinators and designer gowns. The young women headed towards the fountains. Old women wearing simple silk saris whispered loudly and gestured at the young women as if passing judgment on their attire.

Rani saw herself enrobed in a jewel-encrusted sari, wearing a headdress bedazzled with emeralds and rubies. The thirty-pound headdress made it difficult for her to keep her head upright. She was standing under an arch entwined with yellow camellias, her favorite flower. Next to her was a man wearing a formal tuxedo despite the temperature reaching 135 degrees. She shuddered when he gripped her shoulder tightly as if to claim that part of her body.

The young women returned to the shrubs. Images of the old women gossiping faded from view.

She yelled at herself. *Wake up, Rani!* Drifting between consciousness and an oxygen-deprived numbness, she tried in vain to hold her scalpel. She called for the nurse assisting her, but didn't get a response. *Where is my scalpel? Why am I smelling the scent of burning flesh when I'm no longer in the OR? Something's wrong.* The smoke wanted to engulf her. It would be so easy to let the smoke have its way.

Since she kept falling over, she decided to stay on the floor, hands splayed in front. Her body felt as if it had been anesthetized. Her vision was fuzzy and her motor control was off. She placed one hand forward, slid her knee, moved her foot in the same direction. Her eyeballs had the sensation of having been impaled by tiny shards of glass. They shut almost as soon as she opened them. But not soon enough. The image of fire and smoke was seared in her brain. It would never leave her.

The furniture she bumped her head against was smoldering. She knew she had to get out of the room. But the exit was blocked by licks of flame. And she still hadn't found her best friend. She couldn't leave without her.

Jeannie was her idol. Feisty and opinionated. Rani admired Jeannie's self-confidence and her fearlessness. Rani was in awe of Jeannie's refusal to marry the man her parents chose for her when she was a teenager. As an adult, Jeannie rejected men who did not see her as their equal.

Jeannie had an adventurous spirit and was willing to take risks. She booked holidays all over the world and traveled on her own. She was so unlike Rani, who put duty to parents first. On her twelfth birth-day, Rani's parents informed her that she would be marrying a stranger when she turned fourteen. She didn't put up a fight. She meekly acquiesced to her family's wishes, agreeing that her father had been very persuasive when he gave his daughter to the landlord in exchange for free living quarters for the family.

After the marriage, she did exactly what Rajeev, her husband, told her to do. Except when it came to Jeannie. Rajeev couldn't prevent Rani from spending time with Jeannie because the two women were both surgeons in the Little Flowers Clinic, where they reconstructed the mouths of children with cleft palates and tried to give the victims of acid attacks hope by rebuilding their faces.

Jeannie always told Rani that she was too nice, never able to say no. She said that Rani forgave even the unforgivable, that she let people take advantage. Rani listened to her, but halfheartedly. She was afraid of her husband. When Rajeev got angry, he threatened to hit her or turn her parents out onto the street. But she persuaded herself that he wasn't all bad because he'd kept his promise that she could continue her schooling after she was married. He'd even financed her studies to become a surgeon and let her work, providing she came home as soon as her shift ended. Still, he'd told her she was useless as a wife because she hadn't given him an heir. He'd recently threatened to break every finger in her hands so that she would not be able to perform surgery. He reasoned that there'd be no point for her to leave the house if she couldn't work as a surgeon.

Rani called Jeannie, but her voice was whispery thin. Her throat felt as if she had swallowed the dust from a pad of used sandpaper. She wondered why her friend wasn't responding to her calls. While Rani bellowed her friend's name, part of her worried that the cries might be too faint.

Rani continued to scream for her friend, the high pitch of desperation fighting with the hoarseness of a throat scorched by smoke. She caught sight of Jeannie. Her friend was still, sitting upright at the other end of the sofa. She resembled a doll carefully positioned in place. One hand held a mug. The other rested in her lap. She looked untouched by the blast. Except for her neck. It was impossibly twisted.

Rani commanded Jeannie to wake up. She whispered that they had to get out, now, but Jeannie still didn't respond. Rani tried to turn her friend's neck so that it faced forward, but as soon as she touched it, the unexpected rigidity made her fingers recoil as if scorched by flames. There was nothing she could do to help her friend.

Although Rani wanted to remain with her, she knew what Jeannie would have said. She'd say, 'Rani, be strong.' Rani would respond that she wasn't the strong one.

The smoke was overwhelming, and Rani had to fight the urge to let the smoke take her. She wiped away the tears streaking wildly down her cheeks. She wanted to give up and join her friend. But when she hugged Jeannie's lifeless body, she knew that her friend would be aghast if she surrendered to the fire. Rani decided she couldn't let Jeannie down. She would have to fight to survive.

Her mouth hurt. She reached in and pulled out a crown that was hanging loose. She threw it on the floor. When she took one last look at her friend, she spotted a glimmer of gold around her neck. The chain was badly tarnished.

She heard Jeannie's voice. "Rani, this is your shot. Take my name. Use my identity. Take the next step. You can be free." Rani gently removed the gold chain from around her friend's neck and replaced it with her own necklace. Tenderly, she stroked Jeannie's hair and promised that she would try to be strong. Rani vowed to take her friend's name and make her proud.

Rani's lungs were filling with smoke. It was time for her to leave while she still could. She said farewell to her best friend.

Rani pushed forward, fighting the smoke, crawling over the debris, grabbing the leg of a table to move closer to the sink. She hauled herself up and wet the tea towel. The weave acted as a filter.

She was exhausted, but kept going. She mourned as she scrabbled through the wreckage and left her best friend behind.

Day One

Chapter 1

Detectives Harmony Harris and Henry Smith were a study in contrast. Harmony was tall and rangy, while Henry was short and compact. Harmony's black hair was long and curly, pulled back severely to meet departmental requirements. By comparison, Henry's head was shaven, a response to the male-pattern-baldness gene he inherited from his mother.

The differences didn't end there. Harmony spoke so quickly that her words sometimes ran together, at times prompting puzzled looks from those who had just met her. Henry drew out his words, pronouncing each syllable clearly and waiting for a nod or other sign of a response before finishing a sentence. He'd adopted this way of speaking for two reasons. He was from a rural area with a distinct accent that his teachers in the police academy claimed was difficult to understand. In addition, because his mother was hard of hearing and took longer than most to process what was being said, he'd learned from a young age to speak slowly.

As a little girl growing up outside of Kinston, Harmony had wanted to become not only a police officer, but the head of the police. She did not understand why her father suddenly became silent every time he was pulled over while driving the family car. And she was terrified when her brother called their father to say he'd been detained, taken to the county detention center, and strip-searched after being pulled over because the right taillight on the car wasn't working.

Tired of questioning why these things happened, Harmony vowed to end them once she became a senior officer. Since there were no openings in her hometown, she applied to join the nearby Greenville Police

Department the day after her twentieth birthday. By accepting every opportunity for overtime and by volunteering for everything – from soliciting shoppers for a Toys for Tots donation drive, to doling out turkey and sweet potato pie at a homeless shelter on Thanksgiving – Harmony became the 'go-to' person whom the chief could count on whenever he needed a volunteer to represent the department. At twenty-six, she became the youngest detective with the Criminal Investigations Bureau of the Major Crimes Unit. She was well on her way to achieving her goal.

Growing up near Scotland Neck, Henry spent his summers as an unpaid farmhand on his family's tobacco farm. His early-morning job was to feed the chickens, clean out the chicken coop, and retrieve eggs from the hens' nests. He was also responsible for separating bullied chicks from their tormentors. Seeing larger chicks plunge their beaks into the skin of smaller chicks made him see the chicken coop as a microcosm for the larger world. There would always be bullies and there would always be a need for someone stronger to rein them in.

When Henry's parents sold their farm and moved into the city, he decided to become a police officer because it would provide a good-paying job and give him the means and justification to go after those who committed acts of aggression.

During his twenty-five years in the police department, Henry had seen the city of Greenville transition from a rural hub surrounded by farmland to a university town and large health center with forty thousand additional student residents from August to April. While big-city folk from Raleigh might consider Greenville to be a rural stop to drive through on the way to the miles of golden beaches and tony golf courses on the Outer Banks, Henry saw Greenville as a shiny new metropolis springing up in Eastern North Carolina, a beacon of hope for all who embraced the Southern way of life.

Harmony and Henry had been paired together by a police chief who hoped Henry's laconic approach would rein in Harmony's propensity for impulsiveness. Much to the chief's consternation, Harmony and Henry quickly discovered their complementary styles amplified the traits the chief hoped to dim. Henry, the seasoned detective, picked up his pace slightly. Harmony, the new investigator, learned to ask more questions before acting. The chief was thankful that Harmony appeared to be learning restraint. In her years on patrol, she'd received commendations for bravery. She'd also been cited for threatening a pimp who had taken foster children into his family and forced the girls to sell their bodies on the street. When she transported the pimp to prison, her rough handling of the prisoner as he entered the police car was captured on video and formed the basis for a complaint of excessive force that was later dismissed, but not forgotten. Much to the chief's delight, Harmony and Henry's overriding commitment to identifying the bad actors and arresting them based on solid evidence that would withstand the scrutiny of the court meant that the evidence they collected resulted in the highest conviction rates in the department.

They'd been partners for two years when they were dispatched to investigate a murder at the detention center. The long, squat, tan, brick and white building was situated on New Hope Road, across a field and a block up from the County Public Health building and Agricultural Center on Government Road.

"I hate that place," fumed Harmony.

Henry gave his partner a puzzled look. "I love that place. It's where we put the bad guys. Why do you hate it?"

"You're White. You wouldn't understand."

Henry's response was slow and measured. He guffawed gently, keeping his eye on his partner. "Well, I certainly will never understand if you don't tell me why you hate the place. You've got to give me some-thing to work with."

"When-I-was-thirteen-my-brother."

"Hold up a minute," said Henry in his measured voice. "I know what you're saying is very important to you because you're talking as fast as the Amtrak train when it's an hour behind and the politicians in Washington are waiting to board it so they can go home. Slow down so that I can take in what you're saying."

"Henry, I grew up in a nice home. My father worked in a textile fac-tory and my mother was a schoolteacher. They were good parents. They signed us up for music lessons and encouraged us to get our drivers' licenses when we were teenagers. I learned how to play the piano and I was in the glee club. My brother was gifted mathematically. Our par-ents had aspirations for us."

"Harmony, I didn't say, 'Start at the beginning.' I said, 'Slow down.' "

"When my brother was sixteen, he was pulled over on a county road. The cop asked my brother what he was doing out so late in the evening. He said he'd just dropped his girlfriend off at her home after they watched a movie at the cinema. The cop didn't even ask to see the registration papers for the car. He demanded that my brother exit the vehicle. As he was stepping out of the car, the cop pushed him to the ground and held his baton against his neck. The cop warned him that if he said anything, he would snap his scrawny neck in two. Then he cuffed my brother and called his partner to help take him into custody."

"Where was his partner when the cop demanded that your brother step out of his car?"

"My brother said the guy remained in the vehicle. He came out when his partner told him that the driver was resisting arrest."

"What a miscarriage of justice!"

Harmony's voice rose in pitch and she shuddered. "It gets worse. They took him to the county detention center and threw him into a cell. He was strip-searched and left naked and handcuffed to the wall. He wasn't allowed to make a phone call until the next morning. My parents nearly went out of their minds with worry."

"I hope the officers were disciplined."

"They were disciplined for leaving the keys to the car in the ignition. Fortunately, a Good Samaritan stopped the next morning when he saw the abandoned car. He peered inside. When he noticed that the keys were in the ignition, he immediately drove to the closest police station to turn them in and to report that something must have happened to the driver. The officers were never disciplined for how they treated my brother. He struggled for a long time, trying to understand why he was pulled over, strip-searched, and locked up like a dangerous drug smuggler. The incident made me realize that the only way to stop this kind of behavior was by becoming a police officer myself and reforming the police from the inside."

"Whew! I'm sorry this happened to your brother."

"You know, the detention center is located on New Hope Road. But in the Black community, it's known as 'No-Hope Road' because so many of us or our relatives have had bad experiences."

Henry chose a black Ford from the carpool and tossed the keys to Harmony even though it was his turn to drive. She appreciated him giving her something to focus on. Fifteen minutes later, they pulled up to the concrete structure. Several police cars were already on scene, their lights flashing red.

Henry and Harmony pulled out their badges and strode toward the entrance, where Amos Longfellow, the deputy sheriff, greeted them. "The Sheriff is away, so I'm in charge. There was an altercation that started in the recreation center between one prisoner who is usually very quiet, Johnson Johnson, and another, Byron Brown, known as 'Big Boy.' Brown started taunting Johnson, calling his mother terrible names. It escalated, and Johnson plunged his plastic fork into Brown. My guard intervened. But just as Brown reached his cell, he collapsed, and we found a sharpened wooden shiv in his neck. We have several witnesses who confirmed what happened. It's clear Johnson murdered the prisoner who was tormenting him. He must have got tired of being called names. We've locked down the prison and isolated Johnson, the ringleader."

"Alleged ringleader," said Harmony, correcting the deputy sheriff.

"Of course, everyone is innocent until proven guilty."

"Damn straight they are," retorted Harmony.

"There's no call for swearing in my prison. You debase yourself when you use profanity," said the deputy sheriff.

Henry jumped into the conversation, hoping to defuse the tension between his partner and the deputy sheriff. "Thank you for the briefing. We'll take it from here."

"That's all right. We know what happened. It's an open and shut case. All we need is for you to sign off on the report I'm preparing." Longfellow stood and gestured for them to go forward.

They didn't move. "It sure doesn't look like you're interested in finding out the truth," said Harmony.

"Now, now, honey, I'm just trying to save you some paperwork so that you can go home and prepare supper for your husband."

She interrupted the deputy sheriff. "It's Detective Harris. And it's our responsibility to investigate the crime. We will uncover the truth. Send us your accounting of events when you've finished writing up your report. Right now, though, we need to question the suspect and the witnesses. Bring the prisoner to us now," she commanded.

Longfellow glared at her. "Are you ordering me around?" he asked belligerently.

"Detective Smith and I are requesting your assistance so that we can interrogate the prisoner," she said.

"I'm glad you're not bossing me around because I won't stand for no woman telling me what to do. It was a sad day when they allowed women to become police officers," he pronounced.

"Get the prisoner now," she said through clenched teeth.

"This how she talks to you?" Longfellow gestured to Henry.

"You heard the detective. Do what she says."

Chapter 2

Jeannie was on a plane crisscrossing the North American continent. Her journey started in Vancouver. After boarding her second and final flight, in New York, she settled in for a quick nap. But her sleep was anything but refreshing. Even though the bombing was two years earlier, she dreamt that she was trapped in the clinic and couldn't get out.

An insistent trill broke through her nightmare, jarring her awake. Her body involuntarily jerked forward, kept in its place by the lap seatbelt. It took her a few moments to remember where she was. She opened her eyes and closed them quickly, blinking to adjust to the brightness. She felt the cool air flowing from the ceiling. She smelled the sweet scent of milk chocolate. She heard conversations buzz around her.

The passenger next to Jeannie was an older woman. Her hair was bleached blonde and she was wearing a pink polyester safari jacket and matching leggings with crystals rimming the bottom. She savored a chocolate-coated caramel. She used the tips of two fuchsia-colored fingernails to spear a caramel from the sharing-size bag on her tray and offered it to Jeannie. Although repulsed by the action, Jeannie was fascinated by her seatmate's dexterity.

The seatmate gave Jeannie a curious glance. "Honey, that must have been some dream! My name is Wilhelmina Wooten, but everyone calls me 'Willa.' "

Without pausing for a breath, Willa drew out her story. "You were thrashing around in your seat. I wasn't sure if I should leave you alone, try to wake you up, or call the flight attendant for assistance."

Jeannie was horrified that she had drawn attention to herself. She managed a weak smile. "Thanks for your concern. I suppose I'm tired. I left Vancouver last night. It was a long trip."

Willa smiled. "Honey, I'm flying from New York to Raleigh and I find that a long trip. My husband believes that you can find everything you need within fifty miles of where you live. He's never traveled out of the state. You can see he's not traveling with me."

Jeannie looked at the flight tracker. "Not too much longer." She pulled out a paperback copy of a Nicholas Sparks' novel, selected for its North Carolina setting.

Her seatmate didn't take the hint. "Anyway, I'm glad you're feeling better. Unlike that poor passenger. Of course, you wouldn't know anything about that because you were sleeping."

Jeannie's curiosity was piqued. "What do you mean?"

"The flight attendant made a request over the public announcement system. 'If there are any medical personnel aboard, please press your flight attendant call button.' She repeated the request. There don't seem to be any physicians on this flight."

Jeannie guessed that the trilling sounds were what woke her up. Even though she was now working as a quality improvement consultant in a hospital system in Canada, she had trained and worked as a plastic surgeon in her home country.

Jeannie's expression prompted Willa to look more closely at her. "Are you a nurse?"

Jeannie was accustomed to people underestimating her, perhaps because she was petite or because Rajeev always told her she would amount to nothing. For a moment, Jeannie considered asking Willa why she made that assumption. Instead, her social filter kicked in and she replied simply, "No, I'm a surgeon."

The woman's eyes opened wide and she stopped chewing her caramel. Her hands fluttered. She pushed the flight attendant call button before Jeannie could say another word.

As the flight attendant approached, Willa pointed at Jeannie. "She's a surgeon!"

"Are you able to assist with a medical emergency?" asked the flight attendant.

Jeannie nodded.

Her seatmate clapped her hands together and offered a beaming smile. "Go save a life. I promise to save some caramels for you."

The flight attendant directed Jeannie to first class, where a passenger's face had turned bright red and expanded like a round balloon. His eyelids were swollen, and the outer corners were bursting apart. His lips were bulging, as if an untrained plastic surgeon had injected them with one hundred times the prescribed dose of filler. The lower portion of his face was indistinguishable from his neck. He looked like a boxer who had lost a fight after having been pummeled by his opponent.

Jeannie bent down next to the passenger. "My name is Jeannie Johal and I am a physician. I would like to help you. Do I have your permission to treat you?"

While aware that the passenger required medical assistance, Jeannie had learned that she could not provide treatment without the patient's consent. She took the man's nod as consent.

"The flight attendant and I are going to check your vital signs. While she is taking your blood pressure, I'm going to ask you some questions. Are you having difficulty breathing?"

The passenger shook his head.

"Are you able to speak?"

Jeannie heard garbled sounds.

"I need to know if this is your first experience of this kind."

He nodded.

"Your face is quite swollen and I am concerned that your breathing could become compromised. I would like to give you an antihistamine by injection. Before I do, I need to know if you have any allergies."

She passed an iPad to the passenger. "Write down any drugs for which you have known allergies."

She scanned the list: Penicillin, Amoxil, Sulfa, Ciproflaxin.

Medical emergencies occur on about one in every 600 flights. Aviation regulations require aircraft flying domestically or internationally to carry medical supplies that include an approved external defibrillator, first aid kits, and an emergency medical kit. Jeannie asked the flight attendant to hand her a syringe and a vial of antihistamine.

"You'll feel a prick," she said to her patient. "This injection should blunt your response. Your face and neck will cool down, and your eyes and mouth will go back to their normal size."

She carefully watched him. He, the flight attendant, and passengers seated nearby watched her attentively.

Jeannie saw the man jerk in his seat. "Steady. Your heartbeat is accelerating as an immediate response to the antihistamine. Take a few deep breaths. In out, in out. All right. You should feel the antihistamine start to work. I can see your color beginning to improve."

The patient whispered a thank you. He looked tiredly at her.

"I know you feel exhausted. You just went through an ordeal and the antihistamine is also making you drowsy. You're going to be okay. The best thing you can do for yourself is to sleep. We'll continue to monitor you to make sure you're over the worst of the reaction. When you return home, I strongly recommend you get tested for allergies so that you can find out what caused this reaction."

She patted the patient's arm, removed her nitrile gloves, and stood up. Turning, she addressed the passengers craning their heads to get a look at what was happening. "The passenger will be fine," she said reassuringly.

Jeannie returned to her seat, buffeted by a round of applause.

Willa's neck was stretched tautly in the direction of the aisle. "Bless your heart, you're a hero!"

Jeannie turned toward her. "I spent many years training to be a surgeon. What kind of doctor would I be if I hadn't responded?"

"I don't know if I would have your courage. I'd be afraid of getting sued if the passenger's condition worsened. My husband keeps telling me to think things through. I shouldn't have acted so impulsively when I volunteered your service. I'm sorry."

"Sometimes, you have to act quickly. It was my decision to respond. The airline cannot force me to provide service during an in-flight emergency. At the same time, any physician is protected under Good Samaritan laws from damages when providing good-faith medical care during a medical emergency."

Willa was positively beaming. She held up her phone and took Jeannie's photo.

"Why did you do that?" Jeannie's voice must have sounded sharper than she intended because a hurt expression clouded Willa's face. Jeannie shuddered, trying to suppress the memory of what happened after a video of her being rescued after falling onto the subway tracks in Vancouver went viral and was seen by her estranged husband.

Her seatmate was contrite. "There I go again, being too impulsive. I should have asked for your permission. It's not every day I meet a real-life hero, a surgeon who knows what she's doing, and a woman who can explain how medical emergencies work. Wow, my friends aren't going to believe me when I say I've had the most exciting adventures on this trip and met my new superhero. Can I take another photo to show them?"

"Do you take lots of photos?"

"All the time, honey. It's my way of capturing the moment forever."

"Go ahead. When you put it that way, how can I say 'no'?"

The flight attendant came to Jeannie's seat shortly before the pre-pare-to-land announcement was called. "Dr. Johal, the passenger is much better, thanks to you. Would you remain on board until all of the other passengers have deplaned? Our captain would like to speak with you."

"Of course."

Jeannie's seatmate bubbled with excitement. "Maybe they'll give you a pass to fly anywhere for free. You could fly to Rome or Paris."

"I'd be happy to get a free upgrade for my return flight in four weeks," said Jeannie with a smile.

Thirty minutes later, Jeannie had met with airline officials, passed through Security, collected her bags, and arrived at the car-rental bay. She didn't know if she would get a return flight upgrade, but the officials recorded her email address and cell number, and said they'd be in touch.

In Mumbai, Jeannie drove a dark, boxy Volvo station wagon that looked like a tank. It felt enormous and was hard to maneuver. At the time, her husband overruled her objections by explaining that it would protect her if she ever crashed into another vehicle.

In Raleigh, Jeannie selected a scarlet red Ford Mustang. It was sleek and feminine. She liked the curves and how the car made her feel like a rebel. She planned on soaring down the highway as fast as the speed limit would allow. She set out for Greenville, about a two-hour drive.

Beatrix Bach's assistant had booked Jeannie a room at the Hilton Hotel in Greenville. Dr. Bach was the reason Jeannie was going there.

"Norma Dunn and I shared command responsibilities when we served in Afghanistan. She's a brilliant clinician, and I don't understand why she is working in such a small city when she could be a fellow at the Mayo Clinic," said Dr. Bach less than twenty-four hours before Jeannie's first flight.

Jeannie didn't know anything about Greenville, and was annoyed that Dr. Bach felt that she could summon her whenever she felt like it. "I was working on a report when your assistant called my supervisor to request my assistance. Here I am."

Dr. Bach smiled, her incisors giving her a wolflike appearance. "I can tell you're put out that you were called away from your work. Don't be. What I have for you is a thousand times more interesting than writing a report."

Jeannie's curiosity won out. Since Dr. Bach was not known for beating around the bush, Jeannie asked her a direct question. "I'm all ears. What does Greenville have to do with me?"

"Dr. Dunn works in Greenville. It's close to the ocean, not close enough to be considered an ocean community. It used to be a large tobacco center with big farms and a small downtown. The city has grown as the farms have gotten smaller and fewer. The county is trying to diversify. It is a technology hub. The city has a university renowned for its dental and medical programs. There's a Level 4 trauma hospital that admits patients who travel hours to get there. The cancer center is one of a handful across America that provides advanced gamma-knife treatments. The hospital is much larger than St. Barbara's here in Canada."

Jeannie was surprised that Dr. Bach still hadn't gotten to the point of the meeting. "It sounds like a small town in the middle of nowhere."

"A diabetes epidemic is ripping its way through rural North Carolina."

Jeannie shrugged. "Rates are pretty high here, too."

It's not that Jeannie didn't care about the diabetes epidemic, but she didn't understand why Dr. Bach was telling her about the problem in Greenville. "My work involves investigating when patients are harmed after coming into a hospital. In other words, I don't research or investigate chronic lifestyle diseases such as Type II Diabetes. You know this."

Dr. Bach flicked her fingers in irritation. "Of course, I know what you do. Dr. Dunn is conducting a blinded study on the effect of a semaglutide on Type II diabetic patients to see if the disease can be reversed. Half the patients are receiving weekly doses of the drug. The other half are getting sugar pills. Dr. Dunn thinks someone is trying to sabotage the research."

"What does this have to do with me?"

"She asked me for help, and I can't turn her down. I want you to go to North Carolina. Get to know the research team. Find out who's tampering with her research and why."

"I know nothing about rural North Carolina. How could I possibly take a job there?"

"You didn't know anything about British Columbia when you came here from Mumbai," retorted Dr. Bach.

"But Vancouver is a city, even though it's tiny compared to Mumbai. Greenville is just a speck on the map in the middle of nowhere. And the way you've presented it makes it sound as if it's a small, rural city surrounded by tobacco farmers. Why would I want to go there?"

"Because I am asking you to."

Jeannie didn't want to directly refuse the request. Instead, she drew on her limited knowledge of immigration law in an attempt to convince Dr. Bach that she wasn't the right candidate. "I thought I had to have a green card to work in the United States. That can take years to get!"

"We've handled that issue. You'll be going as a researcher with a limited term appointment. The health authority in British Columbia will continue to pay your salary."

Jeannie was miffed that Dr. Bach had all the angles covered. She stifled a howl of protest.

"Stop the whining. This is your opportunity to travel, meet new people, help someone out."

"What about my life here?"

"What life? You ended the relationship you had with that handsome police officer. There's nothing keeping you here other than your work, and I need you to work elsewhere."

Jeannie gasped in disbelief. *I can't believe what I'm hearing. How did Dr. Bach know that I broke up with Jaspreet Singh? Is she keeping a tab on me?*

"You think I don't keep an eye on you? Jeannie, I know what happened at Little Flowers in Mumbai. I brought you into the health authority. And now I'm asking you to do this for me. One month. Thirty days. That's all I'm asking."

Since Jeannie didn't respond, Dr. Bach tried another tactic. "You complain how cold it is here. Greenville is warm and sunny. You won't need to wear boots or a winter coat."

Jeannie remained silent, still trying to process how Dr. Bach knew so much about her.

This time, Dr. Bach took Jeannie's silence as consent. "I'm no longer hearing any protests. Good, that's decided. Now get out of my office. You've got packing to do. It's early summer in North Carolina.

Your flight leaves tomorrow morning. My assistant will forward your e-tickets to you."

"What about my work? I have meetings I can't miss."

Dr. Bach's smile contained a warning. "Do you think you're indispensable?"

Jeannie was momentarily confused. She didn't know how to respond. On the one hand, she'd been selected to go to Greenville. On the other, she was the quality improvement consultant with the least experience.

"You'll learn soon enough that no one is indispensable, not me, not you. The world will not come to an end when we're no longer here. Sure, there'll be a few hiccups, some minor adjustments. But work will go on. Your supervisor will send out a note saying you've been called to work on a special project. She'll arrange for your schedule to be covered. Now time's a-wasting. Get outta here!"

Day Two

Chapter 3

The smell of grease bombarded Jeannie's olfactory senses when she walked into the breakfast lounge. She noticed an open warming oven containing ham, sausage links, scrambled eggs, and hash browns with long curls of fried onions. Steam wafted from an opening in a closed chafing dish. Squirt bottles filled with brown and red liquids, a white plastic bowl brimming with yogurt, and large glass jars filled with cereal, crowded the counter. A waffle iron with premeasured cups of batter had its own table. A coffee urn and hot-water dispenser completed the picture.

As Jeannie looked around, she heard a voice with a distinctive country twang. The voice had a strong accent, with long, flat vowels and drawn-out syllables. "Are you new to Greenville, honey? Is this your first time staying with us?"

She turned and saw an elderly woman smiling at her. The woman had frizzy gray hair pulled back and covered with a hairnet. A crisp, white apron covered the front of her uniform. Jeannie didn't understand why the woman was calling her 'honey' when they were complete strangers. But Jeannie noted that this was the second woman in two days to use that endearment. Since the woman was her elder and Jeannie had been brought up to respect older people, she didn't comment on how she thought it was inappropriate for a stranger to call her 'honey.' Instead, Jeannie quietly answered the question. "Yes, I arrived last night."

The woman walked over to Jeannie's side and smiled at her. "I knew it! I'm Lila-Jean Lamont, and I make sure our hotel guests get a heartwarming, traditional breakfast. I can tell from your appearance and your manners that you're from away." She scrutinized Jeannie's top, suit jacket and skirt, her gaze taking in the hotel guest's appearance from head to toe. "You've come to the right place for breakfast. You'll have to try the chef's award-winning grits and gravy."

She disregarded Jeannie's guarded expression and laughed. "You guessed it. I'm the chef. You'll love my grits."

As if reading Jeannie's mind, Lila-Jean offered an explanation for her greeting. "In the South, we call everyone 'honey' whether we know them or not. It's our way of being friendly. Now, you probably want to know about Southern breakfasts. A traditional breakfast always includes grits or rice. I grew up with grits and gravy. It's a special type of porridge. You'll love it!" She pointed to the closed chafing dish.

Jeannie was reassured by the woman's description because grits sounded similar to breakfast in Mumbai – a spoonful of spicy chutney topping a small bowl of *upma*, a thick porridge made from dry-roasted semolina or rice flour. Sure enough, Jeannie enjoyed the warm, creamy texture of grits, although they were made from corn and sweeter than *upma*. She couldn't say the same for the textured light brown gravy accompanying it. The smell was enough to deter her from tasting it.

"Give it a try," Lila-Jean urged. " It's made with bacon drippings and pork sausages from Smithfield's, just down the road."

Jeannie shook her head and smiled weakly, trying not to grimace because she'd almost sampled gravy made from red meat, something she never consumed.

Breakfast was finished, and Jeannie went out into the parking lot. She was backing her car out when Lila-Jean rapped on the driver's side door. Her face was flushed from exertion. "Girl, are you doing everything in your power to stand out?"

Jeannie's immediate impulse was to grin. "Isn't this a beautiful car? It drives as beautifully as it looks."

Lila-Jean returned the smile. "I packed a little lunch for you, for your first day at work."

She touched the car hesitantly, wiping away an imaginary speck of dust with her apron. "Bless your heart, she's a beauty. My Kia is the saddest, ugliest, boxiest excuse of a car. At least it gets me to work. But this car. You show 'em, girl!" She grinned and scooted back into the hotel.

Jeannie wondered if this is what they meant by Southern hospitality. Lila-Jean's thoughtfulness was touching. She was the first person Jeannie had chatted with in Greenville, and her warm welcome left Jeannie with a favorable impression of the city.

The GPS had Jeannie turning onto Highway 264. Traffic was too busy for her to race down the highway. Instead, she drove at a sedate pace, taking in her surroundings. She saw lots of small shopping malls, a few hotels, a boat-making company, large fiberglass pool shells, agricultural suppliers, many churches, and a long, narrow river.

Turning off the highway, she continued onto a narrow road lined with small, worn houses and untilled fields. A sign listing three buildings and surrounded by flowers got her attention. She briefly wondered which came first – the county detention center, the public-health center, or the agricultural center.

The public-health center was furthest left. It was a squat, single-story structure. As she walked up the steps and opened the door, a raised voice reverberated through the building. A receptionist had her head cocked toward an inner office. Jeannie cleared her throat to get the receptionist's attention.

She slowly turned toward the visitor. Long, curled blonde hair cascaded down her back. Blue eyes were rimmed with navy kohl. Her mascara was thick. Her lips formed the largest pout Jeannie had ever seen, making her wonder if the receptionist supplemented them with fillers. Her nameplate said La Donna Rogers. "Can I help you," she asked politely.

While Jeannie stated her name, the sound of an angry male voice sliced through the wall. "I will not!"

"You will do as I say," commanded a woman with a voice of steel.

The receptionist's tone was sweet as sugar, but her eyes flashed with disdain. "Honey, please repeat your name."

Jeannie was puzzled by the request, but did what La Donna asked.

After the third try, La Donna recorded Jeannie's name. "Thank you so much. We see lots of Hispanics and I understand that accent, but we don't often get people like you in our office." La Donna turned away from Jeannie, intent on catching as much as she could of the argument that was taking place in the other room.

"We don't need strangers meddling in our business. We can take care of our own."

Soon after, a man slammed the office door, strode past the receptionist's desk, pivoted when he saw Jeannie, stopped and stared at her, and then quickened his pace.

"Frank!" La Donna shouted after him, but he ignored her and stomped out of the building.

A petite woman walked briskly toward Jeannie. She wore a bright blue dress with a white jacket and matching blue pumps. A chin-length bob framed her youthful face.

"Dr. Johal?"

Jeannie nodded.

The administrator extended her perfectly manicured hand. "I'm Dr. Dunn. So good of you to come to our little slice of paradise."

Jeannie was bemused by her words. She didn't think of paradise as a place near a prison.

Dr. Dunn smiled at her guest. "It's an insider's joke. The correctional facility is located at the top of New Hope Road. For me, paradise lies below it."

Jeannie was baffled. She had no idea what Dr. Dunn was talking about. She was puzzled over how this woman could be friends with Beatrix Bach, the most direct person she had ever met.

Dr. Dunn walked toward the exit and gestured for Jeannie to follow her.

"Look over there. That's where the real paradise is. They call it the Arboretum – but it's more than just a collection of trees."

Jeannie observed large trees, a green wooden canopy, wide bushes, different shapes and sizes of shrubs, some flowers, a big parking lot, and grass that sloped down to a small pond.

"There's a garden for just about anything you can imagine. And benches everywhere. There's a shade garden for plants that shy away from the light. A butterfly garden that attracts orange monarchs and yellow swallow-tails, as well as bees and hummingbirds. A wet-site garden with banana trees and ginger plants with the most intoxicating scent. A walking trail that will shield you from the summer sun and where you can hear leaves crunch under your feet. An herb garden where your senses will go into overdrive. A memorial garden with fancy roses and benches for reflecting on life. A children's garden with a tunnel, magical mushrooms, and other treasures. The Arboretum is a hidden jewel."

"Dr. Bach said that you and she were close friends," said Jeannie haltingly. "But you seem very different!"

"Chalk and cheese. We are as different as two friends can be. Of course, we served together in medical and surgical hospitals in Afghanistan and Iraq. We are strong supporters of women's rights, too. But Dr. Bach is businesslike and very direct. I prefer to work with people, rather than tell them what to do."

Jeannie's mind immediately revisited the scene of a man almost flying out of Dr. Dunn's office. "That's very interesting," she said. She hoped that Dr. Dunn was unable to discern the insincerity in her tone.

Dr. Dunn laughed. "Well, I usually try to find consensus. Sometimes I have to make a decision that others may not agree with."

Jeannie nodded. In Mumbai, hierarchies ruled. She expected her assisting nurse to do what she was asked to do in the OR. At home, Jeannie had deferred to her husband. Since starting work in Canada, Jeannie had learned that listening made work go more smoothly, especially if you were willing to give a little. Although this was a difficult lesson to master, she'd discovered that this approach got better results and established a foundation for future relationships.

"Let's go into my office. It's unfortunate that you caught the tail-end of my conversation with Frank. He's normally even-tempered, almost easy-going."

"Was he referring to me when he mentioned strangers meddling in his business?"

"I wouldn't take Frank's words to heart. You came highly recommended. Dr. Bach said that you're able to adapt and excel in any environment."

"Your receptionist asked me to repeat my name three times. By way of explanation, she said that she had trouble understanding my accent and that 'we don't get many of your kind here.' "

Dr. Dunn's burst of laughter turned into a sigh. "Well, this is the South. You speak the Queen's English and you're dressed in business attire. La Donna multitasks better than anyone I've ever met. That is, she knows how to chew gum, talk on the phone, and paint her finger-nails at the same time. If I could only get her to learn how to spell or to broaden her horizons. She's never been outside the county, apart from trips to the beach with her boyfriend, and likely never will. She has her opinions, and she will never understand why you are here."

Jeannie was curious as to why Dr. Dunn had hired La Donna when the receptionist seemed disinterested in her job. "Why does she work here?"

"You are forthright!" said Dr. Dunn. "Did you learn that from Beatrix Bach or are you naturally so direct? As a matter of fact, my supervisor recommended her to me."

Jeannie smiled ruefully. She hadn't meant to come on so strong. She probed to learn more about the receptionist. "Does she understand I am here to help identify the problems with your study and correct them?" asked Jeannie."

Dr. Dunn snorted. "I doubt she understands the importance of the study. She likely has relatives with Type II Diabetes, but probably doesn't know who or how many. In some families, it's a hidden disease. Because of the shame associated with being obese, family members often don't talk about it with each other."

"Even in families where some members are noticeably large?"

"Especially in those families. What's more, La Donna would certain-ly never understand the need to bring in someone from the outside to provide their expertise."

Turning, Dr. Dunn addressed Jeannie earnestly. "Someone is out to sabotage my project. I don't know who it is, but I doubt it's La Donna or Frank. She lacks the interest and Frank quit his high-paying corporate job to manage this project because it hits close to home with him. Be careful how you proceed. Keep your wits about you and trust no one."

Chapter 4

Jeannie took deep steadying breaths. She saw the furrowed forehead and worry lines framing Dr. Dunn's eyes. "I survived a bomb blast in Mumbai. In Canada, a White nationalist pushed me off the skytrain platform and then pretended to rescue me. My husband tracked me down in British Columbia and tried to persuade me to return with him to his mansion in India. When I refused, he attempted to douse my face with acid."

"Dr. Bach has told me a little about your background. You haven't served your country in Afghanistan or Iraq as she and I have, but you've certainly experienced significant life challenges. I think you'll find that there will be a temporary burst of inquisitiveness while people get to know you. They may express their curiosity by harping on your accent because it's different from theirs, but when they see you bringing your skills to the table to help move this project forward, they'll come around."

"I hope so, but I'm not here to win a popularity contest," said Jeannie.

Dr. Dunn regarded Jeannie with a wry look. "I can tell," she quipped.

Jeannie looked around the director's office. It was a study in contrasts. A photo of the physician as a young girl doing a deep plié, hair pulled back into a tight bun, back very straight, and knees deeply bent. Another photo, taken a few years later, one hand on the barre, with her pointed foot at a perfect right angle. The third photo showed Dr. Dunn all grown up, with a stethoscope around her neck. She was standing outside an army tent, the drab olive of the shelter blending in with the mountainous scrub and dark brown terrain.

The fourth photo showed her next to another woman. When Jeannie took a step to get a closer look, she saw the other woman was Dr. Bach.

"Yes, that was us when we were young surgeons. We thought we could use our skills to help our soldiers. What we discovered was that we could remove shrapnel from their bodies, but we couldn't heal the deep psychological scars that so many soldiers experienced. "I've always wondered why some combat veterans were more susceptible to psychic trauma than others. Is it linked to brain chemistry? Is there something triggered at the molecular level? Does a hostile environment exacerbate their condition? I don't know the answers to these questions and that's why I shifted from surgery to the behavioral sciences."

"What does Dr. Bach think about physical and psychological injuries sustained in combat?" asked Jeannie.

Dr. Dunn laughed ruefully. "You've been working for Beatrix for how long?"

"About eighteen months."

The director nodded. "Long enough to know that she lives in a black-and-white world. There are no grays for her. She makes a decision based on the available facts and sticks by it."

"I've noticed that she is very direct," agreed Jeannie.

"In reality, nothing is so simple, whether it's why some soldiers return from war with a healthy mindset and others are plagued with post-traumatic stress. Humans are made up of complex systems where a single cell mutation can trigger a host of responses."

Jeannie squirmed because the criticism of Dr. Bach made her feel uncomfortable. Jeannie admired Dr. Bach's decisiveness. Jeannie's supervisor in British Columbia had told her more than once that the world of medicine was filled with nuance, but Jeannie still didn't see it. In Jeannie's world view, every surgeon who saved his or her patient was a hero. Conversely, Jeannie was deeply disappointed every time a physician made a diagnostic or surgical error that harmed a patient.

Dr. Dunn provided Jeannie with a summary of the Greenville health study. "Our subjects are adult females who live here in Pitt County. We've been following them for the past seven months. All are very overweight or obese. Half are prediabetic and the other half were diabetic at the start.

"We give half of the patients enrolled in the study a weekly semaglutide injection. The others get a saline injection. Since it's a blinded study, the patients do not know if they are receiving semaglutides or an inert solution. What's surprising is that all of our patients have lost weight."

Jeannie asked for clarification. "Do you mean 'morbidly obese' when you describe the subjects as 'very overweight?'"

The director chided her. "That term went out of favor a couple of years ago. We don't use it because people associate morbidity with unpleasant subjects. Society thinks people who are severely overweight are lazy and stupid, with no self-discipline. Obesity is a chronic and complex disease with many contributing factors – genetics, environment, income, education, access to healthy food, to name a few."

She continued, as if Jeannie hadn't interrupted her. "Most were referred to us by their primary-care providers or county nutritionists. A few heard about the study in the local newspaper and called to ask if they could join. While the study is taking place, the subjects receive free medical care. They come in once a week for an injection, a weigh-in, a glucose test, and a 60-minute appointment with the nurse or dietitian. They also have free bus passes, free passes to our gym and the local aquatic center, as well as one-on-one sessions with a trainer every two weeks. Those whose movements are restricted receive physiotherapy. Finally, they receive vouchers to buy food from the local farmers' markets."

Jeannie's mouth fell open. "That's a lot of freebies!"

"You seem surprised."

"I am. Is this what it takes to get community members to agree to participate in a medical study in America?"

"Dr. Johal, medical care is not free. Many of the participants do not have medical insurance and cannot afford to pay for these drugs or the lab tests or clinical visits. We don't want to eliminate those who could benefit most from our study."

"No, of course not. When I studied the health of Indigenous women in Canada, I saw they weighed more and had higher rates of diabetes than non-Indigenous women. I don't know if they had limited access to health care, but I do know changes to their traditional diet made them more reliant on processed foods."

"Exactly. It's all well and good that the South is known for its fried chicken and banana pie. Based on population size, Greenville has the dubious honor of having the most fast-food joints in the country. Our barbecued chicken is famous across the South. It's hard to pass up on chicken when it tastes so good, is easy to find, and cheaper to buy than fresh vegetables."

For a moment, Jeannie wanted to disassociate herself from Canada, her adopted country, because she knew that parts of the city she called home were awash with fast food joints, unhealthy food that she shunned. Instead, she signaled her understanding by not saying anything.

"It may sound as if we're allocating a lot of resources to this project, but you have to consider that it costs close to $200 billion annually in the United States alone to treat obesity and related conditions. If we can prevent heart attacks, strokes, blindness, and limb amputation in our subjects, we will have a proven strategy for saving the healthcare system billions of dollars a year. If we can confirm through rigorous testing that a drug turns off the hunger signals in our brains, stops cravings, and makes it possible for participants to lose even ten percent of their body weight, that will have tremendous health benefits."

She paused. "Frank is the project manager. He oversees all aspects of the study – staffing, approving study participants, budgeting, scheduling, communications. I liaise with the three organizations funding the research – the National Institutes of Health, WellStar Pharmaceuticals, a multinational pharmaceutical company, as well as Pitt County. NIH is hands-off. They ask me to provide quarterly progress reports and to highlight any issues the study is experiencing."

"Have you told them you think someone is sabotaging the study?"

Dr. Dunn gave Jeannie a sharp look. "Of course not. Why would I do that? What do you think would happen if I told them there are inconsistencies with the data, some of the data may not have been correctly entered, and I have a feeling someone is out to sabotage the project?"

"They would have serious concerns."

"Exactly. Far better to get to the bottom of the problem and solve it ourselves without having to notify the organizations funding the study."

"You can't hide the irregularities from them forever."

Dr. Dunn's eyes glinted. Her eyes softened when she smiled, helping Jeannie understand how the doctor could charm her opponents into going along with her. "That's why you're here. Dr. Bach is confident that you'll be able to identify the problems and help us resolve them.

She's never let me down on the battlefield, and I have faith that you will be able to fix the database."

"Why do you get funding from a pharmaceutical company? Won't that create a bias in favor of the company's products?"

She shrugged. "Beggars can't be choosers. Pitt County isn't the poorest county in North Carolina but it doesn't have the funds to do large-scale, intensive research projects. The county pays for my salary, as well as La Donna's, and it provides office space. The grant pays the salary of everyone else who works on this study. The grant also covers the cost of a small onsite gym.

"Funding from WellStar Pharmaceuticals enables us to provide the medical care and lifestyle changes to support weight loss and better health. WellStar does not have a say in who participates in the study. We won't allow them to influence the study findings."

"How will you stop them?"

"What a question! This is a blinded study and they do not have access to the names of those participating. They don't know who gets the treatment and who gets a placebo. And they do not have access to participants' files, so they don't know participants' backgrounds or whether they are complying with food and exercise requirements."

Dr. Dunn's response left Jeannie with more questions than answers. "What exactly is the pharmaceutical company getting out of co-sponsoring your study?"

"These are relatively new drugs and it's not clear how long the results will last. It appears that the patients will regain the weight they lose if they stop taking the medication. When the study winds down, WellStar may reach out to participants and offer free medication in exchange for health data. Obesity is a billion-dollar business. If the results are consistently positive, WellStar will use the study results to market their product around the world," she explained.

"And they haven't asked for the patients' identities so they can directly target them?"

Dr. Dunn sighed. "The data we supply to them is anonymized, and they will be able to contact participants only if the participants sign a disclaimer allowing us to share their information with the pharmaceutical company. I have a meeting with the County director and Well-Star's regional sales rep this morning. I guess I'll have to see if the director and the sales rep are content with a verbal progress report because I'm sure as hell not going to put my concerns about data integrity in writing."

She pulled an organization chart from her filing cabinet and pushed it across her desk toward Jeannie. "This will give you a better idea of who does what. Frank supervises a dietitian and three public health nurses who meet with and follow the subjects enrolled in the study. He also supervises a physiotherapist. An epidemiologist used to report to Frank, but the arrangement didn't work out and she's no longer with us. Thankfully, she taught a data-entry clerk how to enter the data. A lab technician comes in once a week to collect the lab tests. Finally, La Donna provides administrative support when she has the time."

"That sounds like a lot of resources for a small, local research project."

She gives Jeannie a quizzical look. "Did Dr. Bach tell you it was a small, local project?"

Jeannie wondered what Dr. Dunn was getting at. "No-o, she didn't exactly say that, but she said Greenville was a small city."

Dr. Dunn's voice rose an octave. She shook her head in disappointment. "She could never get over my accepting a job in North Carolina when I could have worked at the Mayo Clinic. By Beatrix's standard, it may be a small project. But it's the biggest research project this department has ever undertaken and the results could guide healthcare policy across the country."

"How many subjects are enrolled?"

"Six hundred."

Jeannie whistled, "That's not a small project."

"No, it's not."

"How long is the study?"

"The study is scheduled to last twelve months. We've been following our subjects for seven months and all have lost at least ten percent of their total weight."

"That sounds excellent!"

"Yes, but."

"What's the but? Losing ten percent of their weight will give them lasting health benefits," said Jeannie.

Dr. Dunn sounded less certain. "Some of the preliminary results are puzzling."

"What do you mean?"

"All of our clients have lost at least ten percent of their total weight. Some have lost significantly more. But weekly glucose readings are rising steeply for some of the heaviest patients and we don't know why. We don't know if this is directly related to the drug they are being given, if it's related to factors external to the study, or if it's due to coding errors or data interpretation."

"Is it possible those patients are eating a lot of sugary products or drinking a lot of sweet tea?" Jeannie had heard that sweet tea, laden with tablespoons of sugar in every glass, was a Southern staple.

"It's possible," she said doubtfully. "The spikes suggest it's more than that. This is why we need to investigate."

"What do the data tell you?"

"The clerk is conscientious and does what she is asked to do. But she's not a statistician. Unfortunately, it appears that the epidemiologist setting up the database wasn't as meticulous as we thought. We're hoping you can make sense of the data that's already been collected, check for accuracy, and ensure the database captures the variables we need to record. Dr. Bach praised your analytical skills, and Lordy, we need an epidemiologist who knows what they're doing."

Jeannie didn't know how much Dr. Bach had told Dr. Dunn about her. But if there was ever a time to tout her own skills, this was it. "I trained as a surgeon. I specialized in plastics. I worked in a nonprofit clinic that provided services to mothers and children with facial deformities. I also have a graduate degree in epidemiology and enjoy analyzing data."

Dr. Dunn was staring at her.

"I like to know why things happen. It's not enough to fix a problem; I want to prevent it from happening in the first place."

"She said you don't stop your investigation until you understand what's causing the problem and how to solve it. You're just the person we need."

Part of Jeannie wanted to puff up proudly, like a peacock fanning its feathers in front of an audience in a petting zoo. But her pragmatism brought her down to earth. "I will do my best."

"Your immediate challenge will be to win Frank over. He's not happy that I've brought in an external expert."

"Is that why he was shouting at you?"

"You heard that? Yes, I suppose everyone in the building heard us. When it comes to this project, Frank is very protective. He says all of the protocols have been followed to a letter and we don't need an outsider to come in and pick apart our work. He takes his responsibilities very seriously. He's deeply troubled by problems with the data."

"What do you mean?"

"He hired the epidemiologist. I've told him to put the past behind him and to give you full access to our records. I'm sure he'll come around."

Dr. Dunn looked at her watch. "Listen, I have to head out for a meeting. La Donna has set you up with a computer and your own office. She'll show you how to get into the system so that you can read through the research protocols and look at the data that have been collected."

Jeannie rubbed her hands together in anticipation. *I can't wait to get my hands on the data. How is it possible both the data-entry clerk and the epidemiologist would make the same errors? I'm looking forward to getting to the bottom of this and fixing the problems.*

Chapter 5

Jeannie's eyes were skimming through reams of data when she heard the sound of high heels clacking on hardwood floors. She looked up from the computer, surprised that a few hours had passed. Stiff, she rolled her shoulders and stretched her neck from side to side.

Dr. Dunn appeared in the doorway. She looked pale, and a fine sheen of perspiration gave her skin a dewy glow.

"You look hot."

"Meetings with the county's senior director and the pharmaceutical rep always have that effect," she joked. "I know that Bernard Bigelow wants quarterly progress reports and up to this quarter, I have always provided the report spot on time and in writing. The same for the pharmaceutical rep. But I will not provide numbers that don't make sense to me. There's a problem with the data and we need to find its source and correct it. They'll get an update when I'm confident that the numbers are accurate.

"Fortunately for me, Bernard is leaving for vacation later this week. That buys me time."

In Jeannie's experience, bosses tried to clean up loose ends and get as much as possible completed before they headed on vacation. "You're not worried that he's going to press you for results before he leaves?"

"His wife will be keeping him busy with tasks that need to be done around the house," Dr. Dunn responded brightly. "If I know Becky, she'll have Bernard checking the air conditioner and giving the lawn an extra-thorough edging so it continues to look pristine while they are away."

Jeannie had no experience with lawns. "What do you mean by 'edging'?"

"I live in a condo now because I don't want to spend what little free time I have maintaining a yard. But when I owned a home, I had a lawn-maintenance company come in to mow the lawn weekly and dig along the edge of the grass and the flower beds to create a manicured look."

"Why wouldn't your boss hire a lawn-maintenance company to care for his yard?"

"That's a very good question. Becky has tried out numerous lawn-maintenance companies, but none has met her impossibly high standards when it comes to edging. She hires someone to mow the lawn, but expects Bernard to edge the borders and trim the shrubs. The benefit to me is that she keeps him busy at home so that he doesn't have time to pop into our offices unexpectedly. And on the few occasions when he does drop in, it's usually because he's meeting with the arboretum director or decided to go for a walk in the arboretum and thinks I would be disappointed if he didn't stop by my office while in the vicinity."

"I guess he enjoys viewing the flowers and shrubs."

"Bernard has a broad mandate. His direct reports include me and the director of the arboretum. I get the impression that he prefers meeting with the arboretum director because the two have more in common."

"What's that?"

"They both have penises."

"Oh!" This was something Jeannie would have expected from Dr. Bach, but not from a person she'd just met.

Jeannie noticed that Dr. Dunn's voice seemed to fade at the end of her sentences. "Did you have lunch with Bernard?"

"No, we drank herbal tea. But that reminds me. It's lunchtime and you need to take your breaks. There's a Mexican restaurant that makes excellent tacos just a few blocks away. Or you can purchase a sandwich from the food truck in front of the detention center."

"The detention center?"

As if reading Jeannie's mind, Dr. Dunn responded wryly: "No, the County doesn't let prisoners buy food from the food truck. It's for the staff who work in the prison, the agricultural center, and the public-health facility."

She paused. "Don't worry, you'll figure out soon enough how things work around here. After lunch, I'll introduce you to the rest of the team."

Jeannie smiled at her. "Actually, Lila-Jean made me a lunch."

Dr. Dunn shrieked in laughter. "Lila-Jean Lamont from the hotel?"

"The same."

"How did you manage to charm her so quickly! You're going to be such an asset to this team."

Jeannie noticed that Dr. Dunn almost lost her balance when she turned, and wondered if it was because the doctor had donned high heels for her meeting, but usually wore flats.

Jeannie peeked into the brown paper bag. Lunch appeared to be a chicken-salad sandwich on a croissant, a Gala apple, and two sugar cookies. Grabbing her paperback, she stepped outside.

The air felt warm. She removed her suit jacket and folded it over her arm. She walked towards tufts of greenery. Her nose led the way to tall fernlike fronds that smelled of fennel. She inhaled appreciatively and spotted a concrete bench on which she placed her lunch and jacket. A couple of people nodded as they passed by. They were wearing running shoes and pumping their fists. They seemed to be walking with a purpose. Her eyes followed them, watching as they turned a corner and disappeared down a trail.

Jeannie was experiencing sensory overload. She smelled a large bed of rosemary before she could see it. She noticed lantanas with yellow, pink, and orange flowers jockeying for space. She bent down to read a plant sign. A moment later, she reached up to stroke a white petal. For a time, she was lost in memories of visiting the tea farm in Ranikhet with her parents.

She sat on the bench. The sound of her book hitting the ground jerked Jeannie into wakefulness. She heard the wail of sirens filling the air. Through the trees, she saw a stream of vehicles roaring onto Government Road. Her first thought was that there must have been a prison outbreak at the detention center. But, no, the vehicles stopped in front of the public-health building. Emergency Medical Technicians (EMTs) raced up the steps.

Jeannie's training as a physician took over. Grabbing her jacket and lunch, Jeannie broke into a run. While she didn't know why they were there, the presence of EMTs suggested a medical emergency.

A police officer blocked her way.

"Ma'am, you can't go in there."

"I work here," she protested.

The officer repeated himself. "You can't go in."

Jeannie straightened herself to her full height. She might only be five feet tall, but packed a lot of authority into each inch. "I am a physician, a first responder. I can help. It's my duty." She pushed past the hapless police officer before he could even record her name, and opened the door to the building. She looked in, beyond the tangle of people.

She caught a glimpse of Dr. Dunn lying outside her office, splayed out on her back, her head turned to one side. Her complexion was bright red. Her neck was so swollen that it was impossible to tell where her jawline began. Her lips were rimmed with white foam. Her cheek lay on a pool of frothy vomit.

A seasoned-looking officer took long strides toward Jeannie. His face appeared to be carved out of granite. His words were equally harsh. "You. Out."

She protested. "I'm a doctor. I have a duty to help."

"There is nothing for you to do here. You can't help her. You're too late." Jeannie gasped, involuntarily sucking in her breath.

"Don't come any further. You're contaminating the scene of the crime. Now get out."

She shrieked because she was having difficulty taking in what the officer said. She stuttered, "The scene of the crime?"

She found herself propelled off her feet. Two officers grabbed her elbows and forcibly ejected her. "You cannot remain in the building."

"I work here. Can I at least gather my belongings," she pleaded.

The officer followed Jeannie into her office. He recorded her name.

"Give me your shoes. Our crime scene techs will need to process them because you walked through the crime scene. Here are paper booties you can wear instead," he said.

Always quick to process information, Jeannie offered an observation while asking a question. "Why are you calling it a crime scene? Isn't that premature?"

"The doctor herself called it in."

Jeannie wrinkled her forehead in puzzlement. "How is that possible?"

The officer raised his hands as if to fend off her questions. "She called 9-1-1 to report a poisoning – her own."

"How horrible! Good that she had the foresight to make the call," said Jeannie.

"The doctor said she was calling to report a murder. She dropped the phone while the 911 operator was recording the contact information. Now I've told you more than I should and you've had more than enough time to gather your belongings. You'll have to leave and you won't be able to return until the scene has been processed."

He escorted her from the building and told her to wait outside. Jeannie questioned what she had gotten herself into. What was supposed to be a simple assignment – identify the coding glitches and repair the database – had turned into an ominous puzzle. Dread washed over her. Was it possible that her coming to Greenville had precipitated Dr. Dunn's death? Try as she might to put the thought aside, her mind kept returning to her conversation with Dr. Dunn. Someone had clearly decided it wasn't enough just to sabotage the doctor's research results. The doctor herself had to be stopped. Would Jeannie suffer the same fate if she stayed?

Chapter 6

Frank Wright's displeasure resonated with every step he took. His feet made clomping sounds as he stomped down the steps. He kicked stones on his way to the parking lot, sending bits of gravel flying into the air. The long thrusts caused his phone to fall out of a pant pocket, but he was so focused on hitting the rocks that he didn't notice. His jaws were clenched and his lips thinned in a straight line. As he walked, his head shook, mirroring the furrows on his face. *I don't understand why Dr. Dunn is putting this pressure on me. Why does she have to bring in a stranger to review the data?*

His lips curled in contempt. *Why couldn't she have just given me more time to solve the problem instead of calling her old military buddy? If I were a woman, she'd be falling backward to help me solve the problem. But no, she's making it worse.*

He revved the engine of his 2020 Chevy Silverado, causing large clouds of smoke to billow from the dual exhaust pipes. Not even the photo pinned on the dashboard could calm him. *Charlene, you were such a sweet loving child. Your mom and I gave you everything. All we ever wanted was for you to be happy.*

During the hour-long drive home to the Raleigh suburb of Clayton, he reflected on what had brought him to this point. As a project manager, he was expected to be on top of all aspects, but he'd missed the early signals suggesting staffing problems. When he did see the signs and try to make corrections, it was too late. Both the data-entry clerk and the epidemiologist had gone to Dr. Dunn to accuse him of being too harsh a taskmaster. He had terminated the epidemiologist on the spot, while the data-entry clerk had been let go a few weeks later.

He sighed. He should have taken responsibility for their failings. It felt to him as if he wasn't able to do anything right, despite his good intentions. *You know why you took this job. It's up to you to make it work.* His mind ruminated about Charlene's compulsive need to eat everything in sight.

While still a high-school junior, her weight ballooned above three hundred pounds. Fried fast food was a particular problem. She'd try so hard to restrain herself, but a demon inside her had other ideas. After eating the healthy brown-bag lunch her mother prepared, Charlene would stroll across the street to one of several barbecue chicken joints nearby. She developed Type II diabetes before her sixteenth birthday, and a myriad of health problems followed.

Her father remembered the day that Charlene's feet had to be amputated. He would never forget hearing a thud and finding his daughter unconscious on the bathroom floor. Instead of marrying his only child off in a lavish church ceremony, he'd had to bury her. He used his short sleeve to wipe a tear from his face when he remembered the sight of her coffin being carried out of the church.

His daughter's death caused Frank to change his career trajectory, trading his marketing job for the opportunity to project manage Dr. Dunn's research into obesity. While it was too late to help Charlene, he hoped that the research findings would help other young people.

He took a deep breath and exhaled, tapping his fingers on his pants. *I know I shouldn't have cussed when Dr. Dunn told me she was bringing in an outsider to look over the data. Gentlemen don't cuss at women. It's her project. She has every right to do whatever she thinks is best. And I shouldn't have stormed out of the office. I'll apologize when I go back this afternoon. But not until then, because I'm still angry with her.*

Darla Wright was crouching on a bench, weeding a bed of newly planted pink globe amaranths bordering the front of the two-story white colonial when she heard her husband's truck coming into the driveway. Straightening up, she turned and her forehead creased into multiple parallel lines at the unexpected sight. Her fingers danced in the air.

"What's wrong, Frank? Why are you home so early?"

She tore off her garden gloves and moved swiftly toward him.

"I had an argument with Dr. Dunn," he said tersely.

"I thought you liked her. What happened?"

"She told me that she brought on someone from the outside to review the data we've collected. I told her I would find the problem and solve it, but she wouldn't listen. It was humiliating!"

His wife looked at him earnestly. "Frank, it's hard to have someone second-guess your decisions, but remember why you took this job in the first place."

He nodded. "I know. And I know I was out of line cussing at her, but the way she told me what she was planning really bothered me. There was this slip of a thing sitting in the reception area, and I think she's the person who's going to review the data. When Dr. Dunn told me she'd called on her buddy in Canada for help, I didn't realize that the 'help' had already arrived."

"Frank Wright, how could you? You know better than to use bad words. What's got into you?"

He hung his head in shame.

"You know what you have to do."

"I do," he said sadly. "Yes, I owe Dr. Dunn an apology. I just don't understand why she feels the need to bring in an outsider. And not just from outside the county. But a woman, and from a socialist state. We're the United States of America and we know best. We fix things around the world. We don't need help from an outsider."

Darla looked around to see if any neighbors were within hearing distance. "We do know best. I guess Dr. Dunn's tour of duty outside of the country corrupted her."

His wife's insights always amazed him. She could see things so clearly. "That must be what happened."

"Honey, I know you can fix things. Apologize to Dr. Dunn and move on."

"I will. I'll try to help the visiting epidemiologist in every way I can. We all want to get to the bottom of the problem."

Darla's voice was brighter. "Now then, since you're home, join me for an early lunch."

He smiled at her. "That's the best idea I've heard today. But first I'd better call in to say I'll be back after I eat."

He reached for his phone, only to discover it wasn't there. "It appears I left my phone at work. I'll pick it up later."

He took his wife's hand and they walked into the house. After saying a prayer thanking the Lord for their meal and asking for forgiveness for cussing, they ate corn chowder with sausage and toast, oblivious to the mayhem unfolding back in the public-health building.

Chapter 7

Jeannie watched from the sidelines as two vehicles parked at the curb. An ample-sized middle-aged woman briskly stepped out of the driver's seat of a metallic red Ford Escape, a black medical bag clutched in her hand. At the same moment, a skinny young man carrying a tripod and video camera emerged from a dark Dodge van with 'County Coroner's Office' emblazoned on its side. The van contained crime scene tape, orange traffic cones, body bags, recording equipment, and a Stryker power cot for transferring victims from the scene.

The woman and man exchanged words as they donned white coveralls.

"It feels like we were just here," said Jared, who doubled as the coroner's assistant and the videographer.

Dr. Eytan nodded grimly. "It was just yesterday. We were called to confirm a murder next door at the detention center."

They climbed the steps to the building entrance. A police officer carrying a clipboard blocked them from advancing further.

Dr. Eytan flashed her ID card and tried without success to squeeze past the officer.

"The building is closed. You'll have to come back after we've finished processing the scene," he said.

"Bless your heart for being so diligent," she responded.

He blushed, not sure why a person he'd blocked from entering was thanking him.

"Young man, you need to take a closer look at my badge," said Dr. Eytan calmly.

"She's the county coroner," hissed her assistant.

"Oh, Ma'am, I didn't realize you were the coroner. I thought the coroner was a man. May I get your name?" He scrutinized her badge, spelling out the letters. "Give me a moment to record. E-y-e-t-a-n. That's kind of like Italian," he said, while incorrectly recording the coroner's name.

The coroner clenched her teeth together, loosening her jaw to speak. "Jared, my assistant, also needs to see the crime scene."

"Now that's an easy name to spell."

The officer gestured for both to go inside the building. Before entering, they stopped to put on disposable white booties over their street shoes.

The coroner's eyes followed a trail of vomit splatter along a lower wall. "Make sure you capture the fluid," she instructed the videographer as she pointed to the wall.

Dr. Eytan continued her analysis. "She was alert enough to dial 911, but not able to complete the call. She dropped the phone and crawled out of her office. She made it just past the doorway."

"Do you think she was looking for someone?" asked the officer.

Dr. Eytan gave him a piercing glance. "We don't even know the location of the murder scene. I can't speculate on whether she was searching for the killer or seeking help because I don't know if or when she was poisoned."

"You're saying she was poisoned?"

"You're a nosy one. You're supposed to be guarding the scene, not peppering me with questions."

The officer's face turned red and he stepped back.

The coroner continued toward the body. She took another pace, stopped, and sniffed. "I smell cherry cough syrup. I wonder if the victim had a cold and was self-medicating?"

Her assistant knew that the coroner was talking to herself and didn't expect or welcome a response.

She moved next to the body, bending deeply on one knee. The creak it made was jarring in the silence. "Make sure you get close-ups of the victim's face," she instructed. She stared intently, observing the burst blood vessels surrounding the deceased woman's irises. After a long pause, the coroner closed the victim's eyes. She gently detached a vomit-soaked strand of hair sticking to the victim's lips. She opened the mouth, shining a flashlight in the cavity.

She continued her inspection of the face. "Look at her expression. She knew she was going to die. The million-dollar question is: Who wanted her dead and why?"

As she rose, Dr. Eytan could hear the pounding of feet near the entrance. The detectives had arrived.

They pushed their way in, pausing to cover their boots and glove their hands.

Detective Harmony Harris wrinkled her nose and tucked her chin into her chest. A groan escaped her lips. "Augh, that smell reminds me of my nephew, and not in a good way. They say babies eat, sleep, cry, and poop. That's all they do at first."

Henry Smith stared in disgust at his partner. He couldn't believe she would be so crude. How could she describe babies in such an offensive way? He thought of his adorable niece and wanted to give her a protective hug.

He hissed at her. "I can tell you've never had a child."

She nodded. "Agreed. But this smell is terrible!"

He responded. "That's so disrespectful in every way. Your parents got it so wrong, naming you 'Harmony.' "

"You're right, I need to be more respectful. And you need to keep my parents out of this. You have no business mentioning them at a murder scene."

"Let's hear what the coroner has to say," said Henry.

Dr. Eytan walked toward them. "My assistant is videotaping the scene and will be finished in a couple of minutes."

Harmony asked, "Can you confirm that the victim was murdered?"

"You tell me. Don't the police have a record of her calling 911 in which she said that she was reporting her own murder?"

Not to be discouraged, Harmony persisted. "Well, yes, but does the scene bear out what the victim said to the operator?"

"If you mean, does it appear she was murdered? Yes, I can confirm it appears that way."

"What's your basis for making that observation?" asked Henry.

"The victim aspirated fluid. There's a trail of vomit that extends from the desk to the door."

"Did she suffocate on her vomit?"

"It's too early to speculate. I can tell you she reacted strongly to something she ingested. I could smell cherry cough syrup."

"Was she killed here?"

"Your question is an interesting one," responded the coroner. "Her life ended here, making this the murder scene. But there's no indication that whatever she ingested was in her office. Of course, it's your responsibility to look for a sweet red syrup. Once you find it, I can test its contents for you."

"Do you think this killing is related to the detention-center murder?" asked Harmony.

"As a scientist, I don't believe in coincidences. What are the odds of there being two murders in neighboring buildings in two days?"

Henry scoffed at the question. "How can they be related? The murderer couldn't have killed Dr. Dunn because he is incarcerated in the detention center. He has an airtight alibi."

"Unless he arranged for someone to give her a slow-acting poison," suggested Harmony.

Henry gave his partner a doubtful look. "How would he do that? He sat across from us yesterday and refused to say a word. He wouldn't even look at us. You think he then called up his buddy and said, 'Well, I need help killing someone because I just killed an inmate and they're not letting me out. Can you do it?' Prison staff are monitoring anything he says and does, so I don't see how he could have hired someone to kill the public-health director. And why would he?"

"It's not up to me to tell the two of you how to solve your case, but wild speculation and half-baked ideas are not going to lead you to your killer," admonished the coroner.

"No, they won't," agreed Harmony.

"Let my assistant know when your unit has finished examining the crime scene."

"We will. Please let us know when you're scheduling the autopsy," said Henry.

"Though I knew Dr. Dunn only to see her, from all accounts she was an asset to the public-health department and a tireless advocate for better health for the people of Pitt County. She's going to be missed. Jared will let you know when the autopsy is scheduled. I'll do my detailed exam as soon as I can. Dr. Dunn deserves no less. You need to stop the poisoner before she kills more people."

Chapter 8

Detectives Harris and Smith gaped at each other.
"Before she kills more people? Why do you think the murderer is a woman?"

Dr. Eytan looked at the detectives. "Don't you know your crime statistics? Women use poison, men use guns. Of course, I'm speculating when I say this, but the odds are that it was a woman."

She gave her gloves a decisive snap and left the scene.

Henry glanced at the videographer recording the crime scene, taking care not to get in his way. "You don't really think there's a link between the killing at the detention center yesterday and today's murder, do you?" he asked his partner.

"I don't think the inmate killed Dr. Dunn. But it's possible there is a link between the killings. I have no idea what the connection is, though."

Henry acknowledged Harmony's words. "It's a possibility, but it's far too early in the investigation to pursue that angle. You know about that saying in medicine."

"What's that," she asked.

"When you hear the beat of hoofs, think horses, not zebras. In other words, let's get the facts. Find out if Dr. Dunn had any enemies in her work or personal life. Was she generally well-liked or despised by her staff? Did anyone have a recent argument with her? Had she been threatened? What about her personal life? Was she married? Did she have kids? Did she always live in Greenville? Did she get along with her neighbors? Did she have a sizable insurance policy? If so, who stood to gain from her death?"

"Lots of questions."

"Let's get the answers to these questions before we start searching for a zebra in our midst."

"I suppose you're right, but at least admit that this stands out as a murder," urged Harmony.

"Why would I give credence to your need to see zebras everywhere?"

Harmony frowned. "Perhaps I am getting ahead of the game, but around here, just about everyone carries a gun. Most people die by gunshot wound. They are not poisoned."

Henry conceded the point. But the coroner's words puzzled him. "Why do you suppose Dr. Eytan thought that the murderer was a woman?" asked Henry.

"They say that women are more likely to use poison than men, perhaps because it requires more forethought. It has to be planned, and most men are in the correctional center because they made bad choices or acted impulsively. This murder was premeditated," said Harmony.

They walked around Dr. Dunn's desk, taking note of the briefcase next to the desk and a small sheet of paper with handwritten jottings. Henry used his gloved hand to tap her keyboard, but a prompt to enter a password stopped him from being able to see any documents.

Harmony could read three words scribbled on a notepad. "I wonder if these were her last words. 'Jeannie Johal Anitas.' Perhaps Jeannie Johal Anitas is the murderer."

"We'll need to identify this person," said Henry. He straightened up. "There's not much more we can do here. Let's let the crime techs check for prints and the presence of any foreign fluids."

As they approached, the rookie guarding the entrance gestured to Jeannie. "See the girl standing in the corner. She said she works here.

I had her name checked out and she's not listed in the staff directory, although why she'd stick around if she is the murderer is beyond me."

Henry clapped the officer's shoulder in appreciation. "We'll take it from here."

Harmony and Henry could feel the woman's intense stare. As they approached her, she squared her shoulders, her chin jutted out, and she extended a hand.

Harmony flashed her badge and immediately began talking. "Miss Anitas?"

Jeannie looked blankly at her.

Harmony tried again. "Miss Johal?"

Jeannie frowned in concentration, wondering if 'Jo-well' was the North Carolina pronunciation for 'Johal.'

"I am Jeannie Johal," she said.

She saw the detectives exchange a look.

"I'm a physician. I work here."

"We need to take a statement from you," said Henry.

"Where were you when Dr. Dunn was murdered?" said his partner.

"I was sitting over there eating the lunch that Lila-Jean Lamont prepared for me." Jeannie pointed to the green structure at the Arboretum.

"You mean the chef who works at the Hilton?" asked Harmony.

"Yes, I arrived in Greenville last night. I met Lila-Jean this morning when she was serving breakfast. She prepared a brown bag lunch for me. Dr. Dunn told me I could buy lunch from the canteen in front of the detention center or I could go to Anita's to get tacos. I told her I already had a lunch."

The two detectives remained silent, again exchanging a glance.

Jeannie looked up at them. "I was asked to help Dr. Dunn and her team with a research project. Dr. Dunn said there was a problem with the data and she couldn't share the results with her supervisor until the problem was resolved."

"Where are you from? From your accent, you could be a news anchor on the BBC. Are you from England?" asked Harmony.

"No, I traveled here from British Columbia in Canada."

"Is that near Niagara Falls?"

"I don't understand why you're asking me that question. Niagara Falls is in Ontario. British Columbia is on the other side of the country, north of Seattle, Washington."

Henry glared at his partner.

She responded with a shrug, "When I was six years old, we took a road trip to Niagara Falls, Ontario. I went in a boat that went right under the Falls and got soaked by the spray. I think it was called Maid of the Mist. Afterward we had ice cream. That's pretty much all I know of Canada. That, and the fact that it's a communist country that practices socialized medicine."

"Harmony, we wouldn't want Miss Johal to think we're a bunch of country hicks with minimal knowledge of the world outside of Pitt County. Canada isn't a communist country. Although it is socialist and the communists would take over if they could," he admitted.

Jeannie interrupted him. "Actually, it's Dr. Johal. I'm a medical doctor."

He nodded. "We need to ask you a few questions about Dr. Dunn. You may have been the last person to see her alive. How did she look when you saw her?"

Jeannie acknowledged the question. "She had a faint sheen of perspiration on her face. I asked her if she was all right and she dismissed my concerns."

"We would really appreciate your coming to the precinct office to answer our questions," said Henry.

Jeannie looked around anxiously. "When can I get back in my office to begin examining the data?"

"You need to come with us."

As a visible minority, Jeannie had learned not to argue with authority figures. "I'll get my car. It's in the parking lot."

"You're riding with us," said Harmony.

Jeannie let out a murmur of distress. "Am I a suspect?"

"Let's just say that you're a person of interest."

Henry smiled at Jeannie. "What my partner is trying to say is that we're interested in talking to you because you may be a witness to the crime and we need to find out what you saw and heard. We'll bring you back here."

"I don't see how I can help you," said Jeannie. "I ate my lunch, watched a butterfly sipping nectar from a bush, nodded at a couple of people walking on the trails, and I think I fell asleep for a few moments because I woke up to the sound of sirens."

"Nonetheless, we'd like you to come down to the station."

"Am I allowed a phone call?"

Harmony laughed. "Don't be silly. You're not under arrest or anything like that. But if you refuse to come with us, we can charge you with obstructing an investigation."

Jeannie shrugged. "Even though I just met Dr. Dunn for the first time this morning, she struck me as a skilled researcher and a caring person. I will happily accompany you to your station and share with you the little that I know. In any case, I don't know who I would call since Dr. Dunn was my supervisor and I can't call her."

Just as Jeannie was fastening her seatbelt in the back seat of the police car, she saw an object make contact with the window.

"What in tarnation," exclaimed Henry.

Harmony rolled down the driver's window while Henry exited from the passenger side. "Do you know that you just assaulted a police officer's car and, by extension, a police officer?"

She addressed herself to a young woman with long, blonde hair who was barefoot and held one high-heeled sandal in her hand.

The woman raised her arm as if to launch her sandal. Henry pulled his arm around her, preventing her from launching the weapon.

He looked narrowly at her. "No, you don't. Stop it or I'll have to arrest you."

The woman shrieked and pointed at Jeannie. "She's the one you should be arresting. She has no right to be here. Everything was okay until she showed up. Lock her up!"

"I'm here because I was asked to come," protested Jeannie.

"Look at the mess you created. You made Frank walk out on the job this morning. Dr. Dunn was fine when I went out for lunch. And now she's dead. Who sent you here and why are you meddling in something that's none of your business?"

Chapter 9

Jeannie could feel the female detective's scrutiny. Jeannie felt compelled to respond to the unspoken question. "I don't know what she's talking about."

"But you know her?" asked Harmony.

"No, I don't know her."

"It sure seems like she knows you and doesn't like you."

"Let's give the doctor a chance to answer our questions when we get to headquarters," suggested Henry.

"One last question, and then I'll stop," promised Harmony.

He sighed. "What do you want to know?"

She focused on their passenger. "Earlier, you said you'd met Lila-Jean. Would you say you know her?"

Jeannie pondered the question for a moment. "I met her this morning at the hotel and we exchanged pleasantries. We chatted for a little while more when she came up to my car in the parking lot and gave me a bagged lunch. Would I say I know her? I know her name, I know where she works, and I got the impression she has a big heart. Is that enough for me to say that I know her? I guess so."

Henry turned to look at Jeannie. "The woman who threw her sandal at you accused you of meddling where you don't belong. It seems she knows you. Are you sure you don't know her?"

Jeannie stopped herself from clucking in dismay. "I met her this morning. We exchanged a handful of words. That was it."

"Where was this?"

"She's Dr. Dunn's receptionist. Her name is La Donna Rogers."

"Why didn't you tell us this earlier?" asked Henry.

"You approached me and treated me as if I were a criminal. Why didn't you ask her what her name was and why she was standing in the public-health department's parking lot? Why didn't you tell her you were going to bring her in for questioning?"

"We're the ones asking questions, not you. I've a mind to charge you with obstruction," said Harmony.

"Let's have everyone calm down. We'll be at the station in a few minutes, and we will be able to get to the bottom of this situation at that point," said Henry.

Harmony came round to the back seat after they arrived at the police precinct. She opened the door and gestured for Jeannie to get out. When Jeannie felt Harmony's hand pressing down on her scalp, she resisted the impulse to slam her head and Harmony's hand into the roof of the car. Instead, she obediently exited the vehicle, doing everything she could to tamp down the feelings of outrage that threatened to boil over.

Jeannie had the sense that officers in the station were staring at her. That sensation was heightened when a late middle-aged man in a suit jacket walked briskly toward her and extended his hand. She reluctantly took it, gazing up at him in puzzlement.

He took both her hands in his. "Dr. Johal, I'm honored to meet you."

Henry and Harmony exchanged glances and looked at the police captain. "Sir?"

He gestured to a television suspended in a corner of the wall. "The governor is crediting Dr. Johal with saving his son's life."

Jeannie had no idea what the captain was talking about. "I think you're mistaking me for someone else. I don't even know the name of your governor."

"The woman who videotaped Dr. Johal's intervention during an inflight emergency yesterday said that the doctor was on her way to Greenville. Apparently, Dr. Johal administered medical care when the governor's son was having a life-threatening allergic reaction. The woman put the pieces together when she saw the son being picked up at the airport by his father. She ran over to the governor's car and told him what happened. She showed him the video. The story's been playing all day."

"I simply did what any medical provider would," said Jeannie.

"You're a local hero," said the captain. He turned towards Henry and Harmony. "You two in my office now!"

He raised his bushy eyebrows, revealing multiple furrows across his tanned forehead. "What are you doing with Dr. Johal? I assigned you to investigate the murder of the county health director."

"She's not what she seems," insisted Harmony.

Henry rushed in to clarify. "Sir, Dr. Johal was very possibly the last person to see Dr. Dunn alive. We need to take her statement."

The captain stared at Harmony. "Is there something you would like to say?"

"No, sir. It's a complicated situation and we need to talk to everyone who works in that office."

"You do. I'm glad that you're giving Dr. Johal top priority. Please treat her like a VIP."

"Will do, sir."

"Understood, Captain."

Jeannie was standing next to a desk when the detectives returned.

"Let's go into the conference room where we can sit comfortably and get your statement. We don't want to delay you longer than necessary," said Henry.

"Tell us why you are in Greenville."

"My boss in Canada and Dr. Dunn were old army buddies, surgeons who served together in Iraq and Afghanistan. Dr. Dunn is the project leader for a large national study investigating whether Type II Diabetes can be reversed in patients taking a semaglutide. She told my supervisor that someone appeared to be tampering with the data, that the results for this quarter didn't make sense. Since I am a surgeon who also has training in epidemiology, my boss offered my services to Dr. Dunn.

"When I met with Dr. Dunn earlier this morning, she asked me to pore through the structure of the database and check the data to ensure it was properly entered. Dr. Dunn was hoping it was a case of human error – a methodology error resulting from the epidemiologist incorrectly programming a formula, or a typing error – perhaps the data-entry clerk entering wrong information in the wrong field."

"Why would she hope it was human error? Didn't she have confidence in the people hired to do the research?" asked Harmony.

"I can tell you that while Dr. Dunn hoped it was human error, she feared that someone was tampering with the data. I can't speak to whether she had confidence in the project staff. She does have a project manager. I think his name is Frank. But he left before we could be introduced."

"Would you say that you 'know' him the same way you know La Donna," piped in Harmony.

Jeannie flashed her an irritated look. "No, La Donna and I had a direct conversation. When I went up to her desk to introduce myself, she asked me three times to spell my name. She then showed me to the office I would be using during my stay here."

"How much interaction did you have with Frank?"

"None. It sounded as if he and Dr. Dunn were arguing in her office. He left and walked out of the building door."

"Do you know what was the nature of the argument?"

"It might have been me," she shrugged. "I could hear him say that they didn't need an outside expert to come in to tell them what to do, that they could solve it themselves."

"You said that Dr. Dunn left for a meeting?"

"Yes, with her supervisor – the county manager, and a representative from the pharmaceutical company funding the study."

"You remained in the building?"

"Yes, I was reviewing the database."

"When did Dr. Dunn return?"

"I don't know exactly. But I can tell you that she came into my office and we chatted briefly. At that point, La Donna had already left for lunch. Dr. Dunn encouraged me to take regular breaks and reminded me it was lunch time."

"Did she look well when you saw her?"

"She looked hot. I don't know if the drive from one office to an-other location made her overheated or if she was running a fever. She brushed me off when I asked if everything was okay. Perhaps I should have probed more deeply, but I didn't want her to think that I was pry-ing. After all, she's a doctor and would know if she was ill."

The captain entered the room and Harmony could feel his eyes on her. "Thanks for answering our questions. We'll get a squad car to drive you back to the health department so that you can pick up your car," he informed Jeannie before shaking her hand and thanking her for her service.

"When will I be able to go back into the building?"

"Not for a while. The scene needs to be processed and if we find poison on the premises, there will be a further delay before we release the building. In the meantime, please remain in Greenville," said Harmony.

Henry had been listening to his partner. Now he jumped in. "We appreciate that you're here as a favor to the health director, but the offices have to be processed before anyone can be let back in. You'll have to find a different way to conduct your investigation. For now, though, I'll drive you back to the public-health building."

The captain beckoned the three of them into his office. "Dr. Johal, I understand that the governor has been trying to reach you."

Jeannie was speechless. "I haven't received any calls today."

Suddenly she remembered sliding the mute button on her phone shortly after boarding the first plane. "Oh dear! I think I turned the phone off in Vancouver. I'll check for messages when I am back in my hotel room."

On the way to the public-health building, Jeannie rode in the front seat of the cruiser across from Henry. "Now I don't feel like the bad guy," she remarked.

"We never thought you were the bad guy. But you have to understand our perspective. We had to ask you some questions. Your name was on a pad on Dr. Dunn's desk, and we needed to find out who you were. I guess that Dr. Dunn scribbled a note to herself, and that's all it was."

"I guess," said Jeannie.

As they turned the curve leading towards the county buildings, they could see that the steps to the entrance of the county health building had been cordoned off with yellow tape, and a lone police officer stood next to the entrance.

In the parking lot, they noticed a truck parked beside Jeannie's Mustang. A man bent over, crouching on the ground. His head swerved back and forth, eyes intently surveying the pavement. She watched in amazement as he reached under her car.

Chapter 10

"Is there something I can help you with?" asked Jeannie. She looked anxiously at him. "This is my car! What are you doing?"

The man appeared to be in his fifties. His face was red from bending down. He held a phone in his hand. The case was cracked.

Jeannie wasn't certain it was Frank Wright because she'd only got a glimpse of him that morning. But she remembered the aviator glasses and checkered shirt. "Frank?"

He approached her. "That's me. I, er, left the office in a hurry this morning and dropped my phone in the process. When I did 'find my phone,' the radar indicated it was near your car. Thankfully, I found it, although I'll have to test it to see if it still works."

"I remember you leaving the office," said Jeannie dryly. "You were moving very fast."

His face had an embarrassed expression. "Yes, well, sorry about that."

He extended his hand toward her. "You must be Dr. Johal. I'm sorry you had to see me that way. I was angry with Dr. Dunn because she told me she was going to get an external expert in to review our project. And then she told me she'd already contacted an old buddy and arranged for the expert to start that morning. I felt blindsided and I reacted strongly. It wasn't professional of me. I respect Dr. Dunn and I shouldn't have raised my voice. It was inexcusable and I need to apologize to her."

Jeannie wasn't sure how to answer him. Part of her wanted to accept his apology at face value. But the surgeon in Jeannie had taken offense to his comments and wanted to put him in his place. She barely made contact with his hand before withdrawing hers. Then she stepped back a pace and looked him directly in the eye.

"It's too late for that," she said.

"What do you mean?"

He looked at the detective standing next to Jeannie. "Who's this, your assistant?"

It was Henry's turn to step forward. He flashed his badge, giving Frank enough time to read it.

"I said some unfortunate things, Detective! But those words were spoken in the heat of the moment. They didn't mean anything."

"We have witnesses who saw you slam the door and leave – after you threatened Dr. Dunn and her new hire."

Frank was contrite. "I can clear this up. Give me a moment to speak with Dr. Dunn. I was angry because I didn't expect her to have someone new join the project without talking with me first."

Jeannie jumped into the conversation. "I said it was too late because Dr. Dunn was murdered earlier today."

Frank inhaled sharply and took a deep breath. He raised his voice. "That's not possible! She was fine when I left."

Jeannie got in a question. "Let's see. You stormed out of the office. And here you are, six hours later. Where did you go and do you have anyone to vouch for you?"

"I went home. My wife made me lunch. We prayed together. She told me I had to apologize to Dr. Dunn for my blasphemy. I was going to call Dr. Dunn to apologize and let her know I would be returning after lunch. But I couldn't find my phone. Now I don't know how I can make things right between us. I don't know what to do. Dr. Dunn was one of the kindest bosses I've ever had. I can't think of anyone who would want her dead."

He knelt on one knee. His fingertips joined and he raised them to his lips. "Lord, take Dr. Dunn into your arms as you did the Baby Jesus. Welcome her into your kingdom. And show her killer to us that he might be smited and his corpse tossed into a den and ripped apart by one hundred lions!"

Jeannie's eyes opened wide. This was her first experience seeing someone fall on their knees and pray in public. It was also her first experience hearing words promoting violence spoken in the same breath as someone saying a prayer to God.

Henry waited until Frank had finished his prayer. "Do you carry a gun?"

"Weapons aren't permitted in the building, but I keep a .38 in the car for protection."

"May I see it?"

Frank retrieved the gun from the glove compartment.

Henry sniffed it. "Well, I can tell it hasn't been used recently. Do you have any other weapons at home?"

"I sure do. And I keep them locked up in a safe."

"We'll need to see them," said Henry.

"My home is in Clayton, outside Pitt County. You don't have jurisdiction there. Your colleagues can search my home all you like when you get a search warrant," said Frank. "I drove home. My wife and I talked. We ate lunch and we prayed together. Then I drove back to work."

"I'll get a warrant," said Henry. "But you'd let us onto your property and into your house without a warrant if you had nothing to hide and truly wanted to do everything in your power to find Dr. Dunn's killer."

"First, you're asking to search my house without a warrant. Next, you'll be saying that I'm a suspect because I got into an argument with

Dr. Dunn. Under the Constitution, I have the right to free speech and the right to protect my property. You can't take those rights away from me."

"No one's trying to trample on your rights," said Henry.

Jeannie turned to the detective. "How long will the offices be out of bounds? Should I go back to Canada?"

Henry turned to her. "No, you're a person of interest because you were the last person to see Dr. Dunn alive. You need to stay put."

Frank looked somberly at Jeannie. "I failed Dr. Dunn and I can't apologize to her. But I can try to make it up to her by providing you with a project overview, giving you access to the data, and sharing Dr. Dunn's concerns with you. Please stay and work with us."

Jeannie pointed to the briefcase she was holding. "I copied the database onto a flash drive when the officer let me into my office to pick up my belongings. Perhaps the hotel can provide us with a place to work tomorrow."

"That's a good idea. I'll call them in the morning."

Frank looked back at the officer. "Has anyone briefed Bernard Bigelow on what happened?"

"The County business director?"

"Dr. Dunn reported to him."

"Actually, she had a meeting with him this morning," offered Jeannie.

"This morning?"

"Yes," said Jeannie firmly. "When I saw her, she had a faint sheen on her face. When I asked if she was feeling unwell, she replied that meetings with the County business director always left her feeling stressed."

"I'll talk to him, see what he has to say," said Henry. "In the meantime, stay in touch."

Frank turned toward Henry. "Take my gun. You can check the bullets against the bullets that killed Dr. Dunn. I'll call my wife. You can search our house. We have nothing to hide. The sheriff of Johnston County can pick up my guns so that you can eliminate those, too."

"Who said anything about Dr. Dunn being shot?" said Henry.

Frank looked puzzled. "What do you mean?"

"We won't be able to confirm the cause of death until the autopsy and toxicology tests have been performed. But it's likely Dr. Dunn was poisoned."

Chapter 11

When his wife opened the sliding doors of their colonial two-story home and called his name, Bernard Bigelow sighed, put down his edging trimmer, and turned toward her.

He removed his leather gloves and safety glasses. Walking past the hall mirror, he couldn't resist the opportunity to check his appearance. Although he'd been working outside in ninety-degree heat and high humidity, his hair remained perfectly in place. Even his polo shirt still looked crisp.

Bernard was an important man in a small city and he didn't like having his home life disturbed. As the County's chief professional planner, it was Bernard's job to develop and update comprehensive long-term plans for the County's growth, and review and approve land-use permits and development proposals. He'd come a long way from the boy growing up near Fort Bragg, the nationally acclaimed home of the 82nd Airborne Corps and Army Special Ops Command headquarters.

These days, a typical work day consisted of mornings spent ana-lyzing reports, reviewing progress on reports identifying the need for roadway widening, assessing traffic patterns and the impact of bridge renovations, followed by a meeting with his boss, the County senior director. Lunch meant being wined and dined by developers anxious to have their permits expedited and approved. Between meetings with direct reports in the afternoon, Bernard tried to squeeze in time to add his own comments to commissioned reports. What he didn't finish in the office, he brought home.

A few evenings a month, he attended County meetings where businesses, landowners, and concerned citizens expressed their concerns over any number of projects. Bernard exuded confidence and he had little difficulty helping County commissioners and everyday citizens make the right decisions. He was only forty and still had plenty of time to achieve his goal of being selected to represent the people of Greenville and all of North Carolina as the head of government.

"Bernard, someone from the Police Department is turning into our driveway. I can't see who it is, but they're in an official vehicle," she said.

Bernard grumbled because he was almost, but not quite, finished edging his wife's flower beds. For a moment, he thought about asking Becky to entertain their visitor until he finished the job, but dismissed that suggestion as impractical at best, and politically damaging at worst. It was unlikely the Police Department representative was there to speak with his wife. If it got out that Bernard had asked Becky to stall so that he could finish the edging, Bernard might face similar delays when calling for assistance from the Police Department. Greenville was a relatively small city, and memories lasted a long time, especially when it came to holding a grudge.

Instead, Bernard peeled off his protective eyewear and thick leather gloves, unplugged the trimmer, and leaned it against a wall. He kept his baseball cap on. A birthday gift from his administrative assistant, it said, 'I'm Bernard and I'm always right, even when I think I'm wrong.' He entered the house at the same time as the doorbell rang. His wife opened the door.

The man on the other side resembled a linebacker. He was tall and heavily muscled. His head was shaven and his skin appeared smooth, except for five narrow horizontal lines across the forehead. "I'm Captain Colchuk, here to see Bernard. You must be Mrs. Bigelow. Bernard and I regularly cross paths when we're guests at county meetings. He's told me a lot about you."

"Please come in."

Captain Colchuk and Bernard shook hands warmly.

While Becky scooted to the kitchen to prepare glasses of sweet iced tea and a plate of sugar cookies, Bernard and Captain Colchuk got down to business.

"Dr. Dunn was killed earlier today. I believe she reported to you. I am sorry for your loss."

The other man shook his head vigorously. "That's not possible. I saw her this morning for our regular monthly meeting."

"How did she seem?"

"She appeared to be her usual calm, collected self."

"Did she look upset?"

"I wouldn't say that. But she did look resolute."

"What do you mean?"

"Dr. Dunn has – had – an effervescent personality. I'm not the most carefree guy, but her bubbly personality and genuine friendliness won me over quickly. I noticed that she was quieter than usual today. I think she may have had a lot on her mind."

"Was there anything special about this particular meeting?"

Bernard pondered the question. "Well, there was one thing. Dr. Dunn usually provides me with multiple charts. She prepares run charts highlighting cumulative data from the start of the fiscal year to the current month, as well as timelines showing progress to date and milestones met. It was a short meeting. We drank herbal tea and ate cookies that the representative from the pharmaceutical company brought. The tea had a red color and a sweet flavor. I didn't like the taste. Dr. Dunn was a bit more complimentary. The cookies were better, but how can you go wrong with sugar cookies?"

Captain Colchuk stifled a yawn. He'd seen presentations the other man had given, and knew that Bernard could talk for hours without interruption. He tried to help the planner get to the point. "What was different about this morning?"

"There were two things. Dr. Dunn brought a folder with her, as she always does. But she didn't provide any handouts and she didn't do a presentation. She told us that the study registrants have all lost weight, but she had concerns about how the data was being captured."

"What was the purpose of the study?" the Captain asked.

"To see if a new semaglutide drug can help very overweight patients who have Type II Diabetes or are prediabetic lose weight and lower their glucose levels through medication, diet, exercise, and lifestyle changes."

The Captain patted his belly. "Sounds like a plan that would help me. Back in my college football days, I was a solid 235 pounds. Fifteen years later and I'm edging towards the 300 pound mark. Now I sit behind a desk and attend meetings all day. I sure have gotten soft around the middle."

"You don't qualify because you're not a woman."

"Hmph! DEI. It seems all I hear is, you have to be a woman, you have to be a member of a minority. Whatever happened to it being a man's world?" he asked.

"You're preaching to the converted," said Bernard. "The results have been consistently good. But I have to admit that I was a tick annoyed when Dr. Dunn told me she'd brought in an expert to review the data. When I asked her what her project manager thought of the idea, she told me that she hadn't consulted with him. I hear he stormed out of the meeting with her. I'd probably do the same if I were ever blindsided like that."

"About that expert. Her name is Jeannie Johal."

Bernard interrupted Captain Colchuk. "Sounds like she's not from these parts."

"She's a physician from Canada."

"How in God's name did Dr. Dunn find her?"

"Through her army buddy, a surgeon in Canada."

Captain Colchuk was a former marine platoon commander who'd maintained contact with the members of his troop long after returning from Afghanistan. He nodded, "That explains it. And while I can't vouch for her credentials as a data expert, I can tell you that she has the ear of the governor."

"What! How's that possible?"

"I guess you haven't had the television on."

"No, my wife has me trimming the flowerbeds before we leave for vacation."

"The governor's son was on a flight from New York to Raleigh when he experienced a medical emergency. Dr. Johal saved his life."

"Well, I'll be…." It was a rare moment when Bernard was speechless.

"Dr. Dunn's project has suddenly caught the attention of the governor. He appears to be very interested in it. If I were you, I'd encourage Dr. Johal to take a leadership role. She could be your ticket to a state appointment."

Bernard looked deep in thought. "I'm very happy in my current position, serving the people of Greenville and Pitt County. I've no plans to go anywhere," he said.

"For now," corrected Captain Colchuk.

"For now."

"How long will you be on vacation?"

"Almost three weeks."

"Is now the best time to take a vacation?"

"Becky will kill me if I postpone our plans." Bernard corrected his language. "Err, I mean that she'll be very upset. She's been waiting a long time to take this trip."

"I understand. I'll send you updates on the investigation."

"I guess the governor's going to be looking over your shoulder, too," Bernard said. He was on the phone within minutes of Captain Colchuk's departure. Since Bernard was unable to reach Frank, he tried La Donna's cell. She answered on the fourth ring.

"What in God's name is going on at the County public-health office?"

Her voice was reassuring. "Uncle Bernie, it's good to hear from you."

"What happened up there today?"

"Lots. Dr. Dunn was killed, Frank had a big argument with her and walked out. Oh, and a new person, a small woman with a strange accent, started today."

"You met Dr. Johal?"

"The woman who can barely speak a word of English? I had to ask her to repeat herself three times," said La Donna.

"Be careful, young lady. That woman saved the governor's son's life. Treat her like a VIP. Give her all the help you can."

La Donna sighed. "We don't need an outsider to come tell us what to do."

"Enough! We need her help with this project. Remember who got you that job and who can take it away just as easily."

La Donna picked at her fingernails while on the phone with her uncle. She idly wondered why he said they needed the woman's help with the project. She guessed she'd find out soon enough.

Bernard's next call was to Jeannie Johal.

"Dr. Johal, as Dr. Dunn's supervisor, I'd like to welcome you to Greenville. I'm sorry we're meeting under these circumstances."

"Yes, Dr. Dunn mentioned she'd met with you this morning," said Jeannie.

"She told me she was bringing in someone to review the data, but she didn't provide specifics. I am surprised that she felt the need to go all the way to Canada when there are plenty of NC-based epidemiologists."

Jeannie felt compelled to explain. "Sir, I think my coming here was because Dr. Dunn is very good friends with my boss in Canada, Dr. Bach. When she told Dr. Bach that there appeared to be issues with data in her research project, Dr. Bach volunteered my services for a month."

Bernard paused. "I see, that explains a lot. What are your plans now that Dr. Dunn is not available to guide you?"

"It's really up to you, but I'd like to stick around and offer any help I can. Frank and I will be meeting tomorrow, and he can provide me with direction on the project."

"Yes, I suppose he can. Well, I will be on holiday for three weeks. Tell Frank to text me if he needs my help, although I will be out of range for much of that time."

"I'll pass on your message," she promised.

Bernard disconnected the call. He hoped that Jeannie could untangle the data issues. He opened his computer, placed a vacation message on his email, and went back to his wife's flowerbeds.

Chapter 12

After unlocking the door to her hotel room, Jeannie kicked off her pumps, grabbed a bottle of water, and sat at the desk. When she checked her phone for messages, she discovered her mailbox was full. All but one call originated in North Carolina, and she recognized Beatrix Bach as the long-distance caller. The state governor had left two messages. The remaining calls were from people identifying themselves as reporters.

The first call Jeannie made was to Governor Murrell. "Sir, this is Jeannie Johal. I'm sorry, I must have put my phone in airplane mode when I boarded the plane and forgot to turn it back on. I just saw your messages."

His gravelly voice made her think of a Western movie she'd watched about an old-time cowboy who'd spent his day rounding up cattle. "Dr. Johal, I wanted to personally thank you for saving my son's life. If it weren't for your quick actions, I don't know what would have happened."

"Governor, I'm glad your son is better."

Jeannie was surprised when the governor pressed her for more information. "It was the darndest thing. He said he was eating a chunk of cheese when his throat began to tingle. Do you think a chunk of cheese could have caused his reaction?"

She wasn't about to provide medical information without having all the facts, even if he was the governor. Instead, she deflected the question. "I told him to see an allergist, who would try to help him pinpoint the cause."

The governor cleared his throat. "Of course, he's the patient and I'm the father who worries about his son. I can understand how you wouldn't want to discuss your patient's condition without his authorization."

"I'm glad I was able to help your son."

"I understand you're working in Greenville on a research project?" asked the governor.

"Yes, I was invited to lend a hand to look over some data. I'll be here for a month."

"I was talking to Bernard Bigelow about the project. Although Greenville is a small city, it punches well above its weight when it comes to medical research. The study that Dr. Dunn headed has the potential to save millions of lives and even more dollars. It's hard for me to wrap my mind around the idea that Dr. Dunn is dead. It's always a tragedy when a life is cut short, but it's particularly sad when the person who passes is someone who has devoted her whole life to improving care for others."

Jeannie marveled over how well-informed the governor appeared to be. "Although I only met Dr. Dunn the one time – this morning – her commitment to her research impressed me. I was looking forward to working with her. I'm not sure what will happen now."

"Don't make any rash decisions. Bernard and I were discussing the research study, and he thinks that you will provide valuable expertise to the team. I concur, given the leadership you displayed on that flight."

"Governor Murrell, that's kind of you to say, but I haven't even met the team members."

The governor chuckled. "Willa Wooten told me you were a young whippersnapper who prefers to stay out of the spotlight."

"I beg your pardon?"

"Your seatmate."

"Of course."

"When Willa saw me getting out of the car to help my son with his bags, she waved me down and told me about your heroics. She showed me your photo and a video she'd taken, and called you a hero. She sure is skilled at public relations. She's been on local television channels, talking about how a stranger from Canada flew all the way to Greenville, North Carolina, and saved the governor's son during an inflight medical emergency."

"Ah, that explains why I have calls from reporters."

"The story's gone viral, likely because it has a feel-good ending. I hear that the national channels have picked it up."

"We could all use more stories with a happy ending," agreed Jeannie.

"So true. My dear, it's been a pleasure speaking with you. Here is my personal phone number. Please let me know if there is ever anything I can do for you. My son and I are indebted to you, and we Murrells always pay off our debts."

Jeannie looked thoughtfully at her phone. While she felt honored that the Governor of North Carolina had contacted her to relay his appreciation, she was conflicted about being part of a national news story. She had made it clear to Willa that she didn't like being photographed. Jeannie wondered why Willa would appear on television and talk about the incident on the plane. Still, there was nothing Jeannie could do about it. She knew that the story would die down when another, bigger story appeared on the news cycle.

A moment later, her phone rang. Before she could say hello, Beatrix Bach launched into a torrent. "You've been there less than twenty-four hours, and already you're attracting media attention! When I sent you down to Greenville, I was hoping you'd focus on the data, identify what was wrong with it, and make the corrections. I was hoping your presence would be low key, barely noticed. Now you're being portrayed as the heroic doctor who flies across the continent and saves the governor's son!"

"His son was having a severe allergic reaction to an unknown substance. I couldn't let him die."

"Of course not. But did you have to make such a hullaballoo?"

Jeannie sighed. "My seatmate was a very chatty woman who insisted on taking a photo of me with her. She said she takes photos at every opportunity and wanted to show her friends she'd met a real-life hero, as she put it. As you can imagine, I wasn't thrilled about it, but it seemed harmless enough. I didn't know she videotaped it and I didn't know she ran up to the governor when she saw him at the airport. If it had been up to me, there'd be no photos and no one would know about my actions on the plane."

"Well, if the media get hold of you and ask what you're doing in North Carolina, don't give them any fodder they can sink their teeth into."

From the gist of the conversation, Jeannie had the impression that Dr. Bach did not know that her friend had been killed. Jeannie summoned up the courage to tell her, knowing that she might be summoned back to British Columbia immediately. "When I went to the County public-health office this morning, I witnessed a loud altercation between Dr. Dunn and her project manager. It seems she only told him this morning that she was bringing me in to review the data. He sounded incensed and stormed off."

"That's not a good introduction to the research project."

Jeannie knew she had to tell Dr. Bach about her friend, but felt very uncomfortable doing so. "No, it was not. Dr. Dunn reviewed the project with me and then went to meet Bernard Bigelow, her boss. I went out for lunch shortly after she returned to the office. She pointed out a place called the Arboretum that has beautiful trees and flowers. She called it 'paradise.' I ate my lunch there, sitting on a picnic bench and surrounded by aromatic herbs."

"Why are you telling me about trees and flowers? I'm not a botanist and I could care less where you ate your lunch."

"Yes, I am having trouble getting to the point."

"Spit it out, girl. This international call is costing the health authority money."

The words flew from Jeannie's mouth in a torrent. "Dr. Dunn's face was sweaty when she came back from her meeting. I asked her if she felt okay. She said she was a little hot."

Dr. Bach's voice exuded concern for her friend. "I hope it was nothing?"

"Dr. Bach, I'm sorry to tell you that Dr. Dunn was found dead this afternoon. It appears she was poisoned."

Jeannie could hear the sharp intake of breath on the other end of the call.

"Of course, they'll have to do an autopsy."

"Yes, I met the coroner."

"What can you tell me?"

"Dr. Dunn called 911 but couldn't complete the call. The police came, and they insisted I go with them in their squad car. I was really worried for a while because one of them seemed very stern, but the police captain came out of his office as I walked in. He shook my hand and told the detectives I was a hero. As soon as he said that, the detectives became much politer."

"Four years in Iraq and Afghanistan, shells landing all around us, and we both escaped unscathed. She was my best friend. Poor, poor Norma. This shouldn't have happened!"

"I'm so sorry for your loss, Dr. Bach. In the circumstances, would you like me to return to British Columbia tomorrow? I don't see how the study can go forward without Dr. Dunn's leadership."

The sorrow Jeannie heard in Dr. Bach's voice was replaced by her familiar steely resolve. "You'll do no such thing. You're going to be needed now more than ever. I'll contact Dr. Dunn's supervisor and arrange for you to continue to work in Greenville. Let me know when the funeral arrangements have been made and I will book a flight to North Carolina. In the meantime, review the data and find out who killed my best friend."

Day Three

Chapter 13

The Pitt County Detention Center groups together prisoners based on crimes committed, current risk assessment, and behavior. The center was built in 1993 to hold 596 inmates, and like many correctional facilities, is overcrowded.

Detectives Harmony Harris and Henry Smith stepped into the aging detention center, the heavy metal doors clanging behind them. They politely exchanged nods with the guards at the entrance, knowing they were outsiders, intruders with the task of leading a murder investigation that seemed straightforward, yet was anything but.

Deputy Sheriff Longfellow accompanied them. Their first stop was the recreation yard. It had a basketball hoop with a frayed net and a worn picnic table. They could feel dozens of eyes staring at them, daring the detectives to ask questions.

The deputy sheriff pointed to the picnic table. "Big Boy was sitting at the table, holding court with his gang of followers. He was leaning against a wall, by all accounts minding his own business. Suddenly, Big Boy stood up and planted himself in front of Johnson. I don't know what he said, but Johnson responded verbally. Big Boy pushed his thumb against Johnson's chest and muttered more words. Johnson stabbed Big Boy in the face with his plastic fork. It didn't do much damage, but Big Boy looked enraged. A guard intervened by separating them. He must have thought he had the situation under control because he didn't file a report. Instead, he allowed both men to get in line to return to their cells."

The narrator continued. "Much to our surprise, one of the other prisoners attacked Big Boy with a wooden shiv just before Big Boy arrived at his cell."

"Was it Johnson who attacked Big Boy with a shiv?" asked Henry.

"No, Johnson was way back in the line and wouldn't have seen the altercation. But we're confident he had something to do with it."

"How do you know that?" said Harmony.

"Well, it stands to reason. He was witnessed having words with Big Boy and minutes later, Big Boy got killed. It doesn't take a genius to see the connection."

The deputy sheriff's response didn't satisfy Harmony. "Does Johnson know the person who killed Big Boy?" she asked pointedly.

The deputy sheriff shrugged. "What does it even matter? They're all thugs and ne'er do wells."

Catching the expression on his partner's face, Henry jumped in with his own question. "In your esteemed view, do you think prisoners can be rehabilitated and released back into society without posing a threat?"

"It's what we say," said the deputy sheriff. "It would be nice if that were the norm, but it's rare."

"What about Johnson?"

"What about him? He's a small-time loser who's just graduated to the big leagues."

"I still don't understand why he would be complicit in murdering Big Boy."

"Ask him yourself. I won't stand in your way. The sooner you finish your investigation, the better. I'll arrange for the guard to take you to the interview room and you can talk to Johnson directly." The deputy sheriff clicked his heels and tapped the sides of his regulation boots together.

Harmony sniffed as she and her partner walked into the small, dark interviewing room. The room was hot and dusty. It was windowless, except for a one-way mirror allowing observers to watch as suspects were grilled. The room smelled of sweat and despair. Either there was no air conditioning or it wasn't working. The inmate whose hands were shackled and cuffed to the table hung his head down, not even looking up when he heard footsteps.

"Well, who do we have here," said Harmony. She banged her hand on the table to get the inmate's attention.

He looked up, began to say something, and stopped.

Harmony's expression changed and she spoke softly. "Nathan John-son. I forgot your last name was Johnson. You've always been 'Nathan' to me. It's been a long time, a lifetime since we were in school together. I remember you playing basketball. You had a gift. I thought you were going to hit it big, get into the NBA, show everyone what you were made of. What happened to you?"

He looked up at her and remained mute.

Henry decided to jump into the conversation. He read from the inmate's file. "Let's see. Johnson Nathaniel Johnson. Age 31. Born in Kinston. It says here you have arrests for petty theft, drug possession, and fraud."

Henry made a point of counting off the arrests with his hands. "Eight arrests since high school. Why did you attack Big Boy in the recreation area?"

Johnson did not answer.

Harmony used the name she called him when they were kids. "C'mon, Nathan, you can tell me. You and my brother were classmates together. Don't you remember me," she said.

Johnson slowly raised his head and nodded. "You was taller than the other girls. The only thing bigger was that big mouth of yours, always getting you into trouble."

"I was a bit of a hell-raiser," she admitted.

"And now you're the law and I'm the one in prison."

"My brother never got over the shame of being stopped, strip-searched, and thrown in jail. I joined the police to change how Blacks are treated. My brother found solace in fentanyl, and has been in and out of rehab ever since," she explained.

"Aw, I didn't know. I was signed to a contract with the NBA G League a year before I finished high school. I played with the Greensboro Swarm for two years. I never got called up to the big league, and my contract was terminated when I injured my knee during a game. I worked in construction in Fayetteville, as a handyman in Bladenboro, and as an assistant to a man running fishing charters in New Bern, but it's been difficult because some of the places I worked and travelled to were sundown towns. It's been real hard just trying to survive."

Harmony nodded sympathetically. "I decided I would try to change things from the inside. That's why I became a police officer."

"Has that worked for you," said Nathan.

"Well, you tell me. I'm a detective in Greenville and here I am. I have a good job. I keep people safe and I get to put the bad guys in jail. What I'd really like to know is if you're a good guy who was in the wrong place at the wrong time or if you're a bad guy who should be locked up. You can start by telling me why the deputy sheriff thinks you committed a murder."

"I jabbed Big Boy with my fork. I shouldn't have done it, but the things he was saying! I couldn't stop myself. He had no right to say those things about my baby sister. He doesn't know shit."

"They weren't talking about your mother? That's what we heard," said Harmony.

"Naw, he called my sister names that should never come out of anyone's mouth."

"How is Susie?" asked Harmony.

"She's doing well. She lives in Atlanta. She's a makeup artist for a reality show."

"What about the shiv? Did you arrange for Big Boy to be attacked? The deputy sheriff sure thinks so."

"He knows squat. I made a big mistake reacting to Big Boy. I should have tuned him out. But I did not ask anyone to hurt him."

"Do you know who did it?"

Johnson nodded. "Everyone does. Now that Big Boy is out of the picture, The Proud Patriots are going to take over."

"Take over? Isn't the sheriff in command?"

Johnson cringed. "Big Boy's been a dealer for a long time. He used the computers in the library to arrange for orders to be shipped across the country."

"Why did he get killed?"

Johnson looked down and began to speak quietly, as if to himself. He rocked himself, bobbing up and down. "I had a fight with Big Boy. They killed him. They's gonna think I owe them. It's only a matter of time. If I don't give them what they want, I'm a dead man. You've got to help me get out of here."

As a rookie, Henry's naïve idealism had made it easy for criminals to fool him. He wasn't so innocent now. He'd also come to realize the value of looking at a situation from multiple perspectives. His black-and-white world of certainty vanished during an investigation to find a child who had been kidnapped. Although a pedophile had been arrested for producing and selling child pornography, the prosecuting district attorney had been forced to offer a plea bargain in order to find out where the kidnapped child was being hidden. They had to make a pact with the devil to save the child's life.

With more than twenty-five years' experience on the job, Henry had seen and heard many stories. Now, Henry looked dispassionately at the tearful prisoner. "I can't count on my hands how many times a prisoner has asked me to help get him away from a situation. But in order for me to do that, you have to give me something."

Johnson raised his hand and used his fists to wipe the tears from his eyes. "I got nothing, not even a vehicle. That's why I'm here. What could I give you that you don't have?" He began to cry again.

A tic flared under Harmony's right eye. "Johnson, how could you let yourself get in this situation? You had so much potential on the court. What happened to you?"

"I already told you. I injured my knee during a game. They didn't send me for rehab. Instead, they dumped me as if I were a bushel of collard greens turned slimy and spoiled."

"Eight crimes in eight years. Why couldn't you have called me? I would have tried to help," said Harmony.

Johnson summoned up his slight reserves of dignity. "You and your family were nice to me when we were kids. I couldn't let you see how far I'd fallen. I couldn't let anyone from my old life see me like this. Besides, what would you have done? Taken me in and then arrested me for stealing your valuables? No, keeping my distance was the only good decision I've made in the past ten years."

"Well, Johnson, I'm inclined to agree with my partner. Give us a reason why we should help you."

Johnson tried to raise his hand in supplication, but the handcuffs, attached to a mount on the table, prevented the action. He turned to Harmony. "I got no one else to turn to. For old time's sake, can't you help me?"

Harmony had reached her limit. "Stop your sniveling. Man up. Tell us why they killed Big Boy for you."

"That's not it," he insisted.

"Then what is it? Spit it out. We have a murder investigation to solve in here and another one down the road. Stop wasting our time." As soon as the words came out, Harmony realized she'd made a mistake. She could see Johnson's eyes pop open, then narrow.

His eyes shuttered and he gave a slight nod. When he reopened his eyes, Harmony could see they were looking at her with cunning. "I had nothing to do with Big Boy's murder. I've done everything I can to avoid being recruited into a gang. I can tell you the word on the grapevine is that there was a problem with a slowdown at a production facility that supplies much of the Carolinas."

"What problem?" asked Harmony.

"It had something to do with the lab."

Harmony probed for more information. "In North Carolina?"

"Will you get me out of here if I tell you the location?" asked Johnson.

On a hunch, Harmony asked Johnson a direct question. "Do you know the location?"

"No, but I could ask around and find out."

Harmony and Henry looked at each other. Identifying the whereabouts of an illegal drug production facility and shutting it down could lead to special commendations. Most important, it would shut down the supply of street drugs available to local kids, at least for a while. But relocating Johnson to another prison immediately would mean he'd never find out the facility's location. While the two detectives knew they didn't have the power to make a deal with Johnson, he didn't know that.

Henry leaned forward and looked directly at Johnson. "Find out the location for us and we'll look into getting you transferred."

"Hell! If your information results in an opioid production facility being shut down, the state might even drop the charges against you and let you walk out of here a free man," said Harmony.

"If anyone here finds out I'm working for you, I'm a dead man. I won't be walking out of here. They'll take me in a body bag," said Johnson.

"We could ask the district attorney to relocate you. You could get a fresh new start, far away from here," suggested Harmony.

Johnson nodded. "That might work. Where it's warm and dry, and I won't have to look over my shoulder every time I turn around."

"We'll see what we can do. Johnson, I'd like to see you get the chance for a new beginning. In the meantime, keep your eyes peeled and your ears open. Let us know when you find the lab location."

Satisfied that they'd got all the information Johnson had, Henry and Harmony stood up. Henry rapped the door. When the guard unlocked it, Henry turned to Johnson. "You're just a petty thief who's risen above his pay grade. When we get the evidence to connect you to Big Boy's murder, we'll be back to arrest you," he said in a voice loud enough to be overheard.

Johnson's expression looked panicked because he couldn't believe the detective had turned so quickly on him. Harmony quickly and gently turned to him and leaned in. "It'll be okay. If you help us, we'll help you."

He sighed in relief. After everything he had done, he could tell that Harmony still cared about him. He vowed to do everything in his power to find out the location of the lab, no matter the cost to him. He'd prove once and for all to Harmony that her belief in him was justified.

He returned to his cell, seeing prisoners' faces pressed against the bars of their cells. "Murderer!" cried one prisoner. The guard pushed Johnson into his cell. "We know you arranged for Big Boy to be taken out. If you think your conditions are bad now, just wait until you're a convicted murderer."

Chapter 14

Frank Wright, a veteran of ten years of duty in some of the toughest, most hostile spots in the world, knew that his call to the County director, Bernard Bigelow, was nowhere near as daunting as serving as a Marine in Africa. In his work providing logistical support to ships off the coast of Somalia, Frank had to negotiate with ship captains, cajole equipment manufacturers, sweet talk suppliers, and occasionally pay small sums to customs offers to ensure that supplies, equipment, and personnel were protected from piracy threats.

After leaving the Marine Corp with a Medal of Honor, an honorable discharge, and invaluable training in logistics, Frank put his acquired knowledge to good use. The young man from Stedman, North Carolina, population 1,100, became a project manager in his adopted home of Fayetteville, married, and had a daughter. Life was good until his daughter became ill.

Dr. Dunn's research project provided Frank with the opportunity to make some sense of his daughter's death. He and his wife left behind friends and family, relocating to Clayton, a suburb of Raleigh, a culturally diverse and prosperous urban center so different from his tiny hometown. Once a month, he and Darla returned to Fayetteville so that she, a card-carrying member of the local chapter of Moms for Liberty, could get together with her like-minded friends.

As the project manager for Dr. Dunn's study, Frank developed the overarching plan for the project, outlined its objectives and scope, set a budget and deadlines, hired staff, and ran operations on a daily basis.

Frank knew he had to make the call to Bernard Bigelow, but he still hesitated. Frank's knowledge of the County director was obtained through the biased lens of Dr. Dunn, who did not like Bernard, but tried to maintain a civil relationship with him because he was her boss and had the authority to shut down her research project if it didn't align with his goals.

The former Marine looked in the mirror at his reflection. Tall, trim but with the start of a belly, short-cropped hair, weathered skin that had seen more than its share of the sun. A lined face that suggested covert experiences. *You're a Marine. Semper Fi. Always Faithful. Loyal to the cause. Don't let Dr. Dunn's prejudice blind you. Bernard is your new boss. Give him the benefit of the doubt.*

He understood the importance of the call. The meeting could be a turning point in deciding whether the project went forward or was shut down. With a sense of purpose, he dialed the County planner's cell. "Director Bigelow, recent events at the Pitt County Health Center have been tragic."

"Yes, a tragedy. The sheriff informed me of Dr. Dunn's grievous and untimely end."

Frank continued, "Dr. Dunn was my boss and though she was small in stature, she was a force to be reckoned with, passionate about improving the health of the residents of Pitt County."

"She sure was," said Bernard.

"My call is to provide you with an overview of the semaglutide study and give you a progress report."

"I'm glad to hear that, Frank. Dr. Dunn was an excellent physician, but she had difficulty explaining complex concepts to regular people like me. I'm hoping you can do better."

Frank was taken aback by Bernard's lukewarm endorsement of Dr. Dunn but tried not to show his surprise in his voice. "Well, then, I'll begin with the project overview. It's well-known that obesity is a national epidemic, especially among middle-aged women. Obese women are at higher risk of developing Type 2 Diabetes, heart disease, high blood pressure, and stroke. Some cancers have been linked to obesity in women."

Bernard interrupted him. "Tell me something I don't know. For instance, are women more likely to become obese and diabetic because they spend their days baking and eating sweets? Or because they indulge themselves when pregnant and then can't lose the extra weight after the baby's arrival? Or are they just less active than men?"

His words made Frank think that what Dr. Dunn had said was spot on. *Bernard Bigelow is really narrow-minded. I wonder how she responded when Bernard talked about women eating too much or not exercising enough. I would have loved to be a fly on the wall for that conversation! I'm lucky that she dealt with sponsors and the politicos. I'd have trouble remaining polite in the face of such ignorance. Good thing she let me focus on the project itself.*

As a Marine, he'd learned how to compartmentalize. He ignored his misgivings and responded to Bernard. "There are a host of reasons. Women undergo hormonal changes in middle age that lead to weight gain and increase their risk of Type 2 Diabetes. Women prepare most meals for a family, and some nibble while getting food ready to serve to their husband and children. Many women put their children and husbands first. Taking care of their own health only becomes a priority when there is a problem."

"So you're saying most women have no willpower? All they want is instant self-gratification and they don't care if they get so fat that they look like buttered-up pigs ready for slaughter?"

Frank winced. Dr. Dunn had never so much as hinted that Bernard was a self-opinionated government employee with a low opinion of women. "Actually, most overweight women have tremendous willpower, but their willpower is no match for the messages firing in their brains."

"My wife Becky was a size 4 when I married her. She's still a size 4. Now I know Becky is special, but still, what's with women who let themselves go?"

Frank chose to disregard the general message. "Your wife is indeed special and it's possible she has genes that protect her from being overweight."

He soldiered on, aware that the man on the other end of the line wasn't for a moment accepting his words. "I'm saying there are many factors that contribute to obesity. Greenville itself has proportionately more fried and barbecued chicken fast-food restaurants than anywhere else in America. That doesn't help."

Bernard chimed in. "I like B's Barbecue as much as everyone else. But I don't like the lineups. The Starlight Inn in Ayden makes a mean pulled-pork sandwich, and Moore's makes fine barbecued chicken. Then there's Sam Jones on E Firetower. So what if we have lots of places that serve barbecue and fried food? We're in the South, after all."

"Yes, sir, that is true. Dr. Dunn secured a five-million dollar grant to do an intensive study of six hundred women with or at risk for Type II diabetes in Pitt County, which has a high rate of obesity in its general population. The study is jointly funded by Pitt County, the National Institutes of Health, and WellStar Pharmaceuticals. The study provides participants with weekly injections of semaglutides, nutrition information given by a dietician through weekly one-on-one sessions, and access to a physiotherapist or personal trainer. Participants are given money to purchase the recommended foods, and also given transportation vouchers when they don't have a vehicle to bring them to appointments. Their vitals are checked every week."

"That sounds like a lot of 'giving' to me. Whatever happened to hauling oneself up by one's bootstraps?"

"Well, the participants are expected to learn and apply the tools and resources they are given. The thinking is that this kind of intensive support should help them shed pounds, lower their A1C levels and health risks, while paving the way for a healthy future."

"Dr. Dunn was talking about this project years ago, long before she got the funding. How are participants doing?"

"The results are encouraging. Every single participant has lost at least ten percent of their total body weight since enrolling in this study. The study will run for a year, and we're now in the seventh month. The amount of weight lost is statistically significant and will reduce participants' needs for medications and lower their risk of cardiovascular disease."

"That sounds promising, but I don't understand why a big pharmaceutical would support this study. Wouldn't they be worried about people no longer needing their drugs?"

"It's a good question, sir. There are millions of obese people in America and around the world. Having an effective treatment will net Well-Star Pharmaceuticals millions of dollars in profits. I think two of the findings are particularly exciting."

"What are those?"

"Well, twenty percent of the participants are not receiving semaglutides. Of course, they don't know that. But the members of this group have also lost at least ten percent of their body weight. The other interventions may be responsible. Wouldn't it be amazing if low-tech interventions such as structured, supervised regular exercise, meals designed by a dietician, and money to buy groceries and cover transportation had such an impact? From a public-health perspective, these findings could be applied to all of us."

"Are there any other differences between those receiving semaglutides and the control group?"

Frank was very careful to parse his words because recent lab results showed mixed results, and he wanted to know the reason for these results before sharing them. "A1C levels – a marker for Type II Diabetes – have been going up in some participants in both groups, even though their weight is going down. This is something we are investigating now."

"I appreciate your candor, Frank. You've provided me with more information in one meeting than Dr. Dunn provided over the past year. You're an excellent project manager, and I want you to take on a larger role now that Dr. Dunn is no longer here. What do you say? Are you willing to head up the project?"

"Sure thing, I'd be honored to carry on Dr. Dunn's work," he said.

"There's one more thing," said Bernard. "There's the matter of the girl that Dr. Dunn invited to look over the data."

"Dr. Johal, from Canada."

"Yes, it seems she's made an extremely favorable impression with the governor, who wants her to stay on with the project."

"Director, I agree with the governor. Dr. Johal and I met and we are scheduled to review the data tomorrow."

"Just be sure you supervise her closely. We wouldn't want an outsider messing up our data."

Frank was glad that the County director could not see his facial expression. Frank was also relieved that the director did not know that the data was already mixed up. "I'll do my best, sir."

"You're a good man."

There was a pause lasting so long that Frank wondered if the director had disconnected the call.

Then the director resumed the conversation. "I just informed my wife about Dr. Dunn's passing. She sends her condolences. I think she's worried I'm going to postpone our trip. Becky planned this cruise a long time ago. We're boarding a ship that will take us around the Caribbean and to South America. We'll even pass through the Panama Canal. I don't have the heart to tell her that we need to cancel the trip. She had her hair done today, had a mani-pedi yesterday. Her bags are packed and she's rarin' to get on the boat. I can't let her down. This conversation reassures me the research project is in good hands. Call me if you need anything. I'll see you in my office in three weeks." With that, the director pressed the end-call button.

Frank breathed a sigh of relief. He was thankful that he'd called the County director. Mostly, though, Frank was thankful that the director didn't seem to be aware that there were big problems with the data. Frank vowed to get to the heart of the problem and find a solution before the director's return.

Chapter 15

La Donna Rogers was watching *Real Wives of Nashville* when the phone ring alerted her to a call from Uncle Bernard. Although sorely tempted to ignore his call, she knew he would keep calling if she didn't take it.

Hitting the 'on' switch, she feigned enthusiasm. "Uncle Bernie, getting two calls from you in one evening is like winning the lottery. Is there something wrong?"

"Other than your boss being murdered and the project manager walking out of the office to protest the hiring of someone from Canada, no."

"There is that," she said, while filing her fingernails and watching the reality show.

"Young lady, I can hear the sound of you using a file on your fingernails. And the television is blaring. Can you give me your full attention?"

She grinned and laughed. "Sure thing, Uncle Bernie. You know me too well."

He shifted gears. "I've never seen a dead body. It must have been a horrible experience. How are you feeling?"

"I was out for lunch when Dr. Dunn passed. When I came back, the police prevented me from entering the building, so I went to the mall."

"Oh, well, I'm glad to hear you didn't have to see her like that."

"I am, too, although the description I heard was very dramatic, so odd you couldn't make it up."

"What do you mean?"

La Donna took a long swig of her energy drink. "Well, I heard that Dr. Dunn is the person who called in her death."

Bernard bellowed at his niece. "How's that possible? Stop embellishing."

"No, Uncle, I heard that Dr. Dunn called 911 and was reporting that she'd been poisoned as the poison was taking effect. I heard that she collapsed onto the floor while making the call."

"That sounds horrible. The poor doctor."

"While she was a mean –."

He interrupted her. "Don't speak ill of the dead like that. She was your boss."

"Only because you arranged for her to give me a job. She never let me forget it."

"She could be a handful to manage. Sweet as pie one moment, but tough as nails if she disagreed with you. Well, now, I have a favor to ask of you."

"Yes, Uncle Bernie, anything."

Only her uncle's intervention had made it possible for La Donna to avoid working in the family's tanning salon after being sacked from her third job in seven months.

"Frank Wright is going to be your new boss. I've asked him to take on additional responsibilities."

She perked up. "That's an excellent choice, Uncle Bernie. Frank's a great guy, always says hello. And on Mondays, he brings coffee and donuts into the office."

"I can't tell you how many times Dr. Dunn complained that you spent most of your time smoking by the building entrance or sitting at your desk filing your fingernails."

"Oh, Uncle Bernie, I haven't had a cigarette in more than three months." She didn't tell him that she was now inhaling cotton-candy-flavored vapes.

"I'm glad to hear that. You know, La Donna, it's still not too late for you to enroll in a professional program at the college."

"I know, but I'm not interested."

"Well, work hard so that you can save your money. You could buy a car for yourself."

"I know you're joking. I'm happy with the Kia Sportage you gave me for my eighteenth birthday."

"Yes, but isn't there something you would like to do, someplace you would like to go?"

"Will and I have been to Myrtle Beach. We love drinking at the bars on the Boardwalk and watching the tourists with their sunburnt faces walking up and down the strip."

"You don't want to go anywhere else?"

"Well, we've been to Kitty Hawk to see the Wright Brothers Memorial and we enjoyed staying at your place on Emerald Isle. Will has talked about us going to Universal World in Orlando. It'd be cool to go on some of the rides and try out the restaurants. We'll probably take in Disney World as well when we go. But that won't be till next year because Will doesn't get many vacation days where he works."

Uncle Bernie let out a heavy, drawn-out sigh. "If that's what you want."

La Donna didn't understand why her uncle regularly asked her what she would like to do and where she would like to visit. Greenville was perfect for her. She had her own basement bedroom and ensuite at home. Her parents had a pool and hot tub. She could come and go as she pleased, driving the car that Uncle Bernie gave her. A monthly allowance from her parents covered her hairstyling costs, as well as a

manicure and pedicure every month. They also paid for her membership at the local country club. Her salary paid for her gym membership,
as well as her clothes. Will paid for her drinks at TJ's, her favorite bar,
and he sometimes let her buy him a craft beer at Christy's Europub.
She'd offered to pay the time they went to the Starlight Café, but he'd
said it was the man's job to support his woman. She didn't disagree.

"One other thing. Give the new person all the help you can."

"You mentioned that earlier, Uncle."

"Child, promise me that you'll be careful. Becky and I leave tomorrow on our cruise. Your mom and dad will be joining us. I want you
to call if you notice anything out of the usual at work. I want you to
be my eyes and ears. Get Dr. Dunn's daytimer and bring it home with
you so that I can look through it when I'm back. Find out why Dr.
Dunn hired someone from the outside to work on the research project.
Something's going on and I need to find out what it is."

"You want me to spy on Frank and the new person?"

"Aw, La Donna, I wouldn't put it like that. Ask questions. Get to
learn more about what they're doing. And above all else, be careful.
There's a murderer on the loose in the community and I don't want my
only niece to come to harm."

"Uncle Bernie, I'll be okay."

"Just promise."

"I promise," she said.

La Donna's mind was brimming with possibilities following the
phone call. While the police had sealed the office building, La Donna
felt that Uncle Bernie's request gave her the authority needed to enter
the building. She had long resisted the temptation to peek through Dr.
Dunn's personal belongings, but if this is what Uncle Bernie wanted
her to do, who was she to resist? After all, he was Dr. Dunn's supervisor.

She looked forward to finding her supervisor's daytimer to see what was so confidential that she kept it locked in her desk when not on her person.

Day Four

Chapter 16

As they walked into the Pitt County Agricultural Center, Henry stopped to admire the blossoms in two large, round containers. He leaned in to smell the mauve-colored blooms on an herb, and for a moment, his hard features softened.

Harmony smiled at her partner. "Do the plants remind you of your Daddy's farm?"

He nodded. "Momma grew a patch of lavender near the back door. This takes me back to that time."

Although the entrance to the building was open, the door leading to the offices was locked. Harmony applauded the security measure, but Henry objected.

"How are they going to serve the community when the community can't even ask questions to the people who work here," he grumbled. He pushed the call button. The office assistant walked towards him. She unlocked the door, greeted the visitors, and returned to her office. Harmony had to tug on Henry's shirt sleeve when he stopped to read the information sheets lining the wall. The information covered a myriad of topics on growing crops in Eastern North Carolina.

The arboretum director greeted the two detectives as they entered the Horticulture/Arboretum wing. Isaiah Isherwood was a small, wiry man with gelled-back curly black hair. He was dressed in a solid blue polo shirt and chinos. His face was ruddy from years of exposure to the sun. He held out a calloused hand. "Welcome to the Agricultural Center. I am the Pitt County Extension Horticulture Agent, as well as Director of the Arboretum."

He guided his guests into his office and gestured for them to sit. "Terrible business what happened next door at the public-health building," he said.

They nodded in agreement.

"Have you found the killer yet?"

Henry's heart sank. Here he was, at an arboretum whose gardeners coaxed so many plants to grow. Yet the director's question about the death of his colleague overshadowed the gardens' wonders. Henry looked at his partner, who gave an almost imperceptible shake of her head.

"No, sir, we are investigating the crime."

"Got any leads?"

"Yessir," said Henry, without elaborating further.

The director switched topics. "I've known Dr. Dunn since she was a family physician."

"Oh? I didn't know she had a general practice before leading the public-health department."

"Yes, after she received her honorable discharge, she settled in Greenville and opened up a practice. My wife and I were among her first patients. She soon discovered that she preferred to work in public health."

Henry filed this information in the back of his mind. Before he could process the possible ramifications, Isaiah's question brought him back to the present.

"I trust the arboretum is not a suspect?" Isaiah laughed at his own joke.

"Since the arboretum is adjacent to the public-health building and since Dr. Dunn was known to walk in the gardens, we thought it would be helpful to learn more about the facility," said Henry evenly.

"As part of our service to the community, we offer free, guided tours.

You're in luck because one of our most knowledgeable master gardeners is here today. Griselda Grimwade will direct the tour and be happy to answer any of your questions."

"That's an unusual name. Is she from here?" asked Harmony.

"I don't think she was born in America. But she's volunteered with the arboretum since 2002."

"We have a few questions we would like to ask you before we go on the tour," said Harmony.

"Fire away."

"Could you tell us a bit about the arboretum? How big is it? When was it established? Is it run by the City of Greenville or by Pitt County?"

"Good questions. Let me begin by telling you a little bit about myself. I am a horticulture professional and I've been the agent and director here for twenty-two years, since the arboretum was established as an affiliate of the North Carolina State University system by the State General Assembly in 2002.

"I thought the County was responsible for the arboretum," said Harmony.

"Well, it is. The arboretum itself is a seven-acre plot of land that surrounds the Agricultural Center. The County owns the land."

"What's the relationship with NC State University?"

"Many counties in North Carolina have very experienced volunteer gardeners to help with horticulture. These volunteers receive extensive training and certification from NC State Extension, to become extension master gardener volunteers."

"That's a mouthful," commented Harmony.

The director resumed his overview. "The master gardeners conceptualize, maintain, and improve the gardens. They also help educate the public by demonstrating plants that can be grown here, and landscapes people can design for their homes. The master gardeners staff an Info-Line to answer gardening and landscaping questions. They offer workshops, invite well-known guest speakers to give presentations, have an informative website, and a presence on social media. While the County provides some financial support, funds for the gardens come from annual sales and fundraisers organized by the master gardeners. We also get some grants and donations."

"That's a lot of free labor!"

"Master gardeners are passionate about gardening. Until recently, almost all of our members were retired, giving them the latitude to volunteer for as many hours as they like."

Harmony quipped. "I picture a master gardener as a trim, spry older woman who wears long white gloves and a sun hat, and snips flowers to put in vases."

Henry glared at his partner. "Wherever do you get your ideas? Gardens take a lot of work to design and maintain."

The director laughed. "There's a degree of truth in stereotypes. But white gloves would be impractical. Some of our members wear long light sleeves to protect their arms from the sun. Others wear long, sturdy gloves to protect their hands from thorns. Almost all wear hats to protect their heads. Hold on to your image. Wait until you meet Griselda."

Harmony laughed. "I've never given much thought to what goes into creating a nice garden. I admire them when I see them, but I'm not the kind of woman who sits in a chaise with a book and a mint julep, admiring the nearby roses."

"For every woman who does what you describe, there are a hundred others who get their hands dirty by digging up weeds, spreading bags of soil, planting and watering seeds," said Henry.

"Well, I can see myself sitting in a lawn chair in the shallow end of my swimming pool, downing Duck-Rabbit Milk Stout and bon bons after a long day of gardening."

"Except you live on the ground floor of an apartment building and don't have a pool," he scoffed.

"I can dream," she said loftily.

"I like your vision," said the director. He looked from one detective to the other. "How long have you worked together? You sound like a married couple."

While Henry's response was to smile, Harmony looked shocked.

"You'll have the opportunity to make your own impression of what our master gardeners do when Griselda shows you around the gardens. But before that, a bit about what I do.

"My role is to oversee the arboretum, educate and engage the community to appreciate and protect plant diversity and the environment. Our motto is 'gardening that you can do.' We serve the local community by showing people the range of plants that are appropriate for the county – plants they can grow and landscapes they can design."

He noticed Harmony trying to stifle a yawn. "I can see you're eager to experience the gardens. Let's go. Griselda is waiting for us under the green canopy."

Harmony expected she would find the tour boring, if it was anything like the organized tours she'd taken as a high-school student. Little did she know that the tour would unveil a potential suspect. She'd have been even more surprised if anyone had told her that the poison might be identifiable as coming from a plant cultivated by a master gardener in the arboretum.

Chapter 17

From a distance, the woman under the green canopy appeared to have the body of a child. She was tiny and waiflike. Her clothes were so uncoordinated and loose-fitting that they could have come from a new-to-you thrift store. A floppy natural-colored straw hat covered her head, providing protection from the hot sun. An elastic loosely corralled her waist-long straight silver hair into a pony tail. She wore a scoop-necked sleeveless floral tank top, a cowl around her neck, and what appeared to be arm socks that stretched from her wrists to her shoulders. Cropped orange pants were tucked into rubber calf-high garden boots festooned with white daisies against a pink background.

Despite her eccentric attire, Griselda Grimwade exuded an air of quiet authority. She rubbed her hands on her pants and extended one furled fist to each detective. They exchanged hand bumps.

"Detectives, welcome to the Pitt County Arboretum. In my time, I've given tours to school kids and their parents and teachers. I've taken members of gardening clubs around the garden. But this is the first time I've had the pleasure of giving a tour to detectives. Are you looking to see where we bury bodies?"

"Excuse me?" said Henry.

Griselda cackled. "Just kidding. Ask me anything you want."

Harmony stared at Griselda. "Anything?"

Griselda nodded.

Harmony's eyes lit up as she began to speak. "Your name is uncommon. By chance, are you related to Leonard Grimwade? When I was a young child, my grandma gave me a Royal Winton Grimwade teacup to remember our vacation on the Outer Banks. The teacup had the most beautiful color, an iridescent blue. Every time I look at it, it reminds me of the ocean."

A full-throated laugh escaped Griselda's lips. "Isn't it a small world? I was born in England. Leonard, the founder of the family china company, was my husband's uncle. The pattern you are describing is called 'brocade blue.' They were trying to mimic the inside of a seashell. The way you describe your tea cup makes me think they succeeded."

Henry was speechless. He looked from one woman to the other. "All right, then. Harmony, when you've had your *Antiques Roadshow* moment, can we continue with the tour?"

Griselda raised her hands as if in surrender. "Young man, why the hurry? It's not every day that I meet someone from North Carolina who knows my family's business."

Henry had the grace to look embarrassed. "I'm sorry, ma'am," he said, his eyes downcast.

"Another thing," responded Griselda. "Don't call me 'Ma'am.' That's for older people. I prefer 'Miss.' Your partner is welcome to call me by my first name, Griselda."

Henry's cheeks turned bright red. He was embarrassed that he had tried to cut off the reminiscences of an elderly woman who was volunteering to give him and his partner a tour. At the same time, Harmony's response surprised him because her immediate bonding with Griselda belied her usually distant nature.

Griselda gestured to a map of the grounds located in a display cabinet and frowned. "This map shows where our gardens are located. Well, it's not quite up to date. The vegetable garden is not in the right place and the garden in front of the main entrance has been renamed the 'welcome garden.' "

"From the looks of it, the gardens surround the Agricultural Center. Is that right?"

Griselda nodded. "Yes, Detective, we have many gardens, some larger than others. Take the vegetable garden, for example."

She pursed her lips as if to suppress a bad memory. "The arboretum was closed during the COVID pandemic. We weren't allowed to work up here, even though the gardens are outside. The vegetable garden wasn't able to survive without our help. It's taken a lot of time, but it has irrigation and is now filled with a variety of large containers, making it accessible to people who use walkers or wheelchairs. The seedlings have taken hold, and there will be a nice crop."

She continued. "Like most of our gardens, the vegetable garden is a demonstration garden. That means plants were selected that are appropriate for this setting. They can be grown in your backyard and will provide you with lots of fresh vegetables as long as you follow good gardening practices."

Harmony was disappointed. She'd hoped the arboretum would contain exotic tropical plants selected because they reminded someone of far-away lands.

As if reading the detective's mind, Griselda smiled. "We have a plumeria tree that is replanted every year. It's what Hawaiians use to make leis. It's a beautiful plant with an enticing scent, but can't stand up to our winters, even though they are mild. One of our master gardeners digs it up every October before the first frost, and stores it in his garage. We also have palm trees and beautiful ginger lilies."

"Can we see the plumeria tree?" Harmony was like a kid who's discovered her favorite candy.

"Well, since we're standing under this green canopy, let's start your tour with the butterfly garden. It's hard to tell from here, but there are stepping stones that take the form of a butterfly. If we step back, we can see the shape, although that's not what makes it a butterfly garden."

She pointed out large stands of vivid yellow lantana, lantana with yellow, orange, and pink heads, wide clusters of pink and purple coneflowers, yellow and white bursts of yarrow, the golden petals of blackeyed Susans, tall, green spikes with delicate dark blue flowers. "These are all pollinator plants. Butterflies love them."

"What about native plants? Do you grow those?"

"We do. As master gardeners, we try to show our visitors the range of plants that are appropriate for Eastern North Carolina. Some of these are native plants. Every year, proceeds from our big plant sale in May allow us to add to our plants. Where possible, we try to grow native plants."

She pointed to scraggly stalks. "But we're not always successful. These native milkweed plants were gifted to us by a master gardener. Monarch butterflies need them. But with the drought…," she shrugged her shoulders.

"Can't you water them?" asked Harmony.

Henry sent his partner a warning glance. "Irrigation is expensive, Harmony. My daddy's farm relied on the rain."

Griselda nodded her head in agreement with Harmony. "Wouldn't it be nice to know there is a back-up source of water when there's not enough rain? But your partner is right. We draw water from a cistern. But if it doesn't rain…. Irrigation is expensive, and we can only do so much hand watering."

Harmony gestured at ten clay pots attached to a wall. Each was filled with colorful blooms. "What about the flowers in those pots? Where do they come from?"

"I'm glad you asked. Our gardeners comb through the gardens and select different flowering plants each week that are in bloom. They look for plants from the different gardens."

"You're not worried that someone will take the arrangements?"

Griselda's expression darkened and her body stiffened. She pointed a finger at the two detectives. "I have never seen anyone do that. But there is one person I know of who is a flower thief. I tried to get her banned from the arboretum," she barked.

The anger in her voice shocked Henry. "Who would that be," he asked in a voice as smooth as soft butter.

Griselda hesitated. "Well, I really shouldn't say."

"You can tell us," he said encouragingly.

"I really don't like to speak ill of the dead but I saw that woman from the public health department come over here with scissors and a pail filled with water. I knew she was up to no good and I told her she had no right to cut the flowers. She told me it was a public garden, meant for everyone. I reported her to the director, but he didn't do anything."

"Go on. Tell us how it made you feel, seeing her willfully cutting flowers. Did it make you angry?" asked Henry.

She tried to rein in her emotions. "You have to understand. Many of the plants were donated by master gardeners. We're also the ones who do all the weeding, watering, fertilizing."

"Do you think of it as your garden?" asked Harmony.

Grisela nodded. "Well, it really is. If it weren't for the master gardeners, this would be grass and concrete."

"I can see your point," said Harmony. "If I put all that labor into something, I would feel strongly about it, too."

Henry interjected himself into the conversation. "Did you think Dr. Dunn was stealing your flowers?"

Griselda snapped at him. "Detective, don't mock me. They aren't *my* flowers. They belong to everyone. I've volunteered here as a master gardener since 2002 when this was hard, patchy turf. All of our master gardeners are volunteers and we're proud of what we've achieved. If every visitor removed flowers as if this were their home garden, there would be no blooms left to admire."

"I understand how you feel. My daddy was a farmer. He'd have pointed his shotgun if anyone ever tried to steal his crops," said Henry.

His words seemed to mollify Griselda.

"I'm glad you understand. Let's walk over to the CPP." She pointed away from the building and at what appeared to be walking trails between trees.

"CPP?" asked Harmony.

"Certified Plant Professional. Some of us have this highly coveted designation. It means we can recognize plants by the shape of their leaves, thickness of their stems, color of their blooms. We can also identify a plant by closely examining it in the ground, even if the plant is dormant."

Griselda pursed her lips and shook her head. "Again, I don't want to speak ill of the dead, but the woman who died once told me that CPP was an elitist name that no one but master gardeners would understand. She had no idea what effort we put into the arboretum. She had the temerity to suggest we call the CPP area the 'PWP' for the 'People's Walking Paths.' I always knew she was a communist. That proved it to me. We saw what happened in the United Kingdom when the unions called for a general strike that paralyzed the country and the socialists took over the government. We don't ever want to see that happen here."

After walking along the tree-lined paths, Griselda directed her visitors to three gardens bordering the building. "It may not be as showy as the mixed border and perennial gardens, but you can find jewels in the wildflower garden."

Harmony ploughed past the wildflower garden, her eyes caught by the strong shapes and vivid colors of flowering plants in the mixed garden. Hundreds of showy blooms in the nearby perennial garden quickly grabbed her attention.

"My momma would have loved this garden," said Henry.

Griselda nodded. "It was our first garden. We designed it even before the land officially became the Arboretum."

She turned to Harmony. "You were asking about exotic plants. Look at this. *Farfugium japonicum*. The Leopard Plant, so-named because of the yellow spots on the green leaves."

The scents of French, Italian, Greek, and Indian herbs mingled in the air.

"Look at these saffron plants in the herb garden, donated by a master gardener."

Harmony was drawn to a tall purple stalk and touched it, releasing an earthy aroma. "*Salvia leucanthis* – Mexican Bush Sage," murmured Griselda.

Henry's eyes noticed a courtyard dotted by benches and ringed by flowering plants that led to a circular garden. The soothing scents from roses and flowering jasmine on a tall trellis colored the air.

Griselda smiled as if reminiscing. "Mary Jo, one of our master gardeners, used to walk her dachshund around the courtyard. It's hard to say who enjoyed stopping to smell the flowers more, Mary Jo or her dog."

She explained. "That's our memorial garden, where we give thanks to master gardeners who have gone before us. Our oldest master gardeners are in their nineties. Unfortunately, more and more are aging out, and some have passed away. Others have joint problems that make it impossible for them to bend down. This garden looks stunning when the *rosa Meiswetdom* are in full bloom. It's a fitting tribute to the members who are no longer with us."

"Rose bushes?" asked Harmony.

"Yes, drift roses. They climb up the trellis and their perfume is as welcome as their pleasing appearance."

Henry understood that the gardens were extremely important to Griselda. Squinting, he observed a series of metal plaques on a teak structure. Nearby benches provided shade and a place to rest.

"How often do you come up here?" he asked gently.

"I give tours, I curate two of the gardens, and I sometimes help out with office tasks. I guess that means that I'm up here three or four times a week."

"That's a big commitment," said Harmony.

"My husband died fifteen years ago. This helps me pass the time. But as I near my ninetieth birthday, I find myself slowing down. It takes me longer to do things. I can still pull weeds, but it's been a few years since I've felt comfortable climbing a tree with a chainsaw to remove diseased branches."

She looked at her speechless visitors. "You seem surprised. Just because I'm small doesn't mean I'm weak."

"Man, those saws are dangerous! I remember watching an episode of *Jackass* where they had to jump into the air to cut a tree branch. I was sure the guy was going to decapitate himself with his chain saw. I can't imagine myself ever holding a chainsaw, let alone climbing a tree," said Harmony.

Griselda laughed and her eyes twinkled. "You never know what some men will get up to."

"You got that right," agreed Harmony.

Henry quickly changed the topic. "You've shown us beautiful plants and odd-looking specimens. Do you grow poisonous plants here?"

Griselda did not appear to be taken aback by the question. "Yes, of course."

"Can you show them to us?"

"Well, yes, and we've already seen a few. About ninety-five percent of our plants are poisonous."

"What! How's that possible?" squealed Harmony.

The master gardener explained. "It really depends on what you mean by poisonous. The most obvious poisonous plant is poison ivy, which can cause mild to severe dermatological reactions in people who come into contact with it. We don't intentionally grow it, but it pops up now and then."

"I understand that one, but others?"

"NC State has an online plant toolbox that describes the extent to which plants are poisonous. The poison may come from a plant's stem or its leaves. The flowers may be toxic. Reactions can be mild or life-threatening, depending on an individual's susceptibility, the amount and concentration of the poison, whether the poison has penetrated the skin or been ingested."

"I'm surprised you have so many poisonous plants at the arboretum. Is the public aware of this danger?" Harmony asked.

"Do you eat chocolate?" asked Griselda.

"Who doesn't?" rejoined Harmony.

"Did you know it could poison your dog?"

"Yes, but I don't feed it to my dog."

"Do you buy poinsettia plants at Christmas?" asked Griselda.

"Yes, I give them to my older relatives," said Harmony.

"Would it surprise you to know the plant is toxic? You and your pets could become very ill if you ate the leaves."

"I would never eat the leaves."

"But your dog might sniff the plant out of curiosity." Griselda was on a tear. "Did you know that lilies planted in a garden are toxic to pets?"

"Are you saying they could make my dog ill?"

"Yes, it's possible."

She posed a question to Henry. "Do you eat mushrooms with your steak?"

"Yes, but only the ones we get from the grocery store or the farmers' market."

She nodded. "You get my point. Mushrooms grow in all shapes and sizes. Brown mushrooms, shitakes, and oysters are safe to eat, but there are many poisonous mushrooms that mimic these. *Amanita verna –* *Destroying Angel.* They won't harm you if you leave them alone. But they'll destroy your liver if you confuse them with button mushrooms. You will become very ill and perhaps even die. Even mushrooms that appear on lawns after a heavy rainfall can be toxic."

"That's a lot to digest," said Harmony.

Henry raised his eyebrows.

"No pun intended. I've just never thought of plants as being a source of poison as well as a source of pleasure."

"In the hands of an herbalist, a plant can be a source of natural healing. Plants can be made into poultices to relieve pain and inflammation. But some plants can be poisonous if ingested. Someone who doesn't know what they're doing can experience a world of trouble by harvesting the wrong type of plant. It's even worse if someone has know-how and malign intent. They can take the most beautiful of plants and boil the roots, roast the petals, cut them up, or infuse them into a tasteless tincture to take out their enemies. The poor suckers will never see it coming. Within hours, they'll be sweating and writhing in pain, on the precipice between life and death."

"And these plants can be found in the arboretum?" asked Harmony.

Griselda nodded emphatically. "They can be found anywhere. The difference is, because we grow so many different plants, there may be a wider selection of poisonous plants in the arboretum than in your backyard garden. The next time you mow your lawn, check out the far corners of your backyard. Search along any crannies. If you look hard enough, you'll likely find at least one toxic plant in your yard. Touch it at your peril. If you're not careful, it could be your last day on earth."

Chapter 18

Harmony was uncharacteristically silent as she and her partner walked toward their car. Her head was downcast, and Henry could see her grimace as if she'd swallowed something bitter.

"Harmony, what's wrong?" he asked.

"I don't get it. Griselda came from a family that created beautiful china, pieces of art that glisten in the light. But her description of poisonous plants – well, it's sobering."

Henry agreed. "What I found sobering were her references to Dr. Dunn, calling her a thief who should be banned from the arboretum and implying she got what was coming to her."

Harmony giggled. "A thief. A communist. I wonder which is worse, from Griselda's perspective. She certainly knows her plants. But do you think she would go so far as to poison Dr. Dunn just because the doctor took flowers from the arboretum? She's at the top of my list of suspects. I certainly wouldn't want to get on her bad side. I can see her running after me with her chainsaw buzzing. Do you think we'll be that batty when we're ninety years old?"

"I wouldn't use the word 'batty.' I would call her passionate. And I wouldn't mind having her level of energy when I'm her age. Her ability to weed, thin plants, trim branches, and give tours, all in the same day, is remarkable."

"But do you see her as a suspect?"

Henry's phone chimed, saving him from having to provide an answer. At the same time, the two detectives saw an ambulance speeding towards the public-health building. "What gives?" said Harmony.

Henry turned to his partner. "La Donna Rogers just called 911 for assistance."

"What are the odds of two people in the same office being attacked and calling 911 to report it? I ought to buy a lottery ticket tonight," said Harmony.

"You're jumping to conclusions, Harmony. We don't know she was attacked. But I admit, it is unusual for 911 to receive calls from different people from the same office. This is a strange case."

They hopped in their vehicle, tires squealing as they raced across the road to the next building, which was still ringed with yellow police tape.

"Why do you suppose she went into the building when it's still off-limits?" said Harmony.

"Let's ask her."

They ducked under the caution tape and ran up the stairs to the police officer standing guard. They gave him their names and entered the building. Two paramedics gripped a stretcher carrying the still figure of La Donna Rogers.

Henry flashed his badge at one of the paramedics. "Detective Smith. Can we ask her a few questions?"

"She won't be able to hear you. She's unconscious and we need to get her to the hospital immediately."

"Was she attacked?"

"There's no sign of foul play, but her face is clammy, she's sweating profusely, and her pulse is thready."

"Do you know what happened?"

"No, we responded to a 911 call."

Henry thanked the paramedic and then bounded into Dr. Dunn's office. The drawers to her desk were wide open, revealing paper files.

The liquid from an overturned teacup leaked its contents onto a leatherette daytimer. La Donna's cell phone, identifiable by the rhinestones glued onto its cover, was on the floor.

"Are you thinking what I'm thinking?" asked Harmony.

"It looks like she was sitting at the boss's desk."

"Do you think she tried the boss's tea?"

Henry pulled out his phone. He called the EMTs. "Tell the hospital to check for poisoning. The coroner can give them more information."

He carefully placed the teacup in a plastic evidence bag.

Harmony pulled on a pair of plastic gloves. She gingerly opened the daytimer. The pages she flipped open were dotted with handwritten notes, but the pages for the day before and the day of the murder were wet and the writing was indecipherable. "Do you think that La Donna came to pick up Dr. Dunn's daytimer? Why would she do that?"

"Well, perhaps she wanted to know who Dr. Dunn met with in the days and hours leading to her poisoning," suggested Henry.

"If that's the case, why didn't she just take the daytimer yesterday?"

"Good question." He thought for a moment. "She couldn't have because she was at lunch when the doctor made her call. When she returned, she was told she couldn't go into the building."

"I guess she can be ruled out as a suspect in the doctor's death," concluded Harmony.

"Yes, because it's unlikely she would poison the doctor and then poison herself."

"Still, it's too early to jump to any conclusions. She may have had a perfectly innocent reason for coming into the office while the caution tape was still up. She may have fallen ill from natural causes."

"Well, then, what was she doing sitting at the boss's desk?"

Henry shrugged.

Harmony frowned at her partner. "It looks like she was going through Dr. Dunn's personal belongings."

"It does look like that."

He eyed an ornate ceramic teapot on a side table. "Hmm, it's warm. Let's send it to the lab for processing."

His partner looked troubled. "Do you believe in coincidences? Don't you think it's very odd that two women from the same office made 911 calls on consecutive days?" she asked.

"That's gotta be more than a coincidence. We need to talk to La Donna right away. And we need to find out if the toxicology reports on Dr. Dunn have come back."

They drove to the hospital, both silent. Henry maintained a steady pace, refusing to allow his mind to wander down nooks and crannies of possibilities while he was driving. Meanwhile, Harmony's mind was lumbered down with what-ifs. "Do you think? No, it's not possible. What if?" It was as if Harmony was having a conversation with herself and not finding any of the answers satisfactory. She gave out a long sigh.

Henry promised. "We'll get answers to our questions soon enough."

Chapter 19

While the two detectives were making their way to the hospital, Deputy Sheriff Longfellow was plotting how to pry information from Johnson Johnson. Since being interrogated by Detectives Harris and Smith, the deputy sheriff had seen Johnson making greater efforts to exchange pleasantries with other inmates. Still, the conversations seemed short, and the deputy sheriff couldn't glean if Johnson was just making conversation or trying to establish connections.

Inmates in his prison manufactured license plates. Instead of reviewing productivity figures for the previous month, the administrative work he was scheduled to be doing, the deputy sheriff decided to haul the inmate into his office for a little chat.

He spotted Johnson in the recreation area, seated at a table alongside a group of White men listening to a man covered from head to foot with tattoos. "The time is at hand," said Earl. "Just you wait and see."

The deputy sheriff tapped Johnson's shoulder hard enough that the inmate almost fell off the picnic bench. "Get up," he said.

Johnson remained seated, ignoring the command.

He felt air whizzing past his head and instinctively drew his hands up moments before the deputy sheriff clapped the back of his head.

"I told you to get up. If I have to repeat myself, the next place you'll find yourself is in the infirmary. Now what's it going to be? Are you coming for a friendly chat or not?"

Johnson's head was spinning. The slap had made him dizzy. Still, he knew he had to move because the deputy sheriff had a reputation for roughing up prisoners when he didn't get his way. Not only that, but he had threatened Johnson in full hearing of one of the gangs. If he let Johnson ignore him, the deputy sheriff would lose the gang's respect and he couldn't have that.

Johnson slowly turned around and mumbled. "I'm coming."

"I didn't hear you," shouted the deputy sheriff.

"I said, I'm coming."

The deputy sheriff wrenched Johnson's elbow, grabbing it firmly as he frog-marched him inside. The sudden pain made Johnson stumble and fall onto one knee.

"Git up or I'll give you a reason to stay on the floor," threatened the deputy sheriff. He hauled the inmate up and propelled him forward. The guards watched as Johnson was pushed onto a chair in the administrator's office.

The deputy sheriff slammed the door shut. "Now it's just you and me, boy. No prying eyes, no one to report on our little *tête à tête*. What I wanna know is, what are you up to, sitting with The Proud Patriots when you ain't even White?"

"Earl invited me to join him at the table. I sat down. End of story."

The deputy sheriff clapped Johnson on the side of the head. "You do know the Proud Patriots believe in White power? There's no room for a person like you in their group."

Johnson carefully shook his head. "You got it all wrong. They're just what they say they are, proud to be American, patriots to their core. They believe the North Carolina they knew growing up is gone, the tobacco and textile industries killed off by wokism. All they want is a fair shot, but they're not getting it because the politicians keep regulating what people can and can't do. It's got nothing to do with being White or Black, and everything to do with the insiders in Washington who welcome migrants to take our jobs."

This wasn't the first time that the deputy sheriff had seen an inmate indoctrinated by a prison gang. But he was surprised by Johnson's ability to recite the group's mantra. "Well, well, it sounds like you've been drinking the koolaid."

"I've experienced it myself, being passed over for a job because there's a migrant willing to work for less. It's not fair and it's gotta stop."

"You've got a point. There are way too many foreigners in North Carolina. Not to mention the carpetbaggers who sell their swanky homes in Connecticut and move South for the warm weather and low cost of living, driving up our property prices. We're overrun by people who aren't welcome here," said the deputy sheriff, carefully watching Johnson to see his reaction.

Johnson was confused. "It sounds like you understand why The Proud Patriots want change."

"If I were one of them, I'd be stockpiling weapons, robbing banks, getting ready for a revolution," said the deputy sheriff.

"They aren't criminals. They don't rob banks, and the weapons they have are legal."

"Sure, sure," soothed the deputy sheriff. "Where are they getting their money?"

Johnson shrugged his shoulders. "They say they have donors who are doctors, lawyers, pharmacists, even prison guards. There are a lot of people who share their goals and quietly support them."

"If you can help me understand who these supporters are, I'll give you extra privileges."

"The detectives who were here promised they would transfer me out of here if I find out where The Proud Patriots manufacture their drugs."

"They said that?"

"I asked Earl and he told me they don't have any drug labs. What they do have is lab techs who share their beliefs. The lab techs make women's medication – that's what Earl called it – after they've finished their regular work shifts. Earl then arranges for the medication to be shipped directly to the women who need it."

The deputy sheriff thought he'd hit the jackpot. He wondered if the information Johnson was providing would result in a promotion. The deputy sheriff pictured himself managing his own correctional facility, preferably near the coast so that he could fish every morning before going to work.

"That's really good information, Johnson. Now all I need is a name and a location."

"I'll ask Earl. He's been very open about sharing information with me. I don't know why I was afraid of him."

"Don't tell him I was asking you questions," urged the deputy sheriff.

"I sure won't," promised Johnson.

"Be careful. Earl is a convicted murderer. He's ruthless and could hurt you if he thinks you're double-crossing him."

"I would never do that. He's been good to me."

"All right, then."

The deputy sheriff punched Johnson in the face, connecting with his nose. The two men heard the cartilage snap. He passed Johnson a dirty cloth to stanch the blood.

'Why'd you do that?" said Johnson.

"Can't have Earl thinking I'm soft on you."

All eyes were on Johnson as he kept his head down and walked to his cell.

"What happened to your beak, boy?" The inmate across from Johnson's cell clapped his hands to imaginary music. Soon, the other inmates along the cell block joined in. "What you did, what you did," they chanted.

Moments after Johnson entered his cell, a guard opened the door.

Johnson gave the guard a dull look. "You here because the deputy sheriff wants to punch my ribs this time?"

The guard looked sympathetically at Johnson. "No, Earl sent me." The guard passed Johnson a cold compress. "Hold this against your nose and take this pill. Earl said it'll relieve the pain." The guard left as quickly as he'd appeared.

He dry swallowed the blue pill. The icy towel stung Johnson's face. For a moment, he couldn't decide which was worse – the throbbing pain from a fractured nose or the sharp tingling from the ice-filled towel connecting with his skin.

The pain suddenly ebbed and then there was no pain. In his mind, Johnson was sitting on a pier, his feet dangling in the water. His hands held a fishing rod. He was twelve years old and about to snare the largest catfish he'd ever seen. He laughed to himself, unaware that he'd just been given 'women's medication.'

Day Five

Chapter 20

When she inserted the flash drive into her computer a couple of days earlier after leaving the office, she'd received the message 'flash drive not correctly removed' several times. Jeannie was eager to look more deeply at the data. She turned her computer on and waited impatiently for the flash drive to engage. But when she clicked open the document, she frowned because a list of names popped up even though she hadn't typed in a password to access the spreadsheet. *Uh oh, this isn't good. There's a privacy violation here. These files contain confidential patient information. They should be password-protected. Am I being too quick to judge? Kathleen always tells me to look at all the facts before judging.* But Kathleen, who was Jeannie's direct supervisor, was back in British Columbia while Jeannie was on assignment in North Carolina.

Jeannie had expected that the files would be anonymized, with the real names replaced by a number or set of letters. When she came across columns with patients' last names, first names, and street addresses, she googled three patients using the information provided. *Doesn't the data-entry clerk know that you never, ever use a patient's real name and address?* Scanning the columns, Jeannie was appalled to see comments in a box from the referring physician: "Patient is fat and lazy;" "Patient lacks the intelligence to make good food choices;" "Patient lies about what she eats and how often she exercises;" "Patient lives in a poor neighborhood filled with gangs. She says she can't go out because she's afraid she'll be shot."

Jeannie had learned to make decisions quickly when she was a surgical resident. Among the women and children she operated on in

Mumbai, very few were overweight. If anything, most tended to be underweight. But when she moved to British Columbia, she read reports of patients being severely overweight despite their efforts to eat more healthily and exercise more. Initially, she thought they were lazy and needed to be more disciplined when eating sweets.

After a heavy patient presented her with a journal containing daily food consumption and exercise, Jeannie began to question her early assessment. She discovered that so many factors came into play – genetics, the environment, childhood trauma, family income, education, and access to fresh, affordable fruits and vegetables. Obesity was a complex disease, and these were just a few of the elements influencing body size.

When she went downstairs for breakfast, she saw Frank sitting at a table, a half-eaten waffle drenched in maple syrup on his plate. She looked at her watch, wondering if she had mixed up the time.

"Dr. Johal, I got here early. We're not scheduled to meet until eight o'clock. Darla, my wife, insists that I eat a high-protein, low-fat breakfast. I can only eat so many egg-white omelets with gluten-free toast and non-fat 'butter.' I knew that I could get a more substantial breakfast here."

Lila-Jean clucked when she heard his comment. "Frank, you know that Darla is only looking out for you. She wants you to live a long, healthy life."

"I know." He hung his head, a dog-faced expression marring his usual handsome appearance.

"No judgment here," said Jeannie.

"Well, I guess eating waffles every so often isn't a terrible thing. If it were, I'd be out of business. Can I get you a scrambled egg to accompany your waffle?" asked Lila-Jean.

"Only if it comes with maple syrup," he joked.

"Ain't you the comic this morning."

Jeannie couldn't quite suppress a grin. Her breakfast consisted of a scoop of grits, a plastic cup of unflavored yogurt, and a small bowl of fresh fruit. "I'm with you, Frank. My yogurt tastes so much better with a teaspoon of maple syrup."

She looked directly at him and her expression became somber. "It's not good, Frank. I looked at the files and couldn't get past the personal comments. Those are offensive. And I cannot understand why no effort was made to anonymize the data."

He winced. "The epidemiologist set up the spreadsheet for the data-entry clerk. All the clerk had to do was to enter the data provided. We weren't expecting her to analyze the data. But we thought she could follow directions. I guess she wasn't provided with the supervision she needed to enter the data properly."

"Who was her supervisor?"

"Well, the epidemiologist, of course."

"I understand she left the project?"

"Yes, we had to let her go soon after she started. As the project manager, I suppose I was the supervisor but it was really La Donna who provided day-to-day direct supervision."

"Did you hire the data-entry clerk?"

"No, she was already working on the project when I came onboard. Dr. Dunn hired her. The epidemiologist set up the database and showed the data-entry clerk how to enter data. If the database is all screwed up, it's her fault."

Jeannie took in the explanation and offered a comment. "As the project manager, wouldn't you be responsible for the data? Why are you blaming your most junior employee?"

Frank's face turned red. "Your accusations are not appreciated. The fact of the matter is that Dr. Dunn provided the epidemiologist with the project goals and empowered the epidemiologist to design a database to capture the necessary information. I let the data-entry clerk go after it was clear there were problems with data entry."

"Did Dr. Dunn review the database?"

"No, she pretty much let the data-entry clerk do her own thing. La Donna prepared monthly summaries."

"I understand every person enrolled in the study has lost at least ten percent of their body weight."

"Yes, Dr. Dunn was very pleased with this outcome."

"But she told me that A1C levels in some patients were rising, and in some cases, their weight loss was stalled, even though they were the heaviest patients."

"She told me there were issues. I was just about to start investigating them when you arrived."

"Let's finish breakfast and then look at the database."

They ate quickly and in silence. The waffle that had tasted so good a moment earlier turned to mush in Frank's mouth. He pushed the remaining bites aside with his fork and swallowed a mouthful of coffee. After finishing her fruit and yogurt, Jeannie got up from the table, promising to meet Frank in an office the hotel was making available to them.

Arriving first in the office, Jeannie quickly skimmed through the spreadsheet, looking for columns listing A1C glucose readings at different dates. She spotted six columns filled with numbers. Each column had the same heading. None of the columns listed a date. The seventh column was empty.

Jeannie pushed the laptop in his direction before he even had a chance to sit down. "Frank, A1C levels should have been tested every three months, but it's impossible to tell when these readings were taken. It also seems that the numbers were rounded to the nearest whole number. That's just bad practice because it makes the data less accurate. Also, our nurses test glucose readings every week, but I can't find any records showing the results."

Frank tried to save face. "It's possible the columns are in chronological order. We've been collecting data for seven months, and there are seven columns with results."

Jeannie tried not to wince. "Let's say for a minute that is how the data-entry clerk was entering the data. This is worthless. The data are not valid because they cannot be duplicated. How do we even know the data, such as they are presented, were entered accurately? In her mind, the clerk may have been entering the data correctly, but since she doesn't indicate when the readings were taken, no one else will be able to make that determination. What a waste of time and money!"

Frank tried to defend the clerk. "I know that she was sincere when she said she was trying to make a better life for herself. She did exactly what she was told to do. She was instructed to put in whatever was in the notebooks. That's why you see all those comments. She entered them word for word as she found them."

"Garbage in, garbage out. She should have known better."

"Why would you say that? She took her direction from the epidemiologist." He added, in a quieter voice, "I'm not without blame here. She came to me for guidance and I told her to stop bothering me with her silly questions. I should have taken the time to look at a few entries."

Jeannie shook her head. Her voice had a forceful quality. "I think we need to scrap the entire database and build a new one. Extract data from written records. Decide exactly what we want to record and how to stratify it. Decide on a code for anonymizing patients."

"Jeannie, I appreciate your input. If what you're suggesting is true, then months of data entry have to be thrown out. Before we do that, would you at least talk to the data-entry clerk? Perhaps she can enlighten you on how she grouped the entries."

The clerk agreed to meet with Jeannie after being promised a day's wages and a free breakfast.

Chapter 21

Within minutes of her husband's departure, Darla Wright was on the phone, urgently requesting support from members of Moms for Liberty. That afternoon, Darla and two other women sat around her kitchen table, drinking sweet iced tea and eating biscuits infused with berries and cream.

"We are at a crossroads, where, as North Carolinian mothers and wives, we have a choice to make. First, they tried to tell us what our children could and couldn't read in our schools. We put an end to that. When they tried to force our kids to use 'they' to address each other, we stopped that madness in its tracks. Now we've persuaded the legislature to give parents the choice to send their children to public or charter schools by transferring public school funding to the charter school of our choice. That'll show them not to mess with Moms for Liberty!" she said triumphantly. "But now, they're getting into our businesses and forcing our hardworking husbands to do their bidding. This is unacceptable and has got to stop!"

"Well said, Darla," said Jill, founder and president of the local chapter.

"What has the governor and his band of henchmen gone and done now?" asked Jill's daughter, Lexi. "As soon as we fix one problem, they create another."

Darla raised her head high and smiled in relief. "Thank you for your support. I knew I could count on you. You'll never believe what's been happening where my husband works, in Greenville. My husband came home from work early. I was very surprised to see him because he's such a hard worker. He is the first one in and always the last one out the door. But no longer."

"Your Frank? What happened?" asked Jill.

"For the first time in his life, he walked out of a meeting with his supervisor. He was so upset by what she said that he stormed out of the building. When he got home, he had to sit in his truck to cool off because he didn't want me to see him like that.

"Well, his boss decided she was going to bring in an outsider to look through his work. Not just that, but a dark girl from Canada, of all places. And the boss didn't even have the courtesy to tell Frank before she hired this new girl. Can you imagine? He caught a glimpse of her when he was walking out the door and he says she is very young."

"My, my."

"That's what all this illegal immigration is doing, bringing in people from everywhere to take our jobs and rape and murder our children. She probably came over the border from Mexico," said Lexi. Her mother nodded in agreement.

"Well, she came from Canada. It's just as bad as Mexico. Even worse. Their president is a communist and the government controls everything. There's no freedom of speech and they don't let people own guns, only the gangs. They don't have police departments. Instead, they have the Royal Canadian Mounted Police, who wear bearskin hats and ride horses. They also let everyone in. It's a wonder more murderers and gang members don't enter America from Canada," said Darla.

Jill and Lexi clucked in agreement.

Darla continued her screed. "Frank was so upset. He's struggled since our daughter's passing, and I hoped this new job would help him find a clear sense of direction. But now I'm not sure. What do you think I should do?"

"We need to find out how this woman comes to be working in Greenville. Who hired her and is she taking the job a Greenville resident could do?" said Lexi.

"Frank says that the public-health director, Dr. Dunn, hired her for a one-month period, to review the research data. He says there's a problem with the accuracy of the data and it means the project's results may not be any good."

"This is the project he's managing at the public-health center?"

"Yes, he left his job in the Research Triangle to manage this project after our daughter passed."

"Research, my foot! This here's what's wrong. I don't need a PhD from a university to know that the women who are enrolled in this project line up for the buffet at the Golden Corral, get ice cream at Simply Natural, and think exercise means walking from the kitchen to the couch."

"I think their exercise consists of walking into the spa, rolling up their pant legs for a pedicure, and switching on the chair's massage mode," said Lexi.

"Well, that may be true for some of them, but Frank says it's a lot more complicated than it seems."

"You tell him to show that foreigner who's the boss. Can't be having an outsider, especially a dark woman from away, telling people what to do. Darla, we could file a motion to speak at the next Pitt County Commissioners' meeting, but this woman will be on her way out by then. What do you want us to do?" asked Jill.

Now that she had their attention and support, she wasn't sure how to proceed. She'd called them without thinking about what she wanted. She'd contacted them without talking to Frank first. "Well," said Darla hesitantly, "I think I should ask Frank what he wants since the problem is in his workplace."

"True, but as wives and mothers, we have a right to our own opinions. If we waited for men to provide guidance, we'd still be waiting."

"Ain't that the God's truth."

"Let's invite her to lunch. We'll know how to handle her after we've met her," said Darla.

"Should we invite her to lunch in Clayton?"

"No, let's go to Greenville. It has more restaurants. We'll make a day of it," said Jill.

Day Six

Chapter 22

Tanisha James stood hunched in a corner of the restaurant, trying to keep herself as small as possible. She pressed her back hard against the fake wall of ferns in an unsuccessful attempt to make herself invisible. Twice, the waitress had approached her to welcome her to the restaurant. Each time, Tanisha told her she was waiting for someone. She wasn't sure how much longer she could stay near the entrance without drawing too much attention to herself.

Tanisha wasn't accustomed to eating in a restaurant where a hostess or waiter greeted diners in a warm and welcoming manner. Sure, the décor appeared much nicer than IHOP, but the prices! Fifteen dollars for a pancake, and it didn't even come with coffee. Still, the woman with the funny name had invited her to breakfast and said she'd pay for it, too, so Tanisha had agreed to meet her.

But where was the woman who said she would be wearing a red dress? Jeannie Johal was already ten minutes late and there was still no sign of her. Tanisha wondered if it was a prank intended to embarrass her. She'd dressed in her good black polyester pants with a center seam so they always looked freshly pleated. She'd worn her favorite top, a sky-blue T-shirt to which she'd glued on sparkly blue crystals in the motif of a butterfly. And she'd forsaken her usual thongs in favor of her one pair of dress shoes, low-heeled leather Mary Janes that she'd picked up at My Sister's Closet. They were nice shoes, but two sizes too big, causing her feet to float in them. Despite wearing her best finery, she felt out of place.

She breathed a sigh of relief when Dr. Johal opened the door and flew through the entrance. Tanisha was transfixed. The person meeting her was tiny but fast, like a fiery comet that streaks across the night sky. She wore a sleeveless red dress that hugged her form. Tanisha half-expected to see a big black briefcase, similar to what Frank Wright used, but was delighted to be mistaken because her host carried a blocky scarlet bag under her arm. In Tanisha's inexpert view, the bag screamed 'high end' and was the perfect finishing touch to Dr. Johal's outfit.

Jeannie smiled apologetically at Tanisha and held out her hand. After a moment's hesitation, Tanisha shook it.

"I am so sorry I'm late. For a small town, the traffic here is horrendous! The Driving app on my phone said it would take me five minutes to get here, but it actually took me over twenty minutes."

Tanisha's experience with traffic differed because she walked everywhere she could. For her, busy traffic meant she had to step into a dry ditch to avoid being hit by speeding oncoming cars because very few of the roads had sidewalks. She also puzzled why Dr. Johal described Greenville as a small town. To Tanisha, it was a booming city, infinitely larger than her hometown of Kenansville, with a population of 800.

Jeannie and Tanisha followed the waitress and sat at a window corner table with a reserved sign. The waitress provided them with menus. Tanisha's eyes widened and her hands shook as she read through the four-page menu.

"The registration clerk at the hotel said this was her favorite breakfast place. I hope you can find something you like," said Jeannie.

Tanisha's voice was husky. She spoke with a soft tone and a regional accent that dropped the 'g's and 't's off the endings of words. "I can have anything I want?" she asked, as if uncertain of the response.

Jeannie reassured her. "Anything you want," she echoed.

Tanisha's eyes were round as saucers. "'Million Dollar Bacon.' I wonder why they call it that. On the farm where my daddy worked, pigs were called pigs."

Jeannie laughed in agreement.

Tanisha's gaze lingered on the Blueberry Lemon Cream Pancakes. "I know what I'd like. I've never had it but it sounds really good."

As she dug into her granola, yogurt, and fruit bowl, Jeannie marveled how Tanisha could eat a platter of pancakes and a large order of bacon.

"You have a big appetite!"

Tanisha continued to shovel the pancakes into her mouth. After cleaning her plate, she looked up and smiled. "This is the best food I've had in a week. Every bite was delicious. How do you need my help with the data?" she asked.

"Tanisha, Dr. Dunn asked me to come to Greenville to work on her research project. She was concerned that some of the results seemed unusual."

Tanisha looked down at her plate.

Jeannie fixed her gaze on the younger woman. "I understand you entered the data."

"The epidemiologist showed me how. She told me not to leave anything out and not to change the numbers. I put everything in exactly how it was given to me."

"Did she tell you to anonymize the data," asked Jeannie.

Tanisha responded guilelessly. "What do you mean by that?"

"Have you ever worked on a research project where you were told to remove everyone's name so that data cannot be traced back to that person?"

"No, ma'am, the work I did with the epidemiologist was the first time I worked on a research project. It was actually the first time I worked in an office and used a computer."

She looked up to see Jeannie's startled expression and spoke quickly to reassure her. "I was very careful. The epidemiologist had the document open. All I had to do was enter stuff into the boxes."

"And you entered the comments?"

"Yes, that was hard to do because the boxes weren't large enough. I couldn't see what I was entering, but I still put it in."

"And you copied them verbatim?"

"Ma'am?"

"I mean, you typed in exactly what you saw?"

"Yes, exactly what I saw. It's very important to know how people are doing and who's doing what. I would never remove or change that information. After the epidemiologist left, La Donna showed me how to turn the computer on, open a document, save it, close it, and turn off the computer. She also showed me how to put a line or space in the spreadsheet to separate data each month so that it didn't mess up her reports."

Jeannie tried again. "Were you ever told to replace a person's name with a number or a letter?"

"No, ma'am. I was told to copy the information directly from the paper work. I learned to read the nurses' notes, and I am proficient in copying information from laboratory reports."

"Did you ever think about the comments the doctors wrote about patients?"

"No, ma'am, Frank told me I was paid to enter data, not to think. Did I do something wrong?"

Jeannie's expression was troubled. "Perhaps he thought you were questioning the data."

"No, that wasn't it. When I said I'd be uncomfortable if someone said those things about me, he told me my job was to enter the data, not to comment on it."

"From what I'm hearing, you were trying to tell him that there were things said that were upsetting. I'm sorry he said that to you," she said gently.

"I was just trying to help," Tanisha whispered.

"Did you talk to the epidemiologist about it?"

"No, I only ever saw her twice, when I was introduced to her and when she showed me how to enter data. She told me that if she wasn't there and I had any questions, I should ask Frank."

"Did you?"

"Yes, but he said he was too busy to look at my entries, that I should do what the epidemiologist told me. After she left, he told me to ask La Donna for help."

"Did you do that?"

"Ask La Donna? No, ma'am, La Donna told me she was not my supervisor and to put the data in right so that she could get her reports every month. She told me to talk to the big boss if I had any problems."

"The big boss?"

"Dr. Dunn. I tried, but she was always on the way to meetings or running late preparing for meetings."

"Tanisha, it sounds like you didn't have anyone supervising you."

Her reply was tart. "Oh, it felt as if everyone supervised me, telling me what I should and shouldn't do. Only thing is, when I asked a question, they'd say, 'Go ask him, go ask her.'"

"There are bureaucrats everywhere, out to stymie even the most conscientious employee," sighed Jeannie.

"I'm not sure what you mean, but I'd like to get back to work as soon as possible. I need the money, and I only get paid when I work."

Jeannie probed some more. "Did you design the database?"

"No, I was given a spreadsheet with two names and told to use it as a guide. It seemed simple enough at the time. But it got complicated when I added all the names and the information, and was asked to sort the data. There were a few instances when the sorts didn't quite line up, and I had to type in the information manually."

"Do you know the risk of typing in information manually?"

"Well, ya, it's a lot of effort."

"Can you tell me who made the decision not to use numbers with decimal places?"

"The system didn't let me. When I typed in a number with decimal places, the computer refused to put in the decimal places, so I stopped trying. Anyway, many of the patients have a lot of weight to lose. I thought it might affect La Donna's report, but she said that a half a pound here or there isn't going to make much of a difference to their weight-loss efforts."

"What about rounding A1C numbers?"

"I don't know much about those, but thought I should be consistent, so I didn't use decimals."

"I see," said Jeannie.

"I can see that you're upset, but I followed the instructions I was given. La Donna wasn't much help, because she wasn't paid to help me. She was paid to be the receptionist. Is there any chance you'll rehire me? I could use the money."

Jeannie was speechless, but the more she thought about it, the more it made sense. It would take Jeannie weeks to design and populate a new database from scratch. Rehiring Tanisha and getting her trained would accelerate the process. Since Tanisha seemed to be conscientious and methodical, perhaps whole fields of data that had already been entered could be corrected in hours rather than in weeks. Jeannie vowed she would train Tanisha herself if necessary. In the meantime, Jeannie wondered if she should inform Dr. Dunn's boss about the coding errors, but remembered he was away for three weeks. Jeannie hoped that would give them enough time to revise the database, do some preliminary analyses, and ensure that Dr. Dunn's reputation remained intact.

Tanisha interrupted Jeannie's train of thought with an outburst. "I don't want to have to keep hosing down pig carcasses in the slaughterhouse!"

Jeannie interjected. She couldn't stop herself. "Wha-a-a-t?"

"That's what I did before I became a data-entry clerk and that's what I've been doing since Frank let me go. It was either that or picking tobacco, and hosing down pigs pays a lot more."

"How did you meet Dr. Dunn," said Jeannie out of curiosity.

"I was walking along the highway, about two miles outside of Greenville. Dr. Dunn was in an open convertible. She stopped and offered me a ride. We got to talking and she offered me a job. Said I'd have to be trained, but she said there would be lots of people who could help me."

"Hmm, that's interesting."

"Not as interesting as the job. She said the goal was to help people lose weight and keep it off so they could lead healthier lives. I wanted to help her do that."

"I'd like you to continue working with us. But you're going to have to get training first. Can you do that?"

Tanisha shook her head. "No, ma'am, I can't afford college."

"I meant taking an online course."

"I don't have a computer."

Jeannie nodded firmly. "Here's what we're going to do. Come to the office tomorrow at nine o'clock. I will arrange for you to receive one-on-one Excel training so that you can learn how to enter data. I will personally teach you how to protect the privacy of someone's data so that you know who the person is, but only you and I will know their identities."

"Will I get paid during the training?"

"Tanisha, yes, of course. And I'll talk to Frank about making sure you get a paycheck while the office has been closed."

"But I wasn't at work."

"Through no fault of your own."

"Do you think I could get paid for the last month that I worked?"

"What do you mean?"

"Well, I hate to ask, but I sure could use the money."

Jeannie was troubled by what she was hearing. "Are you saying you weren't paid?"

Tanisha held back tears. "Yes, ma'am. I thought it was because y'all weren't satisfied with my work. But I did everything I was told and I was so careful."

"You poor thing! I'll look into that immediately. I wouldn't be able to survive for a month without pay," she said.

"It's been hard. I found a place to stay where they don't charge me anything. They serve breakfast, and then I leave. I walk everywhere."

Tanisha's words struck a strong chord with Jeannie. She pulled out three twenty dollar bills and passed them to her. "Take this money and get yourself some groceries."

Tanisha shook her head. "No, ma'am, I'm not a charity case."

Jeannie immediately realized that she'd offended the young woman. "It's an advance on your salary," she said.

Tanisha's expression was grave as she pocketed the bills. "In that case...."

The wistfulness in Tanisha's expression pulled on Jeannie's heart-strings. She wanted to do more. "I'm also putting in place a system of bonuses. You'll get $100 when you pass your Excel course. You'll get another $100 when I am satisfied that you know how to protect people's privacy."

"I'll end up getting paid more than La Donna!"

"As you should. Data entry is serious business, and I will give you the tools to make you a pro. Now where can I drop you off?"

"I've never been in the Sheppard Library, but I hear they have computers. I'd like to get a head start on my training."

"Sure thing," smiled Jeannie, convinced that with the right support, Tanisha could become an expert data-entry clerk.

Jeannie called Frank to keep him up to date. "It's all set. Tanisha will be coming into the office tomorrow. She's going to start with Excel training."

"But the funeral is tomorrow afternoon," he protested.

"Well, she can work one-on-one with a trainer in the morning. She's eager to learn how to enter data properly."

Frank bristled. "As opposed to how she's been doing it to date?"

"You said it, not me. Do you know someone in Greenville who can sit with Tanisha and take her through the basics?"

"She already knows the basics. She's been inputting data for months."

Jeannie rephrased the question. "Do you know a local trainer who is proficient in using Excel and can review the fundamentals with Tanisha?"

"Not off the top of my head, and not with such short notice," he said.

"Then I guess I'll be her teacher," said Jeannie.

Chapter 23

Tanisha skipped up the steps to the red-brick building housing the Sheppard Library, turning back to give Dr. Johal a wave. She had to tug hard to pull open the glass door, almost losing her balance when it suddenly opened. She was entranced by what she saw. Her neck craned upward to take in her surroundings. The space looked even bigger than the Dollar General where she got her groceries and toilet paper. Unlike the Dollar General, there was no sign warning that shoplifters would be prosecuted to the fullest extent of the law. Nor was there a sign saying that knapsacks and large purses were not permitted. No one was lined up to pay for their purchases, and people weren't jostling each other to grab the daily specials. Instead, a few older women were seated around a table, quietly chatting.

A man sat off to the side, newspaper stretched in front of him. Three people were seated next to computers. Two were reading, their eyes focused on the screens, while the third was rapidly typing. Tanisha marveled over how quickly his fingertips engaged with the keys.

Noticing a woman wearing a nametag marked "Staff" who was talking with another woman, Tanisha timidly veered in that direction. She stopped a few feet from the table because she didn't want to disturb the conversation.

She was near enough to hear the women chatting and could scarcely believe what one was saying. She took a few steps forward and addressed herself to the speaker. "Dr. Dunn wasn't shot with an arrow tipped with poison from a rare Amazonian frog! And La Donna was not pistol-whipped because she tried to prevent an escaped prisoner from shooting at Dr. Dunn."

The speaker looked up. Tanisha could see that the woman had a front tooth broken in a 'V' shape, and was missing at least half of her other upper teeth. Her hair was a frizzy orange, and she wore a large medallion necklace that dangled over her pendulous breasts. She was wearing what appeared to be a horizontal red and white striped beach dress, with Velcro-strapped plastic sandals. "Who's talking to you any-way? You mind your business," she said.

Tanisha's mouth opened and closed in an 'O' shape. She started to speak and stopped when the woman put her hand up and made a swat-ting motion.

The other woman stood up. She smiled warmly at Tanisha. "Don't you mind Nancy. She was just filling me in on the latest news."

Tanisha looked uncertainly at both women. "I'm sorry for interrupt-ing your conversation," she said hesitantly.

Sensing her discomfort, the staff member smiled again. "Is this your first time in the Sheppard Library?"

"It's the first time I've ever been in any library. It's so big," blurted Tanisha.

The woman named Nancy resumed talking, as if Tanisha weren't present. "As I was saying before being so rudely interrupted, there was a big ruckus near the jail. It turns out that the director of the pub-lic-health unit was pretending to be leading a health study into helping fat girls get thin, but was actually injecting them with fatal doses of fentanyl. After learning that his sister was killed, the brother of one of the girls in the study broke out of the detention center and killed the director with a bow and arrow."

"You don't say," commented the librarian.

"Yep, she was poisoned with curare, a poison that comes from a frog in the Amazon."

Tanisha could restrain herself no longer. "How do you know this?"

"I read it on my phone. I regularly receive updates about what's going on in the neighborhood. Also, my neighbor is a friend of a friend of the receptionist who bravely tried to stop the attack."

"Oh! You mean La Donna?"

Nancy stopped telling her story. Her eyes narrowed as she gazed at Tanisha. "You know La Donna?"

"A bit. I've been working in that office for a few months. The doctor was a fine person who cared about the patients in the study. She was not injecting them with fentanyl," said Tanisha.

Nancy backpedaled. "Well, all I can say is this is what was reported."

The librarian interjected herself into the conversation. "Miss?"

"Call me Tanisha."

"Tanisha, welcome to the Sheppard Library. Is there something in particular you are looking for?"

"I'd like to learn how to use Excel better, so that I can enter numbers with decimals and sort data. Can you show me?"

Nancy's eyes gleamed. "Are you the help who takes out the trash and cleans the office restroom? Are you trying to rise above your station?"

Tanisha could sense she was being mocked, but didn't know how to reply, so she did what her mother had taught her to do. "No, Ma'am, I'm not the help," she responded politely.

The staff member gently touched Tanisha's forearm and steered her in the direction of an empty computer. "Watch what I do. See this green box with an X?"

Tanisha nodded.

"Double-click on it to open Excel. Then you can save or edit an existing document or create a new one. You can add rows across or columns down. Make sure you press Control S to save your information."

Tanisha nodded. "Yes, I save every five minutes."

The librarian smiled. "Let me show you how to autosave. You said that Dr. Johal was going to arrange training for you?"

"Yes, I start tomorrow."

"That's good, Tanisha. Now, I'm going to show you how to save changes and store your document in a place and with a name where you can easily find it the next time you need to work on it."

Tanisha watched carefully.

"Your turn," said the librarian.

Tanisha was able to open her document on her first try.

"Let's try sorting information. This will let you sort names alphabetically."

"I sorted the names alphabetically, but Dr. Johal said it's better to separate out first and last names."

"You're a natural! You're a fast learner. Were you working in an office before working in the health office?"

"No ma'am. I worked in a slaughterhouse hosing down pig carcasses. Dr. Dunn saw me walking along the highway. She stopped and offered me a ride. We got to talking. She told me she saw something in me and asked if I would like to learn how to enter data and work in an office. She hired me and I was shown how to type in data. Even though she was a stranger, she was still kind to me. I hope they find who poisoned her."

The librarian was intrigued. "Is it true that an escaped convict struck her with an arrow tipped in poison from an Amazonian frog?"

"No, ma'am. I don't know where that story came from. Dr. Dunn drank something, fell to the floor in her office, and soon after went to her place at the side of the Lord our Savior. The funeral is tomorrow afternoon."

"Bless your heart, Tanisha. I'm sorry for your loss."

Tanisha looked surprised.

"You lost the woman who hired you to work in her office."

"That's true. She was very kind. I hope that I learn to input data properly so that I can be a credit to her."

"You mentioned a Dr. Johal?"

"Yes, I met her this morning. She's a doctor and a scientist who is going to help me learn how to enter the data."

"Is she new?"

"Dr. Dunn invited her to spend a month in Greenville. I don't know much about her except that she's an expert in data. And she doesn't eat much."

The staff member smiled. "Why do you say she doesn't eat much?"

"She invited me to breakfast. I had lemon cream pancakes with million-dollar bacon. They were wonderful! She had fruit with granola in a tiny bowl. It looked okay."

"I can see why Dr. Dunn said she saw something in you. You have something special in you. Don't let anyone tell you otherwise."

"May I come back here if I have any more questions?"

"Tanisha, yes, of course. This is a public library, and my job is to help you find what you're looking for. Come any time."

Tanisha felt hopeful. *I can't wait to go into the office! I'm going to ace Excel and make Dr. Dunn and Dr. Johal proud!*

La Donna was waiting to be discharged from the hospital. Her fingertips were idly sweeping through photos on her Instagram account when her Facebook page alerted her to a new message.

"I hear you're the office administrator for a major research project. I represent WellStar Pharmaceuticals, the company funding the project. I'd love to meet with you to get your insights on how things are going.

What do you say about meeting me for lunch tomorrow?"

La Donna's reply was immediate. "I'd love to, but I'm going to a funeral tomorrow. It would be improper. How about the next day?"

"I'm sorry for your loss. The next day works for me. How does 1 p.m. at The Rickhouse sound?"

"How will I know I'm meeting the right person? A girl can never be too careful."

"So true. I know what you look like so I'll be able to recognize you."

Her Facebook page was filled with images showing her lying on a towel, sipping a margarita under an umbrella on the beach, wearing a skimpy string bikini as she walked into the water. Other photos showed her dancing in the middle of a dance floor in a dark nightclub with her arms wrapped tightly around a man whose hands were groping her.

If La Donna thought it was creepy that this stranger knew her name and what she looked like, she didn't let on. Instead, she responded with a smiley emoji.

Frank was finalizing the logistical challenges of setting up two trailers in the parking lot adjacent to the public-health building. Bernard had been correct when he cautioned that he might be out of phone range. This meant that it was up to Frank to call the police chief, who refused to let Frank and his team back into the building. However, Frank did convince the police chief to let the public-health department set up temporary quarters near the impounded building. Frank arranged for the research trailer to be divided into three sections: chairs and desks for research staff to register participants, interview them, and take their vitals, a section furnished with exercise equipment and a physiotherapy table, and a changing area equipped with water coolers.

Even though the research area had many components, it was the second trailer that proved the most complex to make operational. Long coils of black cables snaked from the trailer to the building. Frank was able to connect three computers and a printer, but not the air-conditioning. And when he got the A/C to work and turned on a pot of coffee, the breaker blew. It took many tries for his workaround to succeed. The office was now ready for work on the research project to resume.

While Frank was setting up the temporary office, his wife and her two friends sat in a booth at The Rickhouse, where they shared a pitcher of old-fashioned cocktails mixed with bourbon. All three had dressed up for the occasion. Darla wore a lavender vee-neck dress with her mother's pearls. Darla appeared matronly. In contrast, Jill looked sporty. Her navy-and-white striped top was paired with a white skirt and cream-colored runners. Lexi wore her usual camo, khaki trousers and hoodie covering most of her body, and Doc Martens on her feet.

They watched in silence as a petite, slender Brown woman entered the restaurant. If they were surprised by her appearance, they didn't let on. Jeannie wore a round-necked white silk blouse with cap sleeves, and a red pencil skirt. Her feet were laced in medium-height red espadrilles. She did not appear to be wearing any jewelry or makeup.

They stood as she approached their table.

"So nice to meet you," said Darla. "We suggested The Rickhouse because of its all-American cuisine."

Jeannie looked around the restaurant, taking in the stuffed moose heads adorning the walls. "Did the owner shoot those?"

Lexi interjected. "Yes, they are recent additions."

"Oh, I see," said Jeannie.

Jill laughed. "Lexi is joking. Those moose heads have been here for as long as I can remember. They probably predate Lexi. There are a lot of hunters in North Carolina, and my guess is that the owners were trying to appeal to their hunting clientele."

Darla tried to steer the conversation to Jeannie and her reasons for coming to Greenville. "Frank mentioned you would be working with him on his research project. What is your role?"

Jeannie smiled as she sat down. "I don't know much about the American South, but I had heard the South was famous for its hospitality. I got a taste of Southern hospitality from Lila-Jean Lamont at the Hilton, and, Darla, I am very appreciative of your lunch invitation."

Jill frowned because Lila-Jean had been her house cleaner before leaving to work at the Hilton. Darla looked twice at Jeannie, surprised by her exotic accent.

"Where are you from?" said Lexi. "You don't sound Mexican."

Her mother shot her a glance.

Jeannie laughed softly. "You are so funny. I live in Canada now, but originally come from India. My teachers were British, so I suppose I have to thank them for my accent."

"It sounds posh, just like the royal family," continued Lexi.

"Well, thank you."

After placing their orders, the Moms for Liberty got down to business.

Darla began the conversation. "Frank was very surprised when Dr. Dunn, rest her soul, told him that she'd hired an outsider – you – to review the research data. In fact, I can tell you he was quite angry."

"And I can understand why. I could hear him arguing with Dr. Dunn. I'd be angry too if my boss hired an outsider without giving me any opportunity to have input into the decision. I don't blame him one bit for being upset."

Jill asked the next question. "What we find surprising is that Dr. Dunn went all the way to Canada to find someone when I'm sure it would have been easier to find a qualified person in North Carolina."

Jeannie smiled for the second time. "Dr. Dunn used to be in the army. She and her best friend – my boss – served together in army hospitals in Afghanistan and Iraq. They've kept in touch over the years. Dr. Dunn mentioned getting unusual results with the research project she's overseeing. My boss, knowing that I'm both a trained epidemiologist and physician, suggested I could go to Greenville and look over the results."

"You look too young to be a doctor and an epidemiologist," said Jill.

Jeannie acknowledged the comment. "I do look young for my age. I'm over thirty."

"Why did you get your other qualification?"

"I studied epidemiology as an add-on. You wouldn't believe the level of ignorance of some of the people I knew in India! It drives me nuts when people make assumptions based on junk science. They don't know what they're talking about, but they repeat what they've heard as if it's the God's truth."

"I know exactly what you mean," said Jill.

"Me too," chimed Darla.

Buoyed by their responses, Jeannie continued her story. "I didn't know how I could possibly work here, especially on short notice, but my boss said the Canadian health authority would keep me on payroll and describe my work as a short research assignment so that it wouldn't cost Dr. Dunn or the people of North Carolina a penny."

"And your boss was able to pull you away from your normal duties and send you here on short notice?"

Jeannie hesitated. "It's not as simple as it sounds. She wields a lot of power. There are three levels between her and me. She asked me to take on this assignment as a personal favor and my direct supervisor recommended that I agree to do it. After all, it's not every day that a senior executive pays much attention to a relatively new employee. Perhaps when this assignment is complete, she'll keep me in mind when there's an opportunity for me to be promoted."

"You sound ambitious. I wish my daughter had even an ounce of your drive," said Jill.

Jeannie smiled soberly, remembering how she'd had to cross several continents in order to get away from her husband.

"I was worried you might be taking work away from someone local, but it doesn't sound like it. Bless your boss for trying to help us out," said Darla.

"I wasn't sure what I'd find here, but so far the people have been very welcoming. I'm sorry that Dr. Dunn has died, and that places an even greater workload on Frank. I hope I can help him."

"Well, I'm glad you're here to help Frank. He was at sea when our only child died. I hope this project makes him feel he has a purpose again."

"That must have been very difficult for you both. I'm so sorry," said Jeannie.

"Yes, we adopted Charlene when she was two years old. Her mother was a drug addict and unable to care for her baby. The father was unknown. She was our angel, taken away far too soon. It's too late for my baby girl, but please do everything you can to help other girls like our daughter lead long, healthy lives."

"I will," she vowed.

The four women walked out to the parking lot. Jeannie was the first to get into her vehicle.

"Wow, that's a bad-ass car," said Lexi admiringly.

"Language, Lexi," said Jill.

"Not exactly a Chevy Suburban," replied Darla.

"We know this woman is an interloper. We have only her word for it that the Canadian government is paying her wages, but we don't know for sure," said Jill.

"Yeah, she could be a spy sent here by a foreign government. They say that there are Chinese spies everywhere. She could be a Canadian spy sent to North Carolina to learn how we do healthcare research here," said Lexi.

"More likely, she wants to figure out a way to get the results Frank was achieving so that she can go back to Canada and claim she has found the cure for obesity. I'll tell Frank to be very careful around her."

"And I'll find out which room she's staying in at the hotel. We need to send her a message she won't forget. Lexi, you know what to do," instructed her mother.

Lexi rubbed her hands in glee. "Yesterday, I extracted poison-ivy sap from the vines twining up the loblolly tree in the backyard. I'll have a welcome package of hand and body lotion ready to go in a jiffy."

"That would be too obvious. Try being a little more subtle. We want to scare her, but not harm her," said Jill. "Give the doctor a memorable Southern welcome that she won't be quick to forget."

"If I dab the sap from elephant ears on her door handle, it will cause severe pain for a few hours, without any lasting effects."

"That sounds better. Honey, be careful. You don't want to get any on your hands," said her mom.

Day Seven

Chapter 24

Tanisha woke to the sound of pelting rain. After eating grainy grits wet with warm water, she grabbed her knapsack and began her trek to work. She walked along the shoulder of the road, taking care to avoid the shiny puddles filled with rain. She'd selected an outfit that had to do double duty. It was her first day back doing office work, and in the afternoon, she would be attending Dr. Dunn's funeral. Her pair of black pants and a dark scooped-necked top would be just the thing to wear.

As Tanisha approached the building, a souped-up pick-up truck blasted past her, proudly flying a Confederate flag. The wheels of the car tossed rain and small pebbles from the drenched asphalt in her direction. She looked in dismay at her soaked clothes, relieved that the dark fabric made the wet patches less noticeable.

The driver wore a black baseball cap jammed low on his forehead. She glared at him because she was tired of truck drivers not slowing down to spare her. She shrugged off her feeling of animosity and walked toward the public-health building, only to be stopped by yellow crime-scene tape.

Jeannie intercepted the younger woman "Over here, Tanisha. Frank has set up a mobile trailer for us to use until we can get back in the building. Also, La Donna was taken ill and may be away for some time, so we will be short-staffed."

Although La Donna had never been nice to Tanisha, the data-entry person still found the grace to show kindness. "I hope she's going to be okay. First Dr. Dunn and now La Donna. I hope she recovers rapidly and everything is smooth sailing from here on."

"I hope so, too. I'm going to be your Excel coach this morning. Frank has set up work stations for us."

Tanisha beamed. *Wowee! This is more attention than I ever got from Dr. Dunn or Frank Wright.* She pulled out her notepad and pen. "I promise you won't be disappointed."

Jeannie looked at her in puzzlement, eyeing the pen as if it were an antiquated instrument. "Why do you have a notepad and pen? Excel is a computerized spreadsheet."

"I took notes at the library yesterday."

Jeannie nodded. "Here's a manual I put together for you as a reference guide. Why don't you jot any notes in here?"

Two hours later, both women stretched their arms wide and yawned. "Time for a break," said the older one. Before she could get a drink, Frank approached Jeannie, requesting an urgent meeting.

"The director of the arboretum has asked if I can write a few paragraphs for him to say at the funeral."

"Why is he asking you for this information?"

"Because he's Dr. Dunn's peer and was the County planning director's designate."

"You worked directly with Dr. Dunn. Why don't you speak?"

Frank hesitated. "That's true, but the planning director is my boss and I have to do what he wants."

"He should have asked you to speak on his behalf about Dr. Dunn."

"You may be right, but he didn't."

"What I'd do if I were you is give the arboretum director one sentence, 'Now I'll call upon Frank Wright to say a few words about his supervisor and colleague, Dr. Dunn.' And then I'd say a few words about Dr. Dunn."

Frank gulped. "Well, that makes sense in a lot of ways. I guess I can do that."

"You'll do fine, Frank."

"Thanks for the reassurance."

"Tanisha is a quick study. She's already identified improvements she can make to the existing spreadsheet."

"Okay, that's good."

"I've taught her how to password-protect documents and I've shown her how to create a code to anonymize patients' names."

"Is that necessary? We're a small office, and no one here is going to get into the database unless they have a good reason."

In the past, Jeannie would have eviscerated Frank with a few choice words. But her Canadian supervisor had taught her to listen before leaping to judgment. "Frank, what is your experience working with patient records?"

"Well, it's limited. I used to work in project management in a manufacturing facility. I'm discovering that health care has its own peculiarities."

Jeannie acknowledged his statement by firmly nodding her head. "I thought that might be the case. As part of her grant application, Dr. Dunn would have had to generate an ethics application for review and approval by the NIH before any participants could be included in the study. She would have had to provide guarantees and examples of how patient data would be protected. The application would have included a mock spreadsheet."

"Oh, I didn't know. The project had already started when I came on board," he said.

"We'll need to see the application so that we know what she promised. In the meantime, Tanisha has just completed a crash course in introductory Excel. She's practicing how to create columns and rows, how to format them, and how to sort data."

"I assumed she knew these things before she was hired," said Frank.

"No, she'd never used a computer before coming here. The epidemiologist created the spreadsheet, turned on the computer for her, and told her to input everything she could. That's what Tanisha did. After you sacked the epidemiologist, La Donna showed Tanisha how to turn on the computer, open the spreadsheet, save it, and turn off the computer. She also taught her how to separate the data by month."

He had the grace to wince. "I'm sounding like a broken record when I say that Tanisha was already here when I joined the group. This explains why she came to me with questions. Instead of listening, I brushed her off. I'm glad La Donna helped her, even though I didn't know La Donna could teach Excel."

"It sounds as if everyone was too busy to help Tanisha. I've told her she'll receive paid training. It may also be helpful to provide her with a laptop that she can use at home."

"That will never work," he said.

"Why not?"

"She lives in a homeless shelter."

"She told me she lives in a place that doesn't charge rent. That brings me to another point. She wasn't paid for the last month that she worked."

"I didn't know. That was La Donna's responsibility."

"But you're the project manager, not La Donna."

"Yes, but I delegated payroll to her."

"I see. Well, please make sure Tanisha gets paid right away. She needs the money."

He nodded. "I'll take care of that immediately."

"Has she been living in a shelter all this time?"

"She moved to Greenville for this job. When she worked in the slaughterhouse, she lived with her mother in Kenansville. But there's no public transport between Kenansville and Greenville."

"Well, this is unacceptable! We need to pay her enough so that she can at least rent a room in someone's house, a room to call her own. Or share an apartment with someone."

"I suppose we could increase her pay," he said grudgingly.

"Let's do that and make it retroactive."

"La Donna's not going to appreciate that. Tanisha will earn more than her."

"She doesn't have to know."

"She'll find out."

"How?"

"I appointed her the office administrator. She makes out all the checks and does the banking."

"Did you give her a raise after you added to her responsibilities?"

He hemmed and hawed. "No, I didn't think of it."

"Frank, you need to take back those responsibilities."

He sighed. "I suppose so. I'm beginning to realize I have delegated way too much. You may not believe this, but I used to be one of the best project managers in the Research Triangle. I lost my way after my daughter died. I took the job here, hoping it would give me answers. Now I need to step up and show that Dr. Dunn made the right decision when she hired me."

"I'm confident you're the right person for the job," she said.

"I'm glad you're here. You're helping us get on track, and I appreciate the vote of confidence."

"Frank, work on the eulogy for Dr. Dunn. Tanisha is creating a dummy spreadsheet and cutting and pasting her existing data into it. I need to drop by the hotel, and then go to the airport to pick up Dr. Bach."

"Another doctor?"

"She's my boss in Canada. She was Dr. Dunn's best friend. She's flying in for the funeral."

He nodded. "I've invited Tanisha to ride to the funeral with me and Darla. I'll be leaving in an hour to pick up my wife at home. We'll swing back to pick up Tanisha."

Jeannie accelerated out of the parking lot, joining other cars speeding on the highway. On arrival at the hotel, she briskly walked into the kitchen area, and asked if she could speak to Lila-Jean.

"I am sorry for disturbing you at work, but you're the only person I could think to ask. There's an employee in our office who lives in a shelter because her family lives in Kenansville and there's no bus between there and here. It turns out there were issues with her paycheck and she hasn't been getting paid. That's been rectified, and I am trying to help find her a place to live in Greenville. It doesn't have to be fancy."

"Why are you asking me?" said Lila-Jean.

"Because you seem to know everyone and because you're kind. This person used to work in a slaughterhouse. Now she's an office worker and if I have anything to do with it, I'm going to transform her into a very competent data clerk. I can teach her computer skills, but I don't know how to help her find a place to live."

Lila-Jean nodded in understanding. "You not worried she goin' to be too big for her britches?"

"No, she's eager to learn new skills. She's mature for her age. She's got so much potential."

"Why do you care? You're only here for a short time."

"I grew up in a poor family. My parents married me off to a man more than twice my age when I turned fourteen. In exchange, he guaranteed them a place to live, and he promised that he would never beat me."

Lila-Jean's quick intake of breath confirmed that she was listening.

"He never beat me, but it was still hard. Tanisha told me that she left school to work in the slaughterhouse. She deserves more than that," said Jeannie.

The older woman nodded grimly. "Jus' cause slavery was abolished in the last century doesn't mean it don't exist."

"Will you help me?"

"I kept my son's bedroom exactly the same way it was before he joined the Army and went to Afghanistan. I figured he'd come back soon enough. But he never did. It's time to pack up his football trophies. Your girl can live with me. He'd be happy, knowing that I gave a girl a chance at a better life."

Jeannie hugged Lila-Jean, prompting a roomful of strangers to look at the Brown woman embracing the Black woman. "Thank you so much. I'll give Tanisha a ride to your place this evening."

Chapter 25

"Thank goodness you've finally arrived," said Beatrix Bach. She pointedly tapped her watch. "I asked the gentleman here to order a limo for me, but he says the Greenville airport is too small to support such a service. Would you believe that he suggested I call Lyft to request a ride?"

"No need to call a ride-share. I'm here. Is this all the luggage you have?" While picking up a small carry-on bag, Jeannie exchanged a glance with the customer-service agent.

"Ma'am has informed me that she brought more than she needs for her quick visit to our fair city. It looks like y'all have everything under control," said the agent. He scurried behind the desk.

A blast of hot air hit them as they walked out of the air-conditioned terminal. "It's hot as Hades here!" gasped Dr. Bach.

"Yes, it's hot, but it must have been hotter in Afghanistan when you served there," mused Jeannie.

"A different kind of heat. Here it feels as if I've stepped into a wet sauna."

Jeannie walked over to her red Mustang. Dr. Bach remained near the building exit.

"You expect me to ride in that death trap? If this was all the rental agency had, you should have held out for another vehicle," said Dr. Bach.

"I chose this car," said Jeannie defiantly.

"Why would you do that? It's low to the ground and has lousy mileage."

"It's a fine car. Rides like a dream," said Jeannie.

"It doesn't hold a candle to my Cadillac Escalade, but I suppose it will have to do," said Dr. Bach grudgingly.

She eyed Jeannie with a mix of curiosity and satisfaction. "The first time I met you, you wanted to blend into the wallpaper and be invisible. Now you're driving a scarlet red Mustang, daring everyone to take you on."

Jeannie nodded. "I've always wondered what it would be like to drive a fast car. Now I know, and I'm never going back to a Volvo."

Dr. Bach looked at the surroundings. "Church, chicken, church, barbecue. Where are the tobacco fields?"

Jeannie glanced at her passenger. "It's the twenty-first century. Greenville used to be farmland. Those days are long gone."

"No tobacco fields? Why is there a big cancer center here?"

Jeannie sighed. She could tell that Beatrix was in an ornery frame of mind. Jeannie took in a deep breath and counted to three. "There are still tobacco fields, just as there are still cotton fields. But you'll find that the crops are outside the city limits. And the big cancer center, as you call it, serves people from neighboring communities as well as Greenville."

She turned into the hotel's parking lot and walked up to the hotel entrance. As she opened the door, a tired-looking Lila-Jean swept toward her. "Here's my address. I'll expect you at eight."

Lila-Jean nodded in Dr. Bach's direction. "This the other Canadian? I understand that the person who has been delivered into the precious, loving hands of our Lord Almighty was your best friend. May her memory be a blessing."

Dr. Bach smiled while Jeannie gaped, her mouth open in surprise.

"Thank you, dear," said Dr. Bach.

Jeannie couldn't restrain herself from asking Dr. Bach how she knew Lila-Jean.

Dr. Bach snorted. "If you could see your expression! It's priceless. Is this the first time you've stayed in a small town?"

Jeannie nodded.

"In small towns, neighbors know each other and they help each other out. That's the nice side of being in a small town. The flip side is that everybody knows everybody else's business. There's no privacy."

"But that doesn't explain how she knew why you were here."

"Perhaps the hotel restaurant is catering the reception following the funeral?" Dr. Bach suggested.

"It's possible. Frank, the project manager, made the arrangements."

"Did you tell him I was coming to the funeral?"

"I did."

"Do you suppose he told anyone else?"

Jeannie exhaled slowly and let out her breath.

"You're catching on fast," said Dr. Bach. "Soon enough, you'll understand how things work."

Chapter 26

Frank moved between the two trailers, checking regularly to ensure computers were working and the research was on track. Around noon, he logged out of his computer and stood up. He stretched his back and neck, rotating his shoulders until he could feel the tendons pop. "Tanisha, don't forget to take a lunch break. I need to go and get my wife. We'll circle back here to pick you up on the way to the funeral."

Since there would be three people in the vehicle, Frank traded in his truck for the Chevy Malibu. Darla smiled at him and patted his arm after listening to him talk nonstop about Tanisha. "Frank, it's been a while since I've seen you this excited," said Darla.

He grinned sheepishly. "You oughta see this girl. She's such a hard worker, and so keen to excel. And then there's the young doctor from Canada, who's been very encouraging. I wasn't sure what I was going to do when I learned that Dr. Dunn was dead, but I'm finding – we're finding – solutions to the data issues and making tremendous progress. Their commitment makes me want to try harder."

"Tell me more about this girl. Does she remind you of Charlene?"

Frank glanced at his wife. "They don't look at all alike. Tanisha is a slip of a girl. But she has the same love of life that Charlene had. She lights up when she talks about learning Excel. She's like an old soul when describing her family. In many ways, she's had a really difficult life – losing her father and young brother in a fire that destroyed the family home, leaving school to work in a slaughterhouse to support the family. Despite those hardships, she's determined to make something of herself. Dr. Dunn made a wise decision when she took a chance on her. It's paying off now."

"Well, I'm looking forward to meeting Tanisha. She sounds so positive."

They drove in companionable silence.

Tanisha already felt as if she were going to burst with excitement. She couldn't contain her enthusiasm when Frank opened the door to the trailer. "Did you know that if you click one key, you can go to the start of your document? Or the end? No more scrolling up and down for what seems like forever! Excel is amazing!"

Despite himself, Frank smiled. "Excel has lots of shortcuts that you'll find helpful."

She took his smile as a cue to continue. Tanisha offered another discovery. "Did you know that healthcare has special rules for protecting the privacy of patients? Did you know that you can password-protect a document so that no one else can open it, unless you share the password with them? Did you know there's a list of numbers that you can use in lieu of a patient's name?"

"Whoa! You're talking so fast I can barely make out a word you're saying." he said. "It sounds like you learned a lot this morning."

"I did. Dr. Johal is an incredible teacher. I'm really looking forward to entering data properly. I'm sorry I didn't know these things when Dr. Dunn hired me. It would have made it so much easier."

He reassured her. "It's never too late to learn. I think you'll be a real asset to this team."

"I'm looking forward to becoming a full member of the team. You won't regret hiring me."

"You're already a full and valued member. Now c'mon. Darla is waiting to meet you and we don't want to be late for the funeral."

She grabbed her knapsack and followed him out.

"I thought my wife's purse was large, but your bag is much bigger. Would you prefer to leave it here?"

Tanisha demurred.

After Frank introduced his wife to Tanisha, they rode in silence until reaching the church. As she entered the edifice, Tanisha marveled at the high ceilings and vast spaces. "When I was growing up, we went to a church that was about a tenth this size. It was a Free Will Church and pretty quiet until Sister Ursula got seized by the spirit and began speaking in tongues."

"This will be a quiet service. Have you ever been to a funeral?"

She nodded solemnly. "When our house burned down, my pappa and my brother died in the fire. The church held a funeral for them."

"Bless your heart, girl. That must have been very difficult for you," said Darla gently.

"You never know what's gonna happen from one day to the next," Tanisha said, with the wisdom of someone far older.

They advanced up the aisle. Frank ushered Darla and Tanisha into the pew in front of Jeannie and the woman with her. Frank and the arboretum director, in the front pew, exchanged nods.

After an opening prayer, the minister presiding over the funeral asked if someone would like to say a few words about Dr. Dunn.

Isaiah Isherwood stood up and introduced himself. He wore a black silk tie and a black, three-pointed handkerchief discreetly peeping out from his breast pocket. He cleared his throat, looked around the room, and began.

"Bernard Bigelow, the County director, was my boss and Dr. Dunn's boss. He championed our initiatives at the County level, and I know he would be here if he weren't circumnavigating the globe with his wife

Becky. Since he couldn't be here, he asked me to say a few words on his behalf. Dr. Dunn and I were colleagues. We supported each other when we could, and we also competed for local funds. She oversaw the Public Health unit, while I serve as the NC State County Extension Director and Horticulture Agent for Pitt County. My first meeting with Dr. Dunn was at a county gathering, where she made passionate arguments in support of those who were unable to speak for themselves – low-income women, especially those grappling with addiction. She said that rather than write these women off, we needed to lift them up, to show them that they could rise above their challenges and become productive, job-holding members of their community. She wasn't a religious woman, but she spoke with the fervor of an old-time preacher. And when the Commissioners gave her some funds but not enough to do what she said was needed, she didn't give up. She looked for support elsewhere and succeeded in securing one of the largest grants this county has ever seen.

"Her passing is a loss not just for the county but for everyone who's ever thought about giving up. Men, women, children. I hope her legacy can continue. I will always remember her as my spirited colleague who made decisions based on what was best for the people of Pitt County."

Frank listened in amazement because the story he'd just heard was so different from what Dr. Dunn had told him. He walked up to the lectern and glanced around the room. He cleared his throat. "Isaiah is correct. When I first met Dr. Dunn, I was reeling from the death of my daughter. I didn't know how I could carry on, but Dr. Dunn gave me the strength to persevere. She invited me to join her team, to channel my grief so that no other teenager would suffer the same fate as my Charlene. Her research was groundbreaking, and I believe she was well on her way to finding a cure for obesity. She was an exceptional physician and a first-rate person, one of the most ethical leaders I've ever met. I've always wondered if physicians are taught to be authoritarian, but Dr. Dunn broke the stereotype. She had a girlish laugh and she used humor to disarm her critics and win them over. She wore clothes she described as 'girly' – bright pinks, scarlet reds, lime greens – no dark business suits for her. And one that had big, red hibiscus flowers against a background of bright green leaves. She looked like her own garden. She once told me she first went to the arboretum to take a close look at the blooms.

"I don't know why anyone would want to kill her. Yes, she enjoyed walking through the arboretum in search of a beautiful flower to pluck and place in a vase on her desk. No, she shouldn't have cut blooms from a public garden, and I admonished her for doing it. She took childish delight in outwitting the master gardener who called her out. At the same time, she was a generous 'Friend of the Arboretum' who made monthly contributions to support the public garden.

"She didn't have much tolerance for companies who put profits above people or for politicians whose goal was to amass personal fortune. Her work was her life. And it's not an overstatement to say that she gave me my life back, she gave me hope. I'm glad to have had the experience of working with Dr. Dunn. I will do everything in my power to carry on her work so that we can achieve her vision."

As Frank returned to his seat, Dr. Bach stood up and made her way to the lectern. She looked around the room before speaking. "Dr. Dunn and I were best friends. We served together as trauma surgeons in Iraq and Afghanistan. Even in the grimmest of situations, Dr. Dunn remained an optimist. She could charm the most cantankerous curmudgeon. And her skills weren't limited to her ability to use her feminine charms. She had a brain and made good use of it. She was a world-class researcher, and fearless in pursuit of her goals. While I never understood her decision to set up shop in North Carolina when she could have been a star at the Cleveland Clinic or the Mayo Clinic, I knew she considered Eastern North Carolina to be her home. She loved the lush flower gardens and respected those who tilled them. She appreciated the farm workers whose toil in the fields made it possible for her to eat what she once called her favorite food – North Carolina butter beans. Above all, she sympathized with rural North Carolinians who felt they had been passed by, left behind by a world that declared a war on tobacco without helping the tobacco farmers and pickers whose livelihoods were taken from them."

She looked around the room at the expressions of surprise on many faces. "You knew her as a capable administrator and a successful researcher. I knew her as the girl who sought adventure while also seeking ways to make a difference. When Norma and I were serving in Afghanistan, we were granted a five-day leave. It wasn't long enough for us to fly back stateside to visit family and friends because the flight itself would have eaten up too much of that time. Instead, we went to Abu Dhabi since it was a mere two hours and forty-five minutes away. Was I in for a surprise! Norma had booked activities for us. I thought we'd do some shopping, enjoy eating at a few restaurants, and go to one of the manmade beaches. Well, there was a little of that. But on our second day, she told me she had a big treat in mind. She told me to pull my hair up and tuck it into a cap, and wear a shirt, jacket, pants, and practical shoes.

"Wouldn't you know it! She booked us to drive Formula 1 racing cars in the Formula YAS 3000. Even though she used the name 'N. Dunn,' and introduced herself that way, no one was fooled. They knew we were women. They made us pay extra and they accepted our money.

They scanned our drivers' licenses and gave us safety briefings. We were fitted with helmet balaclavas and gloves, and assigned instructors who drove ahead of us.

"It was scary and exhilarating at the same time. Norma charmed the pants off of our instructors, who admitted they didn't think a woman could drive the circuit. They told her she'd proved them wrong. The next day, she hired a driver and we drove into the desert. We spent two days providing medical services to the residents of an impoverished village. At night, we prepared meals alongside the women, and we slept on the rugs in their tent. Although only two hours from the glamor of Abu Dhabi, it was worlds apart in every other way. Then it was time for us to return to the base in Afghanistan. Norma had many sides to her, and I've just given you a glimpse into the fun-loving and caring sides."

Dr. Bach's voice hardened and she thumped the lectern with a closed fist. "I have lost my best friend, and in the name of justice, I call upon the City of Greenville to find and punish her killer!"

One by one, the mourners rose to their feet and began to applaud. Dr. Bach stepped away from the lectern and returned to her seat, nodding firmly as she met stare after stare.

Henry and Harmony were seated in the otherwise empty balcony at the back of the church. Henry watched his partner read emails, skim text messages, and reply to those. He jabbed her arm after watching her remove her iPad from her bag and turn it on.

"You're on an assignment. We're supposed to be observing those at the funeral, not using it as an opportunity to play catch-up on personal correspondence," he said.

She looked up. "You do know that women are skilled multi-taskers. Take Dr. Bach, for example. She described her friendship with Dr. Dunn because she wanted the churchgoers to see the doctor as a per-

son. At the same time, she used the opportunity to pressure officials
to solve the murder. I'm sure she's thinking that by getting those in at-
tendance on board, they will exert pressure on us to get quick results."

Despite his initial disapproval, Henry was impressed. "You got all
that by listening to her?"

"And by watching and recording the reactions to her words. I noticed that Isaiah Isherwood did not nod or otherwise react to what Dr.
Bach said about Dr. Dunn. If I didn't know better, I'd think he either
didn't know the victim very well or else was preoccupied."

"Well, Dr. Isherwood had an alibi at the time of the murder. He was
in the arboretum, giving a group of women from a retirement home a
short tour of the gardens. Did you notice anything else?"

"There was a gentleman dressed in a business suit who does not appear to be from Pitt County."

"How can you tell?"

"Look at the other men. Most are wearing polo shirts under their
jackets or dress shirts without a jacket. None of them are wearing a con-
ventional suit and tie. But this guy is in a dark suit with a buttoned-up
shirt and a tie. He has a full head of hair. He's also well groomed, with
no beard or stubble."

"We need to find out who he is," said Henry.

Harmony tried to take the man's photo, but found she could only
get a side profile of his face.

"Does anyone else stand out to you?"

"Well, most of the churchgoers are older. The youngest appears to
be the woman seated in the second-row pew, next to Frank Wright."

"We can ask him who she is when we see him at the reception."

"Aw, do we have to go to the reception? I have plans," she protested.

"Think of all the good ol' Southern food you'll be able to eat. I wouldn't miss the opportunity for Shout Hallelujah Potato Salad, Funeral Potatoes, Tomato Aspic, Pimiento Cheese, and a Jello Salad, not to mention fried chicken and grits."

"We Southerners do know how to use food to comfort those in distress," she said.

"Southerners are known for their hospitality. It's just one of many things that we do well," he agreed.

Once the mourners filling the ground level had filed out, Harmony and Henry descended the steps and exited the church. Henry's phone emitted a low trill. He ignored it.

"Aren't you going to get that? It could be the murderer wanting to confess after hearing Dr. Bach's poignant plea," suggested Harmony.

When the phone rang a second time, he sighed and picked it up. Since they were in his car, he switched the phone to Speaker mode. "Smith here. Who is this?"

"I have information that I'd like to share with you. It may break your investigation wide open," said Deputy Sheriff Longfellow.

"What's that?"

"I'd prefer to tell you in person. See you in my office."

On the way to the Detention Center, Harmony told Henry how La Donna had got past the guard to enter the building. "There's a door in the rear that opens from the back of the director's office near the utility closet. The officer securing the building spoke to everyone in the building, but no one admitted to knowing about the door or the key. Since there appeared to be no key and the door was only used as an exit for a fire drill, the officer didn't seal it. La Donna had a key and entered through that door. La Donna had a key because on her first day of work, she had collected all the keys to the building and kept them. After all, she opened the front door every morning to let staff and visitors in. She opened the waiting-room door on the side of the building so that research participants could enter the building."

Henry said. "That explains how she got in. Now we need to find out what she was searching for in Dr. Dunn's office."

Deputy Sheriff Longfellow was sitting back in the sheriff's office, the spurs on his crocodile boots scratching the desk's top. He gestured for his two visitors to sit.

He started to comment on the 'fine weather,' but Harmony's direct gaze stopped him. He got to the point. "A little birdie told me that there's a lab that produces 'women's medicine' as a sideline in our neck of the woods. The lab is run by a guy who is employed by a multinational pharmaceutical company that supplies narcotics legally to local pharmacies. My contact told me there's a large shipment coming in later this week."

"Who told you this and what do you mean by 'women's medicine,' " asked Harmony.

"I was talking to your partner, not you," said the deputy sheriff pointedly.

"As the only woman here, you should be talking to me when you're talking about 'women's medicine.'"

Henry intervened, placing his hand on Harmony's arm while smiling at the deputy sheriff.

"Thanks for the tip. Did you get the name of the medication or the whereabouts of this lab? Do you know the name of the guy or even his company's name? Do you have any other information?"

"That's all I've got. It's a tip. You guys are the detectives. Isn't it your job to check out leads, run with the information, and identify and arrest the bad actors?"

Harmony formally thanked the deputy sheriff for his information.

The deputy sheriff removed his feet from the top of the desk and stood up. He shook their hands. "Remember me when you have a vacancy in your administrative positions. I'd like to spend my pre-retirement years in an office rather than in a detention center surrounded by criminals who would kill me if they had the chance."

"I hear you," said Henry.

Chapter 27

Even more guests gathered for the post-funeral reception at the Hilton to enjoy sweet tea, grits and gravy, funeral potatoes, Shout Hallelujah potato salad, creamy coleslaw, hush puppies, pulled pork on sliders, pimiento on crackers, and, of course, fried chicken. Key lime pie and banana pie rounded out the offerings.

While Jeannie limited herself to a small serving of coleslaw and a hush puppy, Dr. Bach surveyed the offerings with satisfaction. "Lots of dishes to stick to your ribs. Dr. Dunn wasn't much of a meat eater but she loved key lime pie. I myself favor meat. This is good, solid food, the kind that sticks to your ribs and fills you full up."

The arboretum director joined them at the dessert table. "Please accept my condolences," he said. His wife nodded in agreement.

Dr. Bach gave Isaiah a wary glance. "Are you the director who argued that the County would do better by putting in walking paths around the arboretum instead of providing funds to help women overcome their struggles with food addiction and diabetes?"

"I do think that lunchtime walks around the arboretum's gardens are a great way to get in steps. And gardens are inherently relaxing, so they are a good combination for people who are feeling stress."

"I guess I must have misunderstood Dr. Dunn," Dr. Bach said sweetly.

He looked dismissively at her. "She and I competed for funding from the same limited pool. Although you've got a point. It doesn't matter how good a researcher Dr. Dunn was. Some of the women around here are just plain lazy. Nothing's going to change their behavior." He popped a small powdered donut into his mouth and continued on his way.

Dr. Bach spoke to Jeannie in a stage whisper. "I guess he wears a white jacket so that the sugar from his donuts blends in with his jacket. Dr. Dunn called him a snake. I see what she means. Keep your eye on that man. He'd sell out his mother to get ahead. And with her out of the picture, his ratty little garden will get more funding that would otherwise have gone to Dr. Dunn's very worthy project."

"The garden is not ratty. It's really quite delightful," Jeannie protested.

"No, the Butchart Garden in Victoria is delightful. So is the Van Dusen Garden in Vancouver. The arboretum is a ragtag collection of trees with a few flowerbeds and more than its share of weeds. You can't compare them."

"Greenville does not have the same wealth or population size as Vancouver. It used to be an agricultural center. It's not fair to make the comparison."

"Yet another reason why I told Norma this was not a suitable workplace for her."

"She called the arboretum her paradise," Jeannie countered. "It may not have the flair or sophistication of the Butchart Garden, but it is still a peaceful place. The master gardeners have done a wonderful job creating demonstration gardens filled with beautiful plants and shrubs."

"Enough! I need you to find out who wanted Dr. Dunn dead so that they can be brought to justice. But be careful. There's more than one snake in the grass here."

As Dr. Bach moved toward the exit, her eyes glommed onto a gum-chewing La Donna, whose black leather miniskirt and halter top belied the dignity of the moment.

"You must be La Donna," said Dr. Bach.

The younger woman looked uncertainly at her. "I'm surprised you know my name."

"I'm surprised you are well enough to come and pay your respects," said Jeannie. "How are you feeling?"

Dr. Bach did not give La Donna an opportunity to answer the question. "Dr. Dunn liked to dress up, but she always dressed appropriately. She told me you had very long fingernails and dressed for work as if you were going to a nightclub." Dr. Bach slowly swept her gaze over La Donna, beginning at the head and ending at her feet. "I guess you have no sense of decorum when going to a funeral, either."

They heard the sound of a car screech to a stop next to the hotel entrance. La Donna hissed at Dr. Bach. "You may look more like a business woman in your suit, but you sound just as judgmental as your friend."

La Donna stalked toward the exit. The driver of the truck flung the door open and yelled, 'Get in, Babe." He floored the accelerator, leaving the two physicians speechless as La Donna gave Dr. Bach the finger.

"Whoa! I thought the South was known for its good manners," remarked Dr. Bach.

"I don't think she likes Northerners, and since you're from north of New York, in her mind you definitely qualify as one," said Jeannie.

Dr. Bach glanced at her watch. "I've been in Greenville for less than three hours, yet I will leave with a lasting impression."

"There are some lovely people and some not so lovely people, just as there are in any city," said Jeannie diplomatically.

"Is that so!"

"The people here are justifiably proud of their city. It has a beautiful riverfront. And the Arboretum has walking trails under gigantic trees that provide shade in hot weather."

"With a director who is apparently more concerned with toadying to his boss's wishes than doing what's best for the fair citizens of Greenville. And who's slow as molasses when it comes to women!"

Jeannie was accustomed to Dr. Bach breaking out into blistering diatribes aimed at whoever was unfortunate enough to be in proximity, but she could see that the invective was adding another layer of distress to a community already in mourning. "Dr. Bach, please—," she implored.

Isaiah turned to Jeannie. "Child, don't you pay her no mind. She's lost her soulmate and is responding the only way she knows how. I know she doesn't mean half of what she's saying," he said.

Jeannie looked at him with respect. "Dr. Dunn would appreciate your compassion."

He acknowledged the compliment. "Even though you've only been here for a few days, you seem to have a good understanding of what made Dr. Dunn tick. She'd be pleased to see how quick a learner you have turned out to be."

Dr. Bach glared at him. "Stop trying to butter up Dr. Johal. She'll see your true colors soon enough."

Isaiah's wife clutched his arm. "C'mon, Isaiah, let's go. Now is not the time to try to be reasonable with someone who doesn't understand what caring means. Let's go home."

She turned toward Jeannie. "Make sure your boss gets to the airport safely. We don't need any more perturbations here."

Chapter 28

Frank was moving toward the exit when he felt a pair of eyes drilling into him. He turned around, scanning the room. A man dressed in a dark suit raised his hand in acknowledgment. His wife heard her husband's involuntary intake of breath and looked inquiringly at him.

"It's nothing, honey," he said.

"Who is that man?"

"I've never met him but I saw him in Dr. Dunn's office a few weeks ago. I think he's with WellStar Pharmaceuticals, the company underwriting the study."

"Perhaps you should introduce yourself to him."

Frank grumbled.

His wife persisted. "Dr. Dunn is gone. You can't change that. But think about what she would want. She'd be concerned about losing funding for the study. You told everyone at the service that you would do everything in your power to keep the research project going. Well, this is where you can make that happen." She gave his arm a little nudge.

"Hi there," said Frank, extending his arm toward the stranger. "I am the project manager for Dr. Dunn's research study. I don't believe we've met, but I did see you in her office a few weeks ago."

The two men shook hands while sizing each other up. Anderson Archer was in his mid-thirties. His face was smooth, without even a hint of crow's feet or frown lines. His thick blond hair was slicked back, skirting the collar of his white dress shirt. In addition to being younger than Frank, he was considerably trimmer.

Anderson was the first to break eye contact. He smiled at Frank, displaying two rows of even, ultrawhite teeth. "Call me Andy. I thought I recognized you. I came to pay my condolences. Dr. Dunn was an excellent researcher and a fine woman. I don't know who would have done this to her."

"They say poison is a weapon preferred by women, while men mostly resort to guns," said Frank.

Anderson raised his eyebrows and stared at Frank. "Are you saying she was poisoned? Are you saying the murderer is a woman?"

Frank parried the question with another. "Didn't you know she was poisoned?"

Anderson vehemently shook his head. "No, I didn't know the cause of death. I saw a short piece online. The story reported the death of a prominent physician researcher in Greenville. It mentioned Dr. Dunn's name at the end of the article, as well as a note saying the funeral would take place in Greenville. Here I am, paying my respects."

"I see," said Frank. "I will be continuing to manage the project. There's a physician researcher who just joined the team, Dr. Johal. She and I will share the leadership role. While we can't replace Dr. Dunn, we are both committed to seeing the project through because it's what she would have wanted."

"That's good to hear. My company has a lot invested in this project and we're keen to see the results. I was hoping to ask Bernard Bigelow for a status update but I understand he is on vacation."

A long pause ensued. The two looked at each other, as if trying to gauge the other's expressions. Frank ended the silence. "Becky planned this trip for more than a year. I'm sure Bernard wanted to be here, but couldn't let down his wife."

Anderson nodded understandingly. "Especially if she'd been waiting a long time to travel abroad. My father used to say, 'happy wife, happy life.' I doubt that Bernard wanted to tell his wife to cancel a trip she's been planning for years."

"I guess so."

The two men stared at each other. "If it's not too much trouble, do you think you could provide an update on how the project is going? Dr. Dunn didn't give us a written report the last time we met."

"I don't see why not, but it may take a few days," said Frank slowly. "The building is still closed. We've also been very unlucky with staff."

"What do you mean?"

"Well, our receptionist was hospitalized. She's obviously on the mend, since I saw her a little while ago."

"What happened?"

"She ingested something she shouldn't have."

"Was she poisoned? Lucky that she lived to tell the tale, unlike Dr. Dunn."

"Oh, it wasn't the same. La Donna went into Dr. Dunn's office even though the building is off limits. She flavored her tea with essential oil sitting next to an air diffuser in Dr. Dunn's office. The essential oil carries a warning on its label that says 'harmful if ingested.' It's unfortunate she didn't read the warning before adding a few drops to her tea."

"Why would she ingest essential oil that has such an explicit warning on its label?"

Frank scratched his head and looked uncomfortable. "I don't know. Perhaps she was so intent on combing through Dr. Dunn's personal effects that she didn't notice the warning label."

"Ouch, that's not a kind thing to say about anyone, much less a member of your staff," winced Anderson.

Frank had the grace to look ashamed of himself. "You're right. I shouldn't have said it."

"My pappy taught me that you never insult anyone directly in the South. You can speak generally, but never ever direct your insults at a person."

"Where are you from?"

"I grew up in the finest city in the South."

"Which is?"

"Now I know for sure you're not Southern. Everyone knows Charleston is the finest city."

"Thanks for the geography lesson. My wife is from the South, but my family moved here from Ohio."

"That explains it," said Anderson.

Frank scrambled to change the topic. "You were requesting an update. I can tell you we've hired an epidemiologist with loads of experience analyzing reams of statistical data. She's here. Would you like to meet her?"

Anderson's eyes gleamed in anticipation. "Bring me to her."

Frank watched Anderson's eyes narrow as the two men came in closer proximity to Jeannie and Dr. Bach.

"Why is she standing with that loudmouthed, mannish woman who talked about racing an F-1 in the desert?"

"What happened to Southern manners? Do you consider 'loudmouthed' and 'mannish' to be compliments?" asked Frank.

Anderson sniped. "That woman described how Norma Dunn lied her way onto the race course. She had no business being in that car, much less driving it. Women aren't made to race cars, and she and her friend shouldn't have tried to pretend they were men."

"It was unorthodox, but Dr. Dunn was a leader in a male-dominated community. She was used to playing down her femininity when she had to."

"You mean, when it suited her."

"You could look at it that way, but I've seen Dr. Dunn take down men who stood in her way. I've also seen her be the sweetest, most accommodating hostess you could find, offering visitors a glass of iced tea and dainty cookies."

"She did have a tray of sweets when I met her in her office a few weeks ago," Anderson admitted.

Frank smiled wryly. "As a medical researcher, Dr. Dunn was quiet and reserved. Those who knew her in that regard viewed her as intense and dedicated in her quest to find answers. But as the director of public health, she recognized that she had to play well with politicians and other decision makers in order to get the funds and staff she needed to be able to pursue her research goals. In the short time I worked with her, I came to admire her delicate balancing act, how she was able to give a little to a competing interest so as not to alienate those who shared a different perspective."

He gently placed his hand on Anderson's arm. "Now let me introduce you to Dr. Johal."

"Dr. Johal, this is Anderson Archer. His company is sponsoring Dr. Dunn's research, and I told him you'd recently come on board to help us with the statistical analysis."

Dr. Bach had been standing quietly beside Jeannie. The senior physician's expression was neutral. "Dr. Dunn told me she could use additional technical expertise, so I drafted Dr. Johal into working with my friend for a month. In addition to being an international surgeon and epidemiologist, Dr. Johal is a highly skilled quality improvement specialist with experience leading complex investigations into patient harm."

"Which skills are you finding most in demand?" asked Anderson.

Jeannie dodged the question. "In the short time I've been here, I've learned that the arboretum was a paradise for Dr. Dunn. And in poring through the project data, I've seen there are opportunities for improvement. In fact, this morning I was providing the data clerk with enhanced Excel training. She has the potential to become an expert data analyst." Jeannie gestured toward Tanisha, who was standing a few feet away, gazing at her shoes.

"Perhaps I should be addressing my request for a quarterly status report to you rather than toward Frank," Anderson suggested.

Before Frank could interrupt, Jeannie jumped in. She smiled sweetly at Anderson. "No, I just know bits and pieces. My work is with numbers. Frank knows the big picture. He's managing all aspects of this project. He's asked me to look at the data, and I'm happy to do this. Although I've only been here a few days, he's impressed me with his grasp of the project."

Frank looked mollified. "Andy, as I said a few minutes ago, I'd be happy to provide you with an overview soon. We lost our leader a week ago and the office has been closed. Our receptionist is out on sick leave and won't be back for a couple of days. We're ramping up the data clerk's skills. Dr. Johal just joined us. I will get Dr. Dunn's last progress report, update it, and send it to you."

Anderson pressed the project manager. "In the next few days? It's already overdue."

Frank demurred. "No, it's going to take me longer than that. I can assure you I'll do my best to have the quarterly report ready before Bernard Bigelow's return."

"Well, if that's the best you can do. Here's my card. I'll be waiting for your report. If I don't hear from you before Bernard is back, I'll have a chat with him. He won't be happy to know that you've been stonewalling the project's major donor," said Anderson. He picked up his drink, bowed, and walked away.

Frank seethed, "What a piece of work. He thinks he can boss me around. I'll show him who's in charge."

"I know, I know," soothed Darla. "Just remember, he holds the purse strings, and you don't want him to pull the funding."

He frowned, knowing he would have to tread delicately even though he felt as if he had a one hundred and fifty pound gorilla jumping on his back.

Chapter 29

The funeral reception was winding down. Jeanie signaled for Tanisha to join her. "Where did you put your knapsack?" she asked.

"On the few occasions that I've been in an expensive store, I've worried that I might hit something with the edge of my bag and break it. You see the signs, 'You break it, you pay for it.' Since my bag is on the bigger side, I put it in the coatroom, behind some boxes. It's not visible. I didn't think anyone would mind, and I figured it would be safe there."

"I want to introduce you to someone," said Jeannie. Tanisha followed in silence as Jeannie walked briskly toward the elderly lady cleaning off the tables.

Lila-Jean looked closely at Tanisha, murmuring as she did so. Her voice was gentle when she spoke. "Honey, you're coming home with me tonight. I have a spare bedroom in my house that has your name on it."

Tanisha gasped. "But you don't even know me. How do you know I'm not a thief or a murderer?"

Lila-Jean laughed heartily. "You're a comedian, too, just what the doctor ordered."

Tanisha stood silent and looked puzzled.

"It's a saying. Dr. Johal told me you're working with her on an important project. She and I go way back and if she says you're okay, that's good enough for me."

The explanation puzzled Tanisha. She turned toward Jeannie. "How is it possible you go way back? Didn't you join the research team after me?"

Jeannie smiled at the younger girl's literalness. "It's just an expression. Lila-Jean took me under her wing shortly after I checked into the hotel. She's been looking out for me ever since. You'll be doing her a favor by staying with her. She misses her son terribly."

Lila-Jean agreed. "He went to Afghanistan and never returned."

Tanisha's eyes clouded. "Thank you for raising a son who did his duty. My pappy and brother were called to the Lord recently, and it's been hard for my ma to let go."

Lila-Jean clasped the younger woman's hand. "Stay here with me. You can help me clear these tables. Then we'll head home."

Jeannie turned to Dr. Bach, who'd uncharacteristically remained silent during the conversation. "I have something for you that I think you'd like to have. It was in Dr. Dunn's office. It's in my hotel room."

They headed to the elevators.

"That was a nice thing you did, finding a place for the data-entry person to live."

"You don't know the half of it. Dr. Dunn saw her walking along the highway one day. She stopped and ended up hiring her to be the clerk. But La Donna made a clerical error, which meant that the clerk didn't get paid for a month. Then Frank let Tanisha go. She's been living in a shelter because she can't afford to pay rent. She's back to work with us, and walking to work every day because she doesn't have bus fare. I don't think Dr. Dunn had any idea of the dire straits in which this poor girl found herself."

"It certainly sounds like she's had it rough," said Dr. Bach.

"Lila-Jean will fuss over her. And Tanisha will keep her company. They'll both help each other."

"What happened to her father and brother?"

"I don't know the details. I do know that despite being so young,

Tanisha has had a very tough life. I hope this job and her having a bedroom to call her own will make things better."

Dr. Bach looked approvingly at Jeannie. "You've come a long way from the shy, reserved girl who joined the health authority and insisted on following every policy to the letter. You used to do everything by the book and remind your supervisor and anyone else if they deviated even an iota. You were so inflexible. On more than one occasion, Kathleen came to me and asked what in the world I'd been thinking when I hired you to work in her department."

Jeannie grinned. "I still follow policies, but Kathleen taught me that being right doesn't mean making other people feel bad when they're wrong. She also told me that guidelines are just that. Kathleen told me to learn them and that there was some flexibility in how some are applied."

Dr. Bach grinned. "She did, did she?"

"Kathleen admonished me when I started to correct a new manager who hadn't filled in the incident forms properly. All the information is supposed to be confidential, yet here was this manager putting down the patient's name and address. I was about to ask her if she knew the meaning of the term 'patient privacy' when Kathleen gave me a look."

Dr. Bach laughed. "Yes, I know that look. It conveys more than words ever could."

"Following the meeting with the manager, Kathleen told me to remove the confidential elements. She said it was better to encourage the manager and praise what she'd done right rather than making her feel defensive. I prepared a sample template with fictional information and a half-page primer that we now send out with the blank incident form. This has made it easier for those who do not regularly fill out incident forms to do it properly the first time."

"Did Kathleen recommend you do that?"

"No, I came up with the idea myself. I wasn't going to keep fixing people's mistakes. But Kathleen told me it was a great idea and thanked me for my initiative. She's very quiet, a natural observer and excellent listener. She's adept at picking up on what people are thinking by assessing their expressions and body language. And she's so tactful. As a surgeon, what I said went. I didn't have to worry about hurting anyone's feelings. I miss some aspects of the work I did. But I know that my interpersonal skills are much more developed as a result of working with Kathleen. She's an excellent leader."

She paused as she extracted the passcard to her hotel room from her bag. "Odd, that didn't work!"

She stepped back and frowned.

Dr. Bach was unsuccessful in suppressing a grin.

On the third try, the green light flashed. Jeannie grabbed the door lever and shrieked. "My God! My hand is burning!"

Chapter 30

Jeannie pushed against the open door with all her force. The door finally opened and she almost fell. She saw a piece of white paper on the floor and stooped to reach for it.

"Don't touch it!" bellowed Dr. Bach.

Jeannie's hand felt as if it were on fire. Her mind immediately recalled the explosion in the physician's lounge in Little Flowers Clinic. She moaned as the memories overtook her. Now she smelled the scent of charred flesh and heard the sizzle of burning wires.

Dr. Bach looked worriedly at the younger doctor. "Jeannie, can you hear me?"

No answer. Jeannie's unresponsiveness made her appear to be in a trance.

"Dr. Johal, you're in Greenville, NC with Dr. Bach. I'm going to examine your hand."

She guided Jeannie to a chair and examined her wrist and fingers closely. "You've got raised blisters on the backs of your fingers and the inside of your palm. I can see what look like multiple burn marks. I'm sure it hurts like hell, but it's only temporary. You're going to be okay."

"It's so hot and itchy," moaned Jeannie.

"Get a hold of yourself!"

Jeannie didn't respond. In her mind, she was trapped in the physicians' lounge, powerless to avoid the flames licking her hand.

"Stop it," hissed Dr. Bach. She grabbed Jeannie's shoulders and shook them so hard that the younger woman's teeth rattled. "You're in a hotel room in Greenville, North Carolina. I am with you. You are alive. You are safe and you will be okay. I wouldn't swear to it in court, but it looks to me as if someone laced your door handle with capsaicin or with a plant extract that irritates the skin. I will give you five seconds to snap out of your torpor. Then I will slap your face so hard that it will leave a mark."

Jeannie opened her eyes, blinked, and released a deep sigh. She spoke slowly, with a hint of indignation in her voice. "Did you just threaten to slap my face?"

"That's what you do when someone is hysterical."

"Well, I'm not hysterical."

"You were certainly in your own little world. I called your name repeatedly and you didn't respond. How are you feeling now?"

Her voice sounded strained. "Very tired. And my hand feels as if it's on fire. It really hurts."

Dr. Bach led the younger physician to the sink. "You're going to be all right," she said in a soothing voice. She turned on the cold water. "You need to wash your hand thoroughly with soap and water before you touch anywhere else."

While Jeannie's hand cooled under the running water, Dr. Bach searched through her briefcase. She retrieved a pair of plastic gloves and a tube of ointment. "Your hand's still going to hurt, but this will reduce the burning sensation."

"They let you carry all this on the plane?"

"It's a professional courtesy. Whenever I board a plane, I pass my business card to security personnel and to the check-in counter so that they know there's a medical presence on board the plane in case of an emergency. They like knowing they can count on me and they've never confiscated any of my supplies."

After applying the steroidal cream, Dr. Bach applied gauze to Jeannie's hand. "This will protect the skin. Now, I'm going to give you something to relax you. It'll make you sleepy."

Jeannie nodded mutely. The ordeal had exhausted her. She crawled into the bed, keeping her bandaged hand outside the covers.

While still wearing gloves, Dr. Bach retrieved the note on the carpet. It reeked of curacao and had oil stains on it. The note was handwritten in large, childish printing. She read it out loud. *"You and yore kind aren't wanted here. You think your so smart, well you don't know shit. Git out if you know whats GOOD for you. God bless."*

Although intended to scare Jeannie, the words had the opposite effect. They lifted away the fog of fatigue. She sprang out of bed, wincing when her hand made contact with the covers. "You'd think that someone who writes a threatening letter would make the effort to use correct spelling and punctuation."

"Oh, Jeannie, you're precious! Is it possible that whoever wrote this letter was drunk?"

"Why do you say that?"

"Well, there's a smear of red sauce. It looks and smells like barbecue sauce. And the blue mark smells like curacao."

"What's that?"

"I forgot that you grew up in a sheltered existence. When Nora and I were visiting Saudi Arabia, we weren't allowed to drink alcoholic beverages in public. We bought a bottle of bootlegged curacao. It's a sweet, blue liqueur, a popular component in tropical drinks."

Jeannie's anger was palpable. "They don't know me if they think that covering the door handle with chili pepper oil will scare me away."

Dr. Bach looked at the young woman. "No, they only see that you're a woman and you're Brown. They don't know anything about you."

Jeannie spat out each word in a staccato soup. "They're not going to get rid of me that easily. Something's rotten in Greenville, and I'm not leaving until I get to the bottom of it!"

Dr. Bach nodded approvingly. "That's my girl. They killed Dr. Dunn and someone just tried to poison you. I'll stay with you until you fall asleep. Your hand should feel better when you awaken. Now get back into bed. I want you to find out what's going on here. But do it wisely. Be careful. Use the skills Kathleen taught you. I know you're smarter than this illiterate thug."

Jeannie drowsily corrected her mentor. "Illiterate woman," she murmured.

Dr. Bach turned sharply. "Are you saying it was a woman because of the liqueur?"

Jeannie looked up. "No, what's that got to do with it? I did some research after learning that Dr. Dunn was poisoned. Did you know that women are seven times as likely as men to use poison to murder their enemy?"

"I did not."

Jeannie was on a tear. "Men use guns most of the time, women use guns less than half of the time."

Despite the gravity of the situation, Dr. Bach laughed. "Always the researcher! Where did you get these numbers?"

"An FBI report. Poison is among the weapons of choice and proportionately more women use poison than men."

"That's all very interesting, but you need to rest."

Jeannie nodded drowsily and her words began to slur. "Now I just need to find a woman who eats chicken wings, drinks sickly sweet blue drinks, and doesn't know how to spell."

Day Eight

Chapter 31

Tanisha's whole body hunched forward. Her head was tucked tur-tlelike, the eyes looking straight ahead and darting up and down. But unlike a turtle charting a path to a body of water, Tanisha's eyes were flickering between the written numbers of a notepad and the columns of numbers on a computer spreadsheet.

Back and forth, back and forth. It didn't matter how hard she looked or how much she wanted the handwritten numbers and computer data to match. She just couldn't get them right. The totals didn't match.

She frowned, biting her lip in concentration. She knew she'd made a mistake somewhere, but she didn't know where.

She repeated the manual calculation and still came up with the same total.

Something was amiss.

Slow down. Close your eyes. Take a deep breath. You've got this, girl.

Tanisha typed an awkward sentence into Google, and learned that just because something looked like a number didn't mean it really was a number. She clicked on cell formatting to make sure the numbers were formatted as numbers or currency and not text. She discovered that twelve of the six hundred entries were formatted as text, throwing off the total. After correcting the errors, she ran her total again and discovered it matched with the manual count.

Tanisha was so excited that she could barely restrain herself from bouncing off her seat. She had corrected a problem without having to ask Jeannie for help, and she had discovered a new tool.

Her question to Jeannie was interrupted. "Did you know...?"

Jeannie's eyes swept from Tanisha's computer to the numbers scrawled on a pad. "You're not still doing manual calculations, are you?" she said as she walked into the office. Jeannie's hair looked tousled and the loops on her blouse were uneven. Her eyes had dark circles under them and the thick application of eyebrow pencil gave Jeannie bushy brows. Tanisha was taken aback.

"Are you okay?" asked Tanisha.

Jeannie snapped at the younger woman. "Are you still doing manual calculations?"

"This morning I learned how to check columns of numbers to ensure they are formatted as numbers. Did you know that they can resemble numbers but are really text? Oh boy, if that happens, your totals don't add up. But if you format them as numbers or currency, your total will be accurate. Isn't that cool?"

Jeannie smiled at Tanisha's enthusiasm. "Yes, it is. But it still doesn't explain why you are writing numbers on a pad and pencil."

"It's because I wanted to make sure that I entered the numbers accurately."

"Tanisha, from my observations, you are very careful when it comes to entering information into the computer."

"Yes, but when I double-checked, my numbers didn't match. Isn't it possible that Excel could be adding up the numbers incorrectly?"

"No, it's a spreadsheet programmed to add correctly. But it's only as good as the data entered. Garbage in, garbage out," said Jeannie.

"What do you mean by that?"

"It's a phrase. It means that if you enter inaccurate information, you will get inaccurate results. In other words, if you enter the wrong numbers and use those numbers to analyze your data, you won't be able to rely on your results."

"Is it possible this is what happened when the database was set up? Could someone have formatted the numbers as text?"

"It's possible, yes."

"Well, I am never going to make that mistake," said Tanisha, nodding her head vehemently.

"Alright."

Jeannie's low-key response worried Tanisha because it was so out of character. The younger woman looked at the older woman. "Jeannie, you're normally so bubbly. But you seem tired, even sad."

"Well, the funeral was sad. And seeing Dr. Bach reminded me of my life in British Columbia."

"Too bad she couldn't stay longer."

"I suppose, although she can be very demanding. But yesterday evening, she was very kind to me."

Jeannie held up her hand to show Tanisha a large white gauze bandage covering her palm.

"What happened?"

Jeannie's voice broke. "Someone tried to hurt me."

"Oh my God!"

"My hand came into contact with poison on the hotel-room door handle. Thank God Dr. Bach was with me. She held my hand under cold running water to take away the sting, cleaned and bandaged it, gave me a sedative, and then insisted I get in bed."

"First Dr. Dunn, then La Donna, and now you. Am I next?"

Jeannie smiled wanly. "No, I don't think so. I have a good idea who did this. I think she was trying to send me a warning, not trying to kill me."

"Well, that's a relief! But it's still scary."

"I'm not afraid. I'm angry."

"What are you going to do?"

"She was sending me a message that I'm not wanted here. Well, I'll show her no one threatens Jeannie Johal."

"Are you going to go after her with a gun?"

Tanisha's question surprised Jeannie. "Why would I do that?"

"It's what we do when we have a disagreement."

"Who is 'we' and what do you mean by that?"

Tanisha looked sheepish. "Well, my pa's house was burned down when he lost his job but refused to become a drug mule. I lost my pa and my brother in the fire. Ma says that if Pa had had a gun, he could've shot the guy who came to the door and threw a grenade into the house. The next day, I went out and got a gun."

Jeannie gaped at Tanisha, "That story is awful in so many ways. I'm sorry. Losing your pa and your baby brother must have been awful!"

"And the house. We lost everything," said Tanisha mournfully.

"How did you get hold of a gun?"

"That was the easy part. The man who runs the grocery store sold me a pistol."

"Was it expensive? How did you pay for it? How come he was able to sell you a gun when you were a minor?"

Tanisha suppressed a sob. "Ma and Pa could barely make ends meet when Pa was alive. I had to make a deal with the grocer. He sold me the gun in exchange for personal favors."

"I am so sorry," said Jeannie. "That terrible man!"

"Yes, and then he started to court my mother. When I told her that he was a bad man, she told me I didn't know what I was talking about. When he moved in with us, she told me to be nice to him."

Tanisha spat into the air. "Be nice to a monster? I was just glad that I had a gun because when he came into my room one night and tried to get into my bed, I pushed the rim of the gun into his cheek, cocked the pistol, and told him I would blow him to bits if he didn't get out of my bedroom.

"As soon as it was light, I left home and I haven't been back since."

"Tanisha, when I was fourteen, my father sold me to the landlord. I was forced into a marriage with a man more than twice my age. In return, the landlord promised my parents they could live rent-free in one of his apartments for the rest of their lives."

"Did he make you do things?"

"Not at first. But what he did was legal because I was his wife. It took me almost fifteen years before I had the strength to leave him."

"Do you keep in touch with your parents?"

"No, I haven't seen them in a long time."

"Jeannie, I have an idea."

"Do you mean another Excel formatting tip you would like to share with me?"

"No, nothing like that."

Tanisha looked earnestly at Jeannie, trying to anticipate her response to an unasked question.

"Well, what is it? What are you thinking?"

"You should get a gun."

Jeannie shuddered in distaste. "Guns kill people. I've never even touched a gun. What would I want with a gun?"

Tanisha corrected her. "People kill people. You need a gun to protect yourself in case that person comes after you again."

"I'm a visitor in your country. I could get arrested for having a gun."

Tanisha laughed. "Everyone here has a gun. It's a way of life. You have the right to protect what's yours."

"In Vancouver, I studied self-defense at a gym. I can protect myself."

Tanisha frowned. "You're tough, I'll give you that. But pointing a gun at someone tells them you mean business. They ain't going to mess with you if you threaten them with a gun."

Jeannie was uncertain. "I don't know. And wouldn't I need lessons to learn how to use it?"

"Seven and a half hours of training will qualify you to own a gun."

"One day?" Jeannie was incredulous.

Tanisha grinned. "It used to be that you could go to the hair salon, get a hair wash and set, get your hair dried and styled, all while learning about guns. You'd come out with a fancy hairstyle and a stamped card certifying you were qualified to own a gun."

"It sounds like the Wild West to me."

"I'd like you to think about it. In the meantime, let's take a trip to a gun range where you can learn how to shoot."

"I'm not sure about that."

Tanisha seized upon Jeannie's hesitation. "It'll be like a girl's night, just the two of us. I'll be Stagecoach Mary, and you can be Annie Oakley."

"Who?"

"How about Calamity Jane?"

Jeannie looked blankly at Tanisha. "Who are these people?"

"These are stars of the Wild West. Annie Oakley was born Phoebe Ann Mosey and grew up to become one of America's top sharpshooters. She could shoot a cigarette from her husband's lips, she could split a playing card held in a person's hand. She was a feminist long before women had the right to vote. But my favorite is Stagecoach Mary because she looks like me. Her real name was Mary Fields, and she was the first Black woman to be a Star Route mail carrier. They say she beat out hundreds of applicants for the job by being the fastest to hitch up her six-horse mail-delivery team."

Jeannie's bemused expression drew a laugh from Tanisha. "I can tell you're not from here. Let me show you how North Carolinians have fun. We'll shoot paper targets, you'll learn about gun safety, and I'll tell you about some of America's most famous female gunslingers. We'll have a blast!"

Chapter 32

"Are you sure this is the right direction to the Okay Corral?" It was the third time Jeannie asked the question and the third time Tanisha giggled in response.

Tanisha's giggle sounded like staccato high notes on a xylophone, joyful and unexpected trills. It surprised Jeannie, breaking into her thoughts of being attacked earlier in the week and bringing her attention back to the road and to her passenger.

"Yes, I'm sure. Just keep going straight a little longer. We're almost there."

While Jeannie drove, Tanisha luxuriated in the soft leather seats. "These seats are so soft. Not like my Pa's old station wagon. We never knew if it would start or not. Sometimes, I'd have to get into the driver's seat while Pa was out back pushing the car to get it started. It sure was scary because I'd have to keep it slow so I could shimmy over to the passenger's side and he could jump in while the car was going."

She inhaled deeply. "Your car smells good. I imagine this is what heaven smells like, buttery and rich."

Tanisha paused for a moment. Then she repeated her question, "You're sure you've never heard of the O.K. Corral?"

Jeannie's voice sounded irritated. "Why do you keep asking me that? I've told you I'm not from these parts and you shouldn't expect me to know about a small town in North Carolina."

"Jeannie, I know you're a very smart person. You have all these degrees, but your knowledge is very specific. The original O.K. Corral was located in Tombstone, Arizona, not in North Carolina. It was the site of a very famous gunfight that took place in 1881. Many, many movies have been made about it, and books written about the characters. It's a part of American culture."

"What's so special about the O.K. Corral?"

"I guess you've never heard of Wyatt Earp or Doc Holliday?"

"I have not."

"Well, it's the story of how the Wild West was settled and conquered. Wyatt Earp, his two brothers, and a friend were on the side of the law. The town passed a bylaw making it illegal for visitors to bring weapons into town. A group of outlaws known as the Cowboys had a long-running feud with the Earps. The Cowboys were cattle rustlers and horse thieves. They refused to give up their weapons. The resulting gunfight left three men dead and three wounded, including Wyatt Earp."

"Why is someone being shot to death worth celebrating?"

"Jeannie, you don't get it. We have a long tradition of using guns to protect ourselves. It's even in our Constitution. It's part of the American way of life, and I am trying to help you better understand our culture. We were taught about cowboys and Indians, about men in chaps rescuing damsels in distress, about families traveling in caravans across America, and using guns to defend themselves from attacks."

"Chaps?"

"Suede overpants that cowboys wear to protect their legs."

"Are you telling me that American culture is based on gunfights and conflicts between lawmakers and cattle rustlers, and cowboys who wear extra pants and rescue women?"

Tanisha sighed, disappointed that her charge was not serious about American history. "I was trying to tell you about how the West was settled. If you are threatened, you have the right to defend yourself. If you had a child and someone tried to break into your home, wouldn't you protect your child?"

"By calling 911."

"And if you couldn't get through? You'd stand your ground and do whatever it took to keep your family safe."

Jeannie's response was short and simple. "I don't know what I'd do, and I hope I never have to find out."

Tanisha instructed Jeannie to turn left off the highway and go into Grifton, a village sandwiched between Greenville and Kinston.

The sign for the town was dwarfed by a large rifle-shaped placard advertising the Okay Corral as a place "where you will have a blast." Slogans included "a place for a fun day with the family" and a place to savor "Mom's special apple pie – a bite from paradise." 'Safety training' was written in small ink at the bottom of the sign. The gun range, academy, and eatery were located on five acres of land within spitting distance of the Train Depot in Grifton.

Jeannie pulled up to a sign designating a parking zone. She and Tanisha walked into a trailer with an office sign in the window. She could hear a woman's voice calling loudly.

"Leroy, there's two ladies here. Come and find out what they want."

Leroy Jones appeared from the other side of the trailer. He was a solidly built sixty-five-year old man with close-cropped hair and a precisely trimmed goatee. Years spent in the outdoors had burnished his cheeks to a ruddy red. He walked up to Tanisha and extended his hand. "Retired Master Sargent Leroy Jones at your service, as always. I understand you want safety training for your friend."

Tanisha pulled a card from her pocket. "Thank you, sir, yes. Here is my permit. My friend Jeannie needs a gun to protect her, but she's never even held a gun, let alone fired one."

Leroy scrutinized Jeannie from head to foot, paused, and nodded his head. "I served in the National Guard for thirty years. My closest mate was an Indian from Carolina Beach. You're not related to Kishor Patel, are you? He was a good man."

She smiled. "I know some people named Patel, but not Kishor."

"You have an accent. Where are you from?"

"I'm working in Greenville, but I'm originally from India, as you guessed."

"You've come to the right place. We offer gun safety. Our classroom is air-conditioned. We'll start there, then go onto the range."

"How long is the training?"

"Your friend said you wanted to take *The Well-Armed Woman* course. It's three hours in the classroom and an hour in a shooting station. We'll start with a ten-minute safety video, followed by a fifty-minute lecture. Then I'll show you how to check to see if a pistol is loaded. I'll cover the ABC's of bullets and best safety practices, including how to carry your gun and why to lock it up in a gun safe when not in use. At the end, I'll administer a safety test. If you pass, you'll get your gun certification."

"Can I get in some practice while you're teaching my friend?" asked Tanisha.

"Sure thing. See Darryl. He'll set you all up."

The range resembled tollbooths on new highways. Ten shooting stalls were contained in a concrete frame and separated from each other by acoustic partitions. In the distance, Tanisha could see scrubby grass and further away, paper bull's-eye targets attached to wooden stands.

As she walked to the larger booth on the end, she felt the range supervisor's eyes on her. "Master Sargent Jones directed me to see you."

He nodded ever so slightly.

"Here is my permit. While my friend is taking *The Well-Armed Woman* course, I'd like to get in some practice shooting."

"Did you bring your pistol?"

She pulled it out and uncocked it. "It's not loaded."

"Let's go to my office to get you set up."

They walked to the shooting station on the end. Plastic safety glasses hung from pegs on a side wall, while earmuffs specially designed for shooting ranges were clustered in wire baskets.

She was about to pick up a box of full metal jacket bullets when Darryl held up his hand.

"Not yet. Put your earmuffs and safety glasses on first. Just because you certified here doesn't mean you can walk in and start shooting."

Although eager to practice, Tanisha was not about to argue with the range supervisor. "Yes, sir."

Once she was wearing eye and ear protection, he allowed her to take a box of bullets with her. She followed him to the third stall. He watched while she loaded her gun. Then she picked it up, looked at a target, brought her hands forward, and squeezed the trigger. The bullet hit the inside edge of the outer circle.

"Not bad, but I know you can do better. Show me what you've got."

She pursed her lips and reached into the ammo box to load more FMJs into her pistol. This time, one bullet hit the bull's-eye.

"I told you that you could do better. You showed me." Tanisha allowed herself a small grin as Darryl returned to his post.

Round after round hit the target. She changed hands, holding the weight of the gun in her dominant hand and squeezing the trigger with her left hand. She missed the target.

Darryl called out from his office. "What was that?" As she fired, a low whistle escaped her lips and she missed a second time.

"I tried to lead with my non-dominant hand."

"Is there any reason why you need to be a proficient shooter with both hands?"

"Well, no, but what if I injure my right hand and a shooter tries to get me? It'd be helpful to be able to carry off a kill shot with my non-dominant hand, don't you think?"

He smiled at her. "You're not in the military. You're not in the police. You do know it's unlikely someone will walk up to you and try to shoot you?"

"You know what happened to my pappy."

Darryl's face drooped. "Yes, Tanisha, I know. It should never have happened. It's why I trained you when you came here, even though you were technically not old enough. But you needed protection."

"Thank you. I will always appreciate your helpfulness. I like to be prepared."

"Is that why you brought your friend here?"

Tanisha studied Darryl, wondering how much to divulge.

As if reading her mind, he beckoned her over. "I'm like a priest in a church. This range is my church. People tell me everything and nothing leaves the shooting stall. You can trust me."

A great weight fell from her shoulders. "After my pappy died, I got a job at the slaughterhouse. It was hard work. I was able to wash the blood off, but couldn't get rid of the smell of dead animals. When I was offered an office job, I jumped at it."

He nodded. "I'd never last in an office, but I can see why you prefer it to the slaughterhouse. Go on, tell me what happened in the office."

She swallowed, unsure about confiding in someone she barely knew.

Sensing her hesitation, he tried to draw her out. "Did you witness an active shooting? Was your office shot up?"

"No, my supervisor was murdered in the office. I wasn't there when it happened, but still."

He smiled encouragingly. "It must have been traumatic for you."

"She was poisoned, and then the assistant was poisoned."

"A second poisoning. Where do you work, in the correctional system?"

"No, in public health."

"That can be dangerous, too. A lot of folks blame public-health workers for the COVID shutdown," he said sympathetically.

"It looks like the second person accidentally poisoned herself. She was hospitalized and they were able to pump her stomach. She's getting better."

"That's good."

"But last night, someone threatened my new supervisor. She's been like a friend to me and I don't want to see her killed."

"Gawd, girl, working in public health is dangerous for your health. Especially now. Some of the same folks who were angry about the COVID shutdown are saying that all vaccines should be banned. You've got to get out of that office!"

"Ban vaccines?"

"No, I don't agree with that. One of my aunts got polio. She lost the use of her leg. She dragged it around. She was lucky compared to her friend, who had to be put in an iron lung because she lost the ability to breathe on her own. She couldn't walk, she could barely move. She could talk, but that was about it. My aunt visited her once, and couldn't go back. It was too painful seeing her like that, losing all her freedom. Yes, the polio vaccine prevented many deaths and disabilities after the vaccine was discovered. We don't ever want to go back to a time when a teenager has to be put in an iron lung because of polio.

Still, there are a lot of people who don't have those memories and want to stop immunizing Americans from polio. It sounds as if there may be an extremist in Pitt County who wants to get rid of the public-health office."

"I don't want to go back to the slaughterhouse."

"At least you wouldn't have to worry about someone coming into your office to harm you."

Darryl wasn't the most sensitive of men, but the expression on Tanisha's face made him realize he'd made her even more upset. He tried to soften his words. "Well, offices are generally safe places. Make sure you wear your gun to work. If anyone gets too close to you, you know what to do. Don't hesitate. Show them you mean business."

She gulped. "I will."

He patted her shoulder. "And remember, you have a God-given right to defend yourself. Now go get one of Annie's special cakes while I teach your friend how to prevent herself from being killed."

Chapter 33

Archer easily spotted La Donna because she was wearing a halter top and what appeared to be a rabbit's paw dangling on a gold chain around her neck. When she waved at him, he noticed that her nail polish was Ferrari red.

He shook her hand, covering it with his other hand. "Andrew Archer, but my friends call me Andy. I was at the reception but didn't see you there."

"I stopped by for a moment to pay my respects, but I'm actually recovering from being hospitalized."

"You poor thing! How are you feeling now?"

"Better, thanks. My stomach is still a little topsy-turvy."

"Oh dear. Did you know that The Rickhouse offers forty different brands of bourbon? But of course, with your stomach, you probably prefer tea."

She eyed him without responding.

"I've been winding my way through the bourbons, Basil Hayden, Bulleit, Elijah Craig, and never to be forgotten, Maker's Mark. Even though I always order the same drink, I select a different bourbon and that gives me a new drink every time. Let's see, I think I'll order a Jim Beam Masterpiece for myself and a sweet iced tea for you."

She pouted, drawing attention to her cleavage by petting the rabbit's ear. "Tea, yes, but I was thinking of Marty's Bourbon Tea."

He laughed. "A girl after my heart. Is there anything else you have in mind from the menu? I was thinking of ordering an appetizer for us to share. Seared Scallops looks good."

La Donna pursed her lips. "Maple mustard sauce? Reminds me too much of Canada."

He laughed. "What do you mean?"

"Shortly before she died, Dr. Dunn hired a Canadian to help with the research study, although the woman speaks English with a British accent. If that's not enough, Dr. Dunn's best friend flew down from Canada for the funeral. I expected her to be wearing a fur coat because it's really cold up there, but she had no coat, just a suit jacket."

He was puzzled. "What's the connection with Canada?"

She shook her head and smirked at him. "Duh? Don't you know anything about Canada?"

"What do you mean?"

"Do I have to spell it out? "M-A-P-E-L."

"Oh, I get it. Maple syrup. How do you know it's not from Vermont?"

"Doesn't matter. It's the association."

"Well, then, is there an appetizer you would like?"

"Crab dip is more to my liking, thank you."

They were on their second round of drinks when Andy asked La Donna about the research project. "Do you get a sense that the project is well managed?"

She shrugged. "I don't know. I have to tell you that my role was rather limited. I'm not one of those nerdy, socially awkward researchers and academics who can't hold a simple conversation with someone of the opposite sex. Instead, they channel all that energy into studying and become researchers. My role is more important."

He raised his eyebrows.

She carried on. "I greet people. I'm the first person they see when they come through the door. I also make sure everyone gets paid. I prepare the checks and pay the invoices."

"Are you saying you sign them?"

"No, of course not. Dr. Dunn and Frank had signing authority, but that was a formality. They signed whatever I put in front of them."

"Were there any unusual invoices? Any big amounts that jumped out as odd?"

She narrowed her eyes. "That's a strange question. The invoices were the same week in, week out. We paid our suppliers on time, and those working for the project got paid every two weeks."

"Did you ever hear any discussions about problems with the research?"

She brightened up. "Well, on the day that Dr. Johal, the Canadian researcher, started, there was a big blowup between Dr. Dunn and Frank Wright, the project manager. He accused her of making decisions without consulting him. She accused him of taking a lackadaisical approach to the project as a whole. He ended up slamming her office door and walking out of the building."

Andy leaned in. "Did Dr. Dunn say why she brought in the Canadian researcher?"

La Donna's face grew animated and she raised her hand in a swooping gesture that reminded him of a hawk about to attack his prey. "There may have been problems with the data. She normally had me type up a long progress report and prepare a PowerPoint file to show to Bernard Bigelow."

"The county director."

She corrected Andy. "And my uncle."

"I see."

Andy savored the new information, wondering how he could entice La Donna into providing even more details.

"She didn't ask me to type any report for this quarter. And she didn't ask me to prepare a PowerPoint slide deck, either. She said she'd provide a progress report and send the quarterly report when he returned from vacation."

"Do you have any idea why Dr. Dunn didn't provide the quarterly report as usual?"

She shrugged her shoulders. "Beats me. I figured I'd get it when she needed to hand it in."

"What did your uncle think about this?"

"I don't think he was impressed."

"Why do you think that he wasn't impressed?"

"Because he called me after he learned about Dr. Dunn's death. He asked me to go into her office and find her daytimer, that it might contain information he needed. He told me to keep it secure until I could turn it over to him when he returned."

"Did you find it?"

She avoided answering the question. "Well, when I tried to enter the building, it was cordoned off and a police officer told me I wasn't allowed in."

"Is there anything else you know about the project?"

"It had its ups and downs. Dr. Dunn wanted to have an onsite lab to test the results, but it was too expensive. She wanted a full-time epidemiologist, but that didn't work out. And Frank's mind isn't really on the project."

"But you, you're always on the ball?"

"Yessir. I'm always the first person in. As Dr. Dunn used to say: 'La Donna, you're the face of the organization. You're the first person that study participants see when they come for an office visit.' I took her words very seriously. Did you notice my fingernails? Perfectly manicured, as always. Because I want to make a good first impression."

The pace of her words slowed. "Although, some of those Black girls enrolled in the study have fingernails the length of tiger talons. I wonder how they get them to grow so long. I'd ask them, but it wouldn't be appropriate."

"Why not?"

"Because they are research participants. Dr. Dunn was very insistent when she told me I was not to socialize with them or offer any comments on their appearance. Most of them are fat. Some are really fat. And they look poor. Their clothes probably come from Walmart. What could I possibly say to them?"

"It sounds as if you have a challenging job," said Andy.

"It's all right. Uncle Bernie told Dr. Dunn to hire me and she did. I come in fifteen minutes before everyone else, turn on the lights, crank on the air, check my phone for messages, put on a pot of coffee, and unlock the doors. What I'd really like to do is become an interior designer for the rich and famous, but I'd have to move to Charlotte or Atlanta, and that's too far away. Still, Will and I sometimes take off in his truck and someday we may go as far as Charlotte."

"Will?"

"My boyfriend. He's in transportation."

"How long have you been seeing him?"

She giggled. "Going on nine years. We'll celebrate our tenth anniversary when I turn twenty-four."

"That's a long time."

She turned serious. "It is. I want to marry him, but he says he's not ready. And Uncle Bernie says that Will isn't good enough for me. He says Will has no prospects. But Will has big dreams. He bought a rusted Thunderbird being auctioned off by the police. He restored it and then discovered the car once belonged to Christopher's girlfriend on *The Sopranos.* Will made a big profit selling the car as a result. He fixed up the second one for himself and now he's working on another restoration, of a Thunderbird driven by James Bond. His dream is to refurbish cars that once belonged to famous people and sell them for tons of money. I think he's capable of doing great things."

La Donna pulled her lipstick out of her clutch bag. "If there's nothing else, I'm going to call Will to give me a ride home. I told him I had a business meeting. He offered to pick me up."

As if on cue, Will's voice crackled over the speaker phone. "Ok, babe, be there in 10."

Andy's forehead creased. "Was that your phone or does Will speak with an accent?"

La Donna laughed. "He sure as shit doesn't speak the Queen's English. He's from the unincorporated community of Tick Bite."

"I don't know how to respond to that remark," admitted Andy.

She backtracked a bit. "In fairness, Tick Bite is a pretty place, and it's not fair if people hold where you were born against you. It's what you make of yourself that matters."

Andy waited with La Donna outside the restaurant entrance. When a coral Thunderbird turned into the parking lot, he walked in the opposite direction, careful to stay out of the driver's view.

Chapter 34

Will screeched to a stop, *All American Guy* blasting from his speakers. Will's head was fully shaved and he had a ZZ Top chest-length beard. He stroked it while leaning his head out the window. "Hey babe, jump in."

La Donna gingerly traipsed toward the car, carefully stepping around debris on the ground. Her high heels clattered on the hard surface.

"C'mon, La Donna, we ain't got all night."

She got in and leaned toward Will, her generous lips leaving an imprint on his cheek. "You sure like that song. You keep playing it every day."

"Chris Janson's got it right. He knows what's important. I'm an all-American guy just like him," said Will.

He brought his hand up to her hair and brushed back an errant strand. "You look delectable, like a Waffle House date."

"Silly, I ate at The Rickhouse."

He smiled at her and kept talking, as if she hadn't interrupted him. "That rabbit foot. I want to pet it. It reminds me of my first kill with a slingshot. I was eight years old and practicing shooting at a tree. Pa told me to do something useful, like shooting a rabbit that Ma could skin for food. I went into the woods and got me a nice brown rabbit. I think he heard me or saw me coming because he was still as a statue, not even blinking. He made it easy for me to hit him with a rock up close."

"This is the first time you told me that story."

"It was a long time ago. I've hunted many rabbits since then, but I've never cut off a paw. They say it's a good luck charm."

La Donna beamed. "It gets me a lot of attention, although it's a little hot for this weather. I wore it because I wanted to look especially nice for my lunch meeting."

"Well, you look delicious to me," said Will.

She pouted. "Hmph! The pharmaceutical rep kept asking me about work processes and who does what. And when I told him I prepared the checks, he asked if I also authorized them. As if I would prepare a check and sign off on it. That would be a bad business practice."

"Babe, remind me why you were meeting with him?"

"Will, I already told you. He's the guy whose company is funding the research project. Uncle Bernie told me the project could shut down if the pharmacy company pulled its funding after Dr. Dunn died. I don't want to lose my job."

"You did a noble thing, agreeing to meet with him. A noble thing," said Will.

"I'm glad you see it that way. I gave it my all."

Will dialed up the music, nodding his head to the beat. "I'm a pretty simple man," he sang to the music.

When the last bars of *All American Guy* faded away, Will turned to his girlfriend. "While you were being wined and dined, I was delivering packages. I have one last delivery to make. It'll only take me a few minutes, and then we'll have the rest of the day to ourselves."

"It was a business meeting, nothing more than that."

"If you say so. But my business meetings never take place over dinner."

His tone surprised La Donna. "You just called it a noble thing to do, to have lunch with this stranger who holds the purse strings. That means you picked me up from work."

He corrected her. "Well, I picked you up at The Rickhouse."

"Where I was working."

He sighed, "Yes, dear, where you were working. Anyway, as I was saying, I have a package to drop off."

They drove along Greenville Blvd. and Memorial Blvd., the Thunderbird's headlights casting long shadows. A North Carolina-style barbecue offered drive-through service, and Will did a sharp turn to enter the drive-in lane. He gobbled his pulled pork sandwich, swallowing it with a mouthful of Mountain Dew. He turned onto Hwy. 11.

"Where are we going?" asked La Donna.

"Kinston. We'll be there in no time."

Thirty minutes later, Will turned into Kinston, the city on the Neuse River, and parked behind a brick building that dominated Herritage St. and North St.

"Isn't this Mother Earth Brewing?" said La Donna, an enthusiastic note entering her voice. "I've never been, but I saw a YouTube video on it."

"Yes. You wait here. I won't be but a minute," instructed Will.

She watched as he opened the door to the Tap Room. She squinted but the dim lighting prevented her from being able to see where Will had gone. Shrugging her shoulders, she climbed out of the Thunderbird and made her way in.

"I'll have a mojito," she said.

The bartender looked quizzically at her. "You do know this is an establishment where we sell beer, not spirits?"

She pointed to a menu. "Yes, and it says 'mojito' here. I'll try your mojito beer."

The bartender gave a little flourish, as if bowing to his customer. She watched him muddle mint into the bottom of a tall glass and add a twist of lime peel. He poured a pint of Mojito Berlinerweisse into the glass and passed it to her.

La Donna tentatively brought the glass to her lips, hesitating before taking a sip. She let out a gasp of pleasure. "It does taste like a mojito, my favorite drink," she exclaimed.

The bartender laughed. "So glad you like it. We aim to please."

Halfway through drinking the prepared beer, she heard raised voices from a corridor next to the bar.

"Where's the rest of the product?"

"I don't know what you mean," was the puzzled response.

La Donna made direct eye contact with the bartender. "That's my boyfriend. He was supposed to drop off a package here."

She paused. "And that's Andy Archer. I met him earlier today. What's he doing here?"

The bartender's eyes narrowed. "There must be some sort of misunderstanding. There is no Andy Archer here."

She heard a loud clang that sounded like out-of-tune cymbals. Then a short cry, cut off. Another loud clang. Another cry, this one more pronounced. She tried to ignore the sounds.

"Have another beer mojito." The bartender pushed a second drink toward her.

She swallowed the rest of her drink and ignored the new one. The bartender placed his hand over her arm when she stood up from the bar. "Stay out of it. It has nothing to do with you."

She shook his hand off and stalked in the direction of the voices. The corridor contained restrooms and a room with a window in the door. She could make out two profiles. "Will? Andy? Are you in there?"

Silence.

She tried the doorknob. It was unlocked. The room was lined with lab equipment and packaging supplies.

She saw Andy hovering over Will, a large gong beside him. Will's hands covered his ears.

"La Donna, what are you doing here?" Andy's voice was very calm.

Will looked up, his eyes pleading with her.

She said the first thing that came to mind. "I can see you've met my boyfriend. It looks as if his earache has returned."

Will looked angrily at La Donna. "I told you to stay in the car."

"And miss the opportunity to try a new kind of mojito? Not a chance," she replied.

While Andy stared at her, she stepped to Will's side and held out her hand. She said gently, "C'mon, Will. I'll get you a salve for your ear. You've delivered your package. You've finished your work for the day. Now it's time to leave."

Will and Anderson's eyes were locked in an unspoken battle. Suddenly Andy's hand made a dismissive gesture. "You heard the lady. Go on, get out of here!"

Chapter 35

Will reached across the front seat and gave La Donna's knee a squeeze.

She yelped. "Ouch, that hurt! What did you do that for?"

"I told you to stay in the car," he said in his slow country drawl.

"It was a bar. And not just any bar, one we've talked about trying out. What did you think I would do?"

"What I told you to do. You should have listened to me."

"And missed the opportunity for a beer mojito at one of the top places for craft beer in North Carolina?"

He paused as if to consider her words. "Well, when you put it like that."

"My drink tasted very good and the bartender gave me a second one for free. But when I heard your voice, and then Andy's voice, I knew something was up."

"How do you know him?"

"He's the man I met with at The Rickhouse."

"What! I thought that was a business meeting."

She sighed impatiently. "Will, you've got to pay more attention. I told you I was meeting with the pharmaceutical representative whose company is funding the public-health study."

"You mean Anderson Archer?"

She pouted. "Yes, he told me to call him Andy. He kept asking me how the project was going. He didn't seem at all interested in my work."

Will reached over and caressed her cheek with his hand. "Well, babe, I'm interested not just in your work but in everything about you."

She gave him her warmest smile. "I told him you refurbish vintage cars driven by Hollywood stars. I told him you have big dreams."

"I sure do. One of them is to get out of this small town, go somewhere new, where your uncle isn't always peering over my shoulder, and people don't know that my parents were poor White farm workers without a penny to their name. I want to own my own car restoration business and be known from Fayetteville to Myrtle Beach for being the best in the business."

"And you will be. I believe in you." She nuzzled his ear, causing him to momentarily swerve.

He pulled off the highway and they embraced. He stopped when she tugged at his belt and tried to unzip his pants. "Honey, there's nothing I would love more than to love you right here, right now, but we're almost at my place. We can wait a few minutes. We have the whole evening ahead of us."

Will's forehead furrowed in disbelief as they approached his house. Parked in front was a car with Archer slouched against it, a cigarette in his mouth.

"What the – " said Will.

"Will, what's Andy doing here? Was he following us?"

"I didn't see him. And I left before him, so I don't know how he could have got here."

"What does he want?"

"I don't know, but I'm about to find out."

Archer stood upright when Will approached. "I bet you're wondering why I'm here," he said.

"Damn straight."

"I'm here to collect the rest of my product. The package was short a couple of bricks."

Will responded evenly. "I don't know what was in the box I delivered to you. The box was sealed and I didn't open it. I don't know anything about bricks. I gave you the box, and that's all there is to it."

"Boy, think carefully before you walk away from here. You don't know who you're dealing with!"

Will gave Archer the finger and walked back to his car.

La Donna slid across the seat and opened the door for Will. "What did he say?"

"Nothing much. It was just a little misunderstanding."

"What kind of misunderstanding?"

He snapped at her. "There you go again, asking and asking your questions. Nagging me when I've made clear it was nothing."

"Well, if it was nothing, why are you sniping at me? If I didn't know better, I'd say you're displacing your anger with Andy by yelling at me."

"What do you mean by that?"

La Donna blushed. "You can't yell at him because he's your boss. So you yell at me."

"That's silly. What makes you think that?"

"When work is slow, I sometimes watch *The View* on my phone."

"*The View?* That show where a bunch of crazy old women gossip and give their opinions on everything? Why would you watch a bunch of communists from the deep state fill your head with nonsense? Is this what working in a public-health department has done to you?"

"I don't generally agree with their views, but one of the hosts said she was angry with her daughter, but didn't know what to do about it. Instead of telling her daughter how she felt, she yelled at her husband. One of the other women on the show said the wife was 'displacing her anger.' Is it possible you're displacing your anger with Andy onto me?"

In response, Will placed his foot flat against the accelerator and gunned the Thunderbird. The sports car tore down the road, far exceeding the speed limit. The brakes squealed as they arrived at La Donna's house.

'Get out. Go and 'displace' your opinions on someone else."

"But Will, all I meant was–."

He interrupted her before she could come up with an explanation. "La Donna, it's been a long day and I'm tired. I'll see you tomorrow."

She dispiritedly walked toward her front door. Upon entering the foyer, she looked in the mirror and tugged off the rabbit's paw. 'Lot of luck you brought me today,' she sighed.

She headed into the kitchen and reached into the cupboard for a bottle of bourbon. Before she could pour herself a glass, she heard the doorbell ring.

"Will, I knew you'd come back. I'm so glad you changed your mind. I'll be right there," she called loudly.

As she opened the door, a hand clad in a black glove reached in. "Don't make a sound," hissed the man whose face was hidden by a baseball cap low on his forehead and a mask that covered most of his face.

He pushed his way in and shut the door.

She thought she recognized him. "Andy, is that you? What do you want?"

In response, he peeled off the face mask. His lips were flattened into a thin line. "Will took something that belongs to me and I want it back."

La Donna could feel her heart thumping in her chest. "Your beef with Will has nothing to do with me. Why are you here?"

"He says he doesn't have it. I need to show him I mean business."

She tried to distract him. "I was just about to pour myself a drink. I know you like bourbon. Would you like Maker's Mark on the rocks?"

"I'll have it straight."

She measured two jiggers and poured the whiskey into a squat glass. She was starting to add ice cubes when he placed his hand over the glass. "You don't need ice with that. Drink up."

"I made it for you."

He grabbed her wrist. "I said, 'Drink up.' Now!"

She gulped the dark whiskey, feeling it burn in her throat.

"More! This time pour yourself a full glass. And don't bother with water or ice."

For the first time in her life, La Donna felt frightened. Andy no longer appeared to be the suave, urbane pharmaceutical representative who had sat across from her over lunch. He seemed like an angry man intent on vengeance.

When she brought the glass to her lips, he pushed it against her mouth and told her to swallow. She hesitated for a second time and he yanked her hair, pulling her chin upward. "Drink it!"

She whimpered. "I'm trying."

He grabbed her head between his hands and pushed her face into the wooden counter. She cried out.

"Stop your whining or I'll smash your head in," he threatened.

"Don't hurt me," she pleaded.

In response, he poured the rest of the drink down her throat, holding her mouth shut so that she was forced to swallow.

Although La Donna was an enthusiastic social drinker, the neat whiskey seared her throat. She began to cough.

In response, Andy slapped her face and slammed her mouth into the counter. "You're a whore! You'd sell yourself for a few free drinks and an expensive meal. You have no shame!"

She whimpered, slowly raising her head so that she could eye her tormentor. She raised her hand and lifted a finger as if to point.

"Will is the only man I've ever been with."

He glared at her. "One more glass, I think." With one arm, he supported her head. With the other, he poured the remaining liquid in the bottle down her throat. She gagged as he forced her to swallow the liquor. Rivulets of mucus ran from her nose, mingling with tears that coursed down her face. As soon as she began to vomit, Andy pressed his hand firmly against her lips.

It was becoming harder and harder for her to breathe. She could taste whisky and bile in her mouth. She could smell vomit. All she could make out was the black glove pressed against her lips. She tried to edge away from his hand, but couldn't move. She began to see small stars shooting in the darkness.

"That's it. Let the whiskey do its job."

He watched as her body went still. Her head banged against the edge of the counter. She slid onto the floor. He checked her neck. Satisfied that she no longer had a pulse, he went to the sink and washed out the second glass, returning it to a shelf. Next, he wiped her glass with a Lysol cloth, pressing her fingers to the cleaned goblet. He used a smear of blood to write "WILL" in large letters. He calmly walked out of the apartment. He closed the door softly, not wanting to draw any attention. Then he took off his gloves.

Andy quietly opened his car door and slid in. Keeping the headlights off, he coasted down the street, turned, and doubled back, parking about half a block away from La Donna's house so that he could see anyone coming. He sat back and waited.

Chapter 36

Will would never admit to La Donna that she was right and he was wrong. After all, she was just a girl and it was her role to build him up, not tear down his confidence. Sure, she'd gone to college for one semester and he'd dropped out of high school before he could graduate, but that didn't make her his superior. It bugged Will when La Donna corrected him. It made him feel small. She sometimes corrected how he pronounced words. "If you want to be my boyfriend, you can't say 'ain't' and you have to pronounce the endings of your words." Every time she corrected him, he felt a small part of himself die, like the flame of a candle burning dimmer and dimmer.

In his eyes, she'd gone beyond the pale by admitting to watching women who were infamous for their loud mouths and liberal positions. How could she listen to a communist program where nothing was off-limits? He didn't know for sure, but the women were probably lesbians or, even worse, men dressed as women. Not only was she watching this garbage, but she seemed to believe some of it. She even tried to use psychology on him. If he wasn't careful, next thing she'd be doing would be telling him what he should do to make his dream come true. It couldn't come to that. Will was his own man. Proud and free, just an ordinary American trying his hardest to make a good life for himself.

No, Will was going to lay down the law, remind her that her place was behind him or at his side, not in front. He was the boss and she needed to know that. After all, this was North Carolina, and everyone in Pitt County, including the girls, knew that the men were the breadwinners, the ones who brought home the bacon. Sure, she had a job, but she earned chump change, barely enough to cover her manis and pedis.

He deliberated whether to text her or head directly over to her place. His irritation grew when she didn't respond to two texts. After waiting another five minutes, he sent her a short, curt text. 'WTF?'

Three minutes later, he sent another text. "Babe, why aren't you responding? Are we so done that you don't even want to have a conversation?"

He vented his anger in his fifth and final text. "I'm coming over. We're going to have this out once and for all. You'd better let me in."

He got into his Thunderbird, turned on the ignition, jacked up the speakers, and accelerated, leaving a trail of fumes behind him. He was so intent on reaching her house that he didn't notice the car parked on the opposite side of the road, and the man in the front seat, a ball cap pulled tightly down over his forehead.

Will turned into her driveway and sat for a moment, second-guessing himself. He knew she liked him, even loved him. She'd told him she wanted to marry him. And she'd said she believed in him. He noticed that she'd become more short-tempered since working for the public-health director. But he figured that could be the stress of the job – and the stress of having Uncle Bernie always watching her, telling her to work harder, to go to school, that she could do so much better than Will.

He couldn't wait to become a famous restorer of vintage cars. In the meantime, he knew he had to apologize to his girlfriend for coming down so hard on her.

He climbed the steps to the porch and rang the bell next to the front door. There was no answer. Since he couldn't hear the bell ring, he rapped on the door instead. There was still no answer. Will frowned, wondering if La Donna had gone to bed. But it was so early. He thought she might have called a girlfriend in search of a sympathetic ear. Perhaps they'd gone out for a drink or two or three. But it wasn't like La Donna to drink heavily on a week night because she had to go into work early every morning, and she took that responsibility very seriously.

The evening was overcast, drenched in dark grey clouds. The neighbors' porch light was off, not surprising because they were elderly and in bed by eight every evening. Everything was still.

Will felt a growing sense of unease. He couldn't put a name to it, but it felt to him as if something was wrong. It was just too still. He pushed his foot against the lower part of the door, nearly losing his balance when it opened.

He called into the blackness, "La Donna, are you here? You mean a lot to me and I'm really sorry I yelled at you."

His words echoed in the dark. He reached for the light switch just inside the door. His olfactory senses were alerted at the same time that his eyes were blinded by the bright light. Earlier in the evening, Archer had punched him in the face and bloodied his nose. He could smell the same bitter, salty tang in the air, mixed with the sour smell of vomit and the overpowering smell of spilled bourbon.

Will hesitantly walked toward the kitchen, eager to find La Donna but worried about what he might find. She'd had a few drinks during her business meeting at The Rickhouse and she'd told him she was on her second drink at the bar. He hoped she hadn't come home and helped herself to a few more ounces of whiskey.

A moan escaped his lips and he instinctively swallowed and covered his mouth when he turned on the kitchen light and entered the room.

La Donna lay on the floor, curled in what looked to him like a protective position. She was lying face downward, her hair splayed about her shoulders and muddled with vomit. An empty bottle of Makers' Mark lay on its side, teetering precariously on the edge of the counter.

He went to her side and kneeled beside her, searching for a pulse. He couldn't find one. Her eyes were closed and whisky drool continued to dribble from the corner of her mouth. He wiped it gently away and stroked her hair. "Why, La Donna, why? We would have accomplished great things together, you and me. Why did you do this?"

He dialed 911 and when the operator answered, he choked out a few words, "My girlfriend, She's on the floor." He hung up, not knowing what to say.

He crouched beside La Donna, wiping her face with a wet cloth. His eyes glazed with horror when he saw his name written in red. He didn't understand why she would write his name. Was it her way of apologizing, of expressing regret at what she'd done, of saying she hadn't meant to harm herself and would take it back if only she could? He was still mulling over the significance when he looked closer and saw that the letters were printed, not written in flowing, girly script. It wasn't her handwriting. Someone had written his name intentionally.

That same someone had taken his girlfriend from him. Who would want La Donna dead? She was an all-American girl, out to have a good time but not out to hurt anyone. While less-beautiful girls might envy her, he doubted they would go so far as to murder her. He didn't think anyone in her workplace would want to hurt her. They might not like how she polished her fingernails and chomped on gum while answering the phone. But they would never do anything to incur the enmity of her Uncle Bernard because he had the power to shut down the research project, and they needed their jobs.

Could a man have become angry with La Donna because she refused his advances? Will thought this was possible, especially if someone had bought her a few drinks on the expectation that she would put out. But she'd said that Andy hadn't seemed interested in her, that all he wanted was to find out information about the research project.

What other reasons would there be to kill her? Will thought hard and was shocked by the realization that someone might have murdered La Donna to get back at him.

Someone was trying to frame him for her death. He had to find out who murdered the love of his life. He swore he would find the person and exact his revenge even if it took his last breath.

The realization that he was being framed meant that he had to get away before the police arrived on the scene. After all, he'd called them.

He wasn't going to stick around waiting to be arrested for a crime he didn't commit.

He ran from the house into the drizzle, slamming the door shut. He clambered into his car, ignoring the vomit on his clothes. He'd always given La Donna a hard time for eating in his car. Now was not the time to worry about staining the leather. He had to get away before the police arrived. He gunned the engine, pressing hard on the accelerator. The calm, monotonous thudding of the windshield wipers contrasted with the thoughts hurling helter-skelter through his mind.

Will was so intent on getting away that he didn't see the driver in the ball cap start up his engine and follow the Thunderbird. All he could hear was the wail of sirens. All he could see was his girlfriend's face and his name etched in scarlet letters.

Chapter 37

Only when his seatbelt dug deeply into his shoulder and yanked him backwards did Will realize he had been hit. Instinct prompted him to grab the steering wheel tightly, fingers clutching it like the claws of a hawk just after it snatches its prey.

"Now what!" he exclaimed. He began to shake his head, but the movement elicited a sudden jolt of pain that stopped him in his tracks. His vision blurred and he closed his eyes.

He reopened them when he saw a dark figure crouched next to the driver's door. His mind registered that someone was there, but he didn't wonder why. A fist wrapped on the window. Will looked at it, unresponsive.

The hand tugged at the driver's door. Will caught a glimpse of a young woman's hand with manicured red fingernails. He saw a red heart tattooed on the inside of her wrist. He looked up and made eye contact with the woman. She looked at him and gasped, "My God, you're covered in blood! I'm so sorry. I was chatting on my phone with my girlfriend and all of a sudden saw you stopped even though the light was green. I wasn't able to stop on time. Are you hurt? Are you okay? Of course, you're not all right."

He tried to respond but his initial attempt failed. His head felt disconnected from the rest of his body. He raised his hand toward his forehead and watched, perplexed, as pieces of the windshield trickled from his hair. "The windshield's smashed," he remarked.

He knew he had somewhere to be, something urgent to do, but couldn't summon the energy to move. He had lost all his momentum and sat silent and unmoving, seatbelt still attached. With an excruciatingly slow motion, he undid the seatbelt. He didn't know if seconds or minutes had passed by. "My head hurts and my chest hurts," he mumbled slowly, as if speaking through a thick wad of gauze stuffed in his mouth.

The woman who opened the driver's door paused when she heard his slurred words. "You smell. Are you drunk? Is that why you were stopped at the bottom of the hill? Is that why you just sat there after the light turned green? You caused this accident, not me. It's all your fault."

She fled back to her car and flooded the gas. She gunned the engine and jerkily reversed her SUV. She hit the partially open door on the driver's side when she passed Will's car, pushing it in. She flipped him a finger and roared away.

The impact of the second hit had a more severe impact because he wasn't wearing his seat belt. He felt his head snap backward, and the steering wheel dug deeply into one side of his chest.

He slowly repositioned himself in the driver's seat but couldn't figure out how to buckle up the seat belt. The windshield resembled a crystal abstract painting, but the engine still turned over. "Thank God. I have to go home." He repeated this mantra as he drove, head craned forward to see through the shattered glass.

About 10 minutes later, he veered to a halt. He pushed against the door, wondering why it wouldn't open. His third try was successful, and he nearly fell out. Regaining his balance, he positioned one leg after the other onto the pavement, in the same way that tipsy drivers take tiny, careful steps, planting one foot in front of the next. But Will wasn't drunk and he wasn't able to stand upright. He had no strength. His fingers slipped from the door handle. He toppled onto the pavement, his hands moving too slowly to absorb the impact.

Get up! Get up! Since he couldn't stand, he crawled over the curb and up the walkway. By the time he arrived at the front door, he was able to half-stand. He lurched into the house and balanced himself by jamming his shoulder against the wall.

He made it as far as the bathroom. Without thinking, his hand reached up to turn on the light switch. His head felt as if it were being stabbed by lightning bolts. He quickly turned off the light and lay his head on the counter. Slowly, he turned the sink tap on, wet a towel, and pressed it against his face.

He couldn't see any blood, but he could smell it. Everywhere. On his head, covering his shirt, on his hands. He crawled into the shower, yowling when the fine needles made contact with his battered skin. Just when he didn't think he could take it any longer, his eyes came unstuck and he regained his awareness. He used all of his physical and mental powers to stand up and peel off his sodden clothes. He let the water run over him until the smells of blood and vomit were washed away.

He couldn't lift his arms to put a T-shirt over his head, so he zipped on a hoody. He gave up trying to put on socks because it hurt his head too much to bend down. He was as fully dressed as he was going to be by the time he heard a knock on his door.

Detectives Harris and Smith brought their vehicle to a stop behind the Thunderbird. They walked around Will's car, observing the crumbled rear bumper, the bent frame on the driver's side, dent in the roof, and the cracked windshield. Harmony's flashlight captured signs of blood inside and outside the vehicle.

"Do you think he'd be stupid enough to drive home after calling 9-1-1 from his girlfriend's home?" queried Harmony.

"No telling what someone in shock might do," said her partner in a level tone.

"Do you think he murdered her?"

"I'm not sure. He was likely the last person to see her. He was on the scene and his fingerprints are everywhere."

"Not to mention she wrote his name in red."

"I don't know about that clue. It seems too obvious. And why would he call 9-1-1 to ask for help if he just killed her?"

"Remorse? They got into an argument. He got angry and hit her. He called 9-1-1 hoping the paramedics would get there in time to save her."

Henry eyed his partner with skepticism. He said, "That's a lot of suppositions. We need the facts. Let's take this one step at a time."

The door to the house was partly open. Henry and Harmony looked at one another and nodded. She rang the doorbell and, without waiting for a response, they walked in. "Will Davis, son, we need to talk to you. Come out where we can see you," said Henry.

They could hear labored breathing and the sound of irregular footsteps.

Harmony switched on the hall light. She heard a high-pitched scream and a thud as Will toppled to the floor, clutching his head in his hands.

"Did you kill La Donna,?" asked Harmony.

"No," he grunted.

"Why'd you call 9-1-1?"

"To get her help."

"Did you get into a fight with her and knock her to the floor? Tell us what happened, Will. We know you didn't mean to hurt her."

"I didn't hurt her."

"But she's dead."

"I loved La Donna. We were going to get married."

"If you loved her, why did you leave her alone on the kitchen floor?"

He grunted a response. "I came to her place to talk to her. But she didn't answer the door. When I opened it, I saw her slumped over. She wasn't breathing. I called 9-1-1 for help and while I was waiting, I saw my name written on the floor. I was afraid I would be blamed. There wasn't anything I could do, so I left. I came home because I needed to clear my name."

He began to wail. "My head hurts so much and I've lost my girl."

Harmony screamed at him. "You worthless son of a bitch. To leave your girlfriend lying in a puddle of blood. You're nothing but a craven coward. She deserved better than you. How could you leave her all alone like that?"

"Call for a bus."

She looked at Henry without responding.

"Harmony, we'll talk later. I don't know what's eating at you, but now is not the time. We need to get Will to the hospital so that his injuries can be assessed and treated."

Harmony hissed and her voice took on a shrill tone. "His injuries. What about hers? Oh, wait, it's too late for her. He killed her and now we're worried about how he's feeling?"

"I'll call for a forensics team. I'll go with Will in the ambulance to make sure he doesn't go anywhere. You can follow in the car. We'll meet at the hospital and take his statement there."

When Harmony didn't act, he raised his voice. "Call for a bus now," he thundered. The loudness of his instruction galvanized her into action.

Harmony watched as the paramedics strapped Will onto a gurney and wheeled him into the ambulance. She saw her partner climb into the back of the ambulance. She got into the squad car as the ambulance tore away from the sidewalk, lights blazing and siren wailing.

Neither noticed a man slouched in the driver's seat of a car almost directly across from Will's driveway. Only later, when the guard posted outside of Will's hospital door reported a dark-clad figure hovering over the patient, would they wonder if a third party with malign intent had been watching them.

Chapter 38

Although she tried, the paramedic was unable to mask her disdain for the detective riding with her and the patient in the back of the ambulance.

"Something's on your mind," observed Henry.

The paramedic looked up from the IV she adjusted and stared at the detective.

"Is there something you would like to say to me?" he asked.

"You said he was in a motor vehicle accident?" she asked.

"Yes, we were able to determine that his car was hit from behind while he was in a stopped position. The driver's door was also hit. He was able to drive away from the scene, but later collapsed in his home."

"I get the head injury. His hair is wet and his scalp is cut up. There's swelling and he may have a concussion or worse."

She pointed to the patient's torso. "From the bruises, it's clear he was wearing a seatbelt. It saved his life. The belt prevented him from being ejected, but he may have a very serious head injury. The doctors will have to evaluate it when he gets to the hospital."

Henry offered a suggestion. "It's possible he hit his head on the roof of the car, against the door frame, or against the windshield."

She nodded. "It's possible. The grains of glass in his face tell me his airbag didn't deploy."

"No, he drove a vintage sport car that did not have an airbag."

She shook her head. "He's lucky to be alive. Did you catch the driver of the vehicle that hit him or was it a hit and run?"

"The driver hit him, twice, and then left the scene of the accident without reporting it."

"Was it a she and did she get out of the car?"

Henry tried to redirect the paramedic. "We don't know. I'm sure in your line of work that you've seen many horrific scenes. In my line of work, most of what I do is interview and reinterview people, examine crime scenes, read documents, and skim through databases in search of information that may tie disparate clues together. Oh, and I spend too much of my time writing reports."

The paramedic gave an uncertain smile. "Put like that, your work sounds boring."

"It's rewarding when we're able to catch the bad guys and reassure the victim that she or he is safe."

The paramedic thought back to the cases she'd treated over the past week. They included a pregnant woman shot by her jilted lover, a bullet that whizzed through the glass in a residential area and became lodged in the brain of a seven-year-old girl practicing piano, and a young driver who wrapped his car around a utility pole on his way home after vaping and drinking. "Perhaps boring isn't so bad."

The ambulance pulled up to the Emergency Department and the paramedic and her partner wheeled the gurney directly to the treatment area while Henry stood near the Triage desk. Soon after Harmony joined him, they watched as the patient was wheeled up to the MRI suite for a brain scan.

Henry was on his phone reviewing notes with his partner when the patient was admitted to the surgical ward. "I'll stay with him in case he regains consciousness. We need to find out more about the person who rammed his car. Was it intentional or an accident? If it was an accident, why didn't they call it in? It's possible this person murdered the victim's girlfriend and wanted to take him out too. If that's the case, then he may be a target in the hospital. We can't take that risk. Call the captain to see if he can assign a protective detail to make sure Will is safe."

Harmony relayed her partner's instructions to the officer assigned to guard Will's room. "Your sole job is to ensure Will's safety. You need to prevent anyone but authorized personnel from entering Will's room. Am I making myself clear?"

"Yes, Detective."

Day Nine

Chapter 39

Henry remained in Will's room through the night, hoping he would regain consciousness so that he could answer questions about the crash. Henry listened to the slow drip of fluids and the beeps and buzzes of the monitors capturing Will's vital signs. Henry looked for, but didn't see any signs of Will regaining consciousness. When an officer showed up in the morning, Henry called Harmony to request a pick-up at the hospital. She said she would be delayed.

In his dreams, Will kept replaying the sight of La Donna splayed on the floor in her kitchen. He felt a gentle touch on his shoulder and opened his eyes to find a nurse at his side, taking his pulse with a stethoscope. He could smell the bitter scent of antiseptic.

"Mr. Davis, you're safe. You're in the hospital. You've been through a lot, but you're going to get better. It's good to see you're back with us. You had us worried for a while."

When Will tried to lift his head, he groaned and lay back on the bed. Beads of sweat shone on his forehead.

"Mr. Davis, don't try to move. You were in a car accident and sustained a fracture of your skull. It'll take time, but you will recover. The police want to talk to you, and I'll send them in."

His eyes widened in panic. "What do they want with me?" he asked.

The nurse scanned his face, noting with concern that his heart rate had surged upward and his blood pressure was following suit. She sought to reassure him. "They're searching for the driver who rammed your vehicle. They want to know if you can identify this person."

She watched as his vital signs returned to near-normal.

"It was a woman and she had bright red fingernails," he said.

"You can tell the detective all about it," she said encouragingly.

"The detective," he said anxiously.

"He sat with you through the night. You don't remember him being here?"

"No."

"Well, he's one of the good ones, and he'll make sure you get justice." Will smiled weakly.

Moments later, Henry walked into the room. "I'm glad to see you've regained consciousness. I'd like to ask you a few questions, if you're up to it."

He moved the chair closer to the bed and sat down. "Did you see who hit your vehicle?"

"It was a woman."

"You're sure?"

"Yes, she had long painted fingernails, scarlet red."

Henry processed this information, wanting to focus on the woman's overall appearance first. "Was she short or tall, young or old?"

"I think she was in her forties, on the smaller side."

"Did you get a good look at her face?"

"No. My eyes really hurt and it was hard to open them. But I saw her hand."

Henry sounded perplexed. "What about her hands stood out?"

"She came right up to the driver's side and knocked on the window. Her fingernails were long and perfectly groomed, a scarlet red. She had a red heart tattooed above her right wrist."

When Henry finished jotting down notes, he looked more closely at Will, wondering how the injured man could so clearly recall details. "Are you sure?"

"Yes, her fingernails were as red as any polish La Donna has ever worn. La Donna likes glamor. I'm very simple. Give me a beer and a football game and I'm all set. La Donna likes the bright lights, being the center of attention. I'm happy to know she will always come back to me. How is she doing?"

Henry glanced at the nurse worriedly.

"Dear, you need to get your rest." She turned off the overhead light and gestured for Henry to leave the room.

The nurse whispered to Henry. "It's not uncommon for patients who've suffered severe head trauma to forget what happened leading up to the trauma. It's the brain's way of protecting a patient who has seen or felt too much. Give him time to recover. He'll remember soon enough."

Henry re-entered the patient's room. "I have just a few more questions. We need to find out if your car accident was intentional or not. Did the driver ram your car more than once?"

The patient responded slowly, in a low tone that suggested he was deeply fatigued. "Yes, it was the strangest thing. I was stopped at a light and she rammed right into me. Then she came to the driver's side door and asked if I was okay. She said she'd been chatting on the phone with her friend and told me she couldn't stop in time. I had trouble getting words out and when I did, she got angry and accused me of being a drunk driver. She said the accident was all my fault. She backed out and accelerated, hitting the driver's side of the car on her way. She gave me the finger as she rode past."

"Do you know what kind of car it was?"

"A gray SUV. It looked newer. The first three letters of the license plate were "FDM," same as mine. I chose 'FDM' to show everyone that I live in the land of the free."

He looked anxiously at the detective. "Do you know what happened to my Thunderbird?"

Henry leaned in. "A Thunderbird! I thought it was some kind of vintage car."

"I restored it myself. I am a courier for a pharmaceutical company. It's not exciting, but it pays the bills while I work on growing my business as a restorer of vintage cars. My plan is to become the best car restorer between Raleigh and Myrtle Beach. I just want to go home, to see La Donna." Will began to mewl like a fearful cat.

Henry awkwardly patted Will's shoulder. "Son, let us find out what happened. Focus on getting better. We'll get to the bottom of this. I promise you that we'll find the driver who rammed your car."

Will closed his eyes and was soon asleep. Henry observed the even breathing and hoped the young man could find some respite from the terrible events of the past eighteen hours.

Henry stepped outside the hospital room, gently closing the door behind him. He spoke to the officer assigned to guard Will's room. "Someone may try to get to him. Make sure you check everyone's ID before you let them in. Call me immediately on my cell if you see anything unusual."

Harmony picked Henry up outside the hospital entrance. She remained unconvinced that Will was an innocent party. Nothing Henry said could persuade her.

"Henry, he left her all alone, bleeding to death on the kitchen floor."

"Wait, Harmony, that's not necessarily true. He said that she was dead before he got there."

Harmony's response was scornful. " 'He said.' Why would you take his word for it? Most wives are murdered by their spouses. How is this any different?"

"Let's wait for the coroner's report before we jump to accusations. I can tell you, though, that I found him very genuine. He answered my questions and was very forthcoming. He may be a little naïve, but he's not a murderer."

"Well, if you say so. He may not be a murderer but by abandoning his girlfriend, he's the lowest form in my books."

Chapter 40

Will was dreaming about how he'd located his first Thunderbird. He'd found it in a junkyard. Its fender was folded like the bellows of an accordion. The frame of the roof was badly dented and the windshield and two headlights were missing. The interior was covered in grime.

After taking photos, he'd pulled the Thunderbird apart, removing the engine and transmission, documenting every piece so that he would be able to reconstruct the car. He rebuilt the engine from the cylinders up. He began working on the frame, removing large swathes of rust and replacing metal that couldn't be repaired. He used a stud welder to fix large dents. He applied paint and polished the chrome fender until it gleamed.

He smiled, remembering La Donna's insistence that the interior of the car had to match the pristine exterior. Only when she gave her approval to the new upholstery was he confident that the car was ready to be sold.

He frowned in his sleep as a grey cloud obscured his vision. Dread seized him and he began to choke. He could hear the reassuring words of the detective and feel the comforting touch on his shoulder. His breathing slowed. He and La Donna were rocketing down the highway in the newly restored Thunderbird, as free as eagles soaring in the treetops.

Outside the hospital room, the officer stifled a yawn. He regretted bringing a thermos filled with coffee. After seven hours without a break, he needed to relieve himself. He squirmed, hoping that the detective would return soon.

A trim man with blonde hair combed straight back and held in place with gel approached the officer. The man wore a monogrammed white jacket labeled 'Dr. Whyte, Neurosurgeon.' Hospital ID hung around his neck. He extended his hand. "I'm a big fan of the men in blue. Thank you for protecting this patient."

The officer waved him into the room, then walked toward the rest room to relieve himself.

Will was in a twilight zone, half asleep, half awake, when he heard the door click and saw someone enter. He initially assumed it was the nurse, but smelled aftershave lotion.

Inside the room, 'Dr. Whyte' surveyed the machines monitoring the patient before approaching the bed.

Will whispered to his visitor. "Hello, I'm thirsty and I'd like some water, please."

Silence.

The lack of response troubled Will, prompting him to swivel his head so that he could get a better look at the person. Something about his demeanor prompted Will to speak more forcefully. "Who are you?"

Dr. Whyte turned and smiled at Will. He pointed to his jacket. "I'm here to check your neurological functions."

Will's face was swollen. When he squinted, his eyes appeared to disappear in the inflamed folds. "Do you think you could give me some water?"

"Of course," responded Dr. Whyte smoothly. After filling a cup with water, he waited expectantly for Will to raise his head.

"Can you raise the bed so that I can take a sip," asked Will.

The doctor looked dismissively at Will. "That's nurses' work."

Will reached for the call button.

Before his hand could make contact, Dr. Whyte pulled the button away.

The action sent alarm bells ringing for Will. "What are you doing?" His voice trembled. "I want to see the nurse now."

"Shhh. You can have water after the neurological exam. It'll only take a moment."

Dr. Whyte pulled what appeared to be a stainless steel pen from his jacket pocket. From his other pocket he extracted a vial filled with a clear liquid.

"What's that for?" asked Will. He could feel his heart thudding.

When the neurosurgeon extended the pen, Will saw that the end was a needle tip and not a tip meant for writing. The doctor filled it with liquid from the vial. "It'll enlarge your pupils so that I can see behind your eyes. I'll be able to tell if there's nerve damage."

"Stop. I don't want anything put in my eyes," said Will. In response, the doctor edged closer to Will's side. When the doctor began to lean in, Will screamed. With a strength borne of fear, he lifted up his arms and pushed the doctor away. The silver pen slipped from the doctor's grip and fell onto the floor, making a clinking sound.

Will screamed again. This time, it came out like a growl, low and guttural, as if he were an animal protecting himself from an attack by a larger prey.

The doctor placed his hands around Will's collarbone and began to push him back against the pillows.

When the officer returned to his post, he was more relaxed. He leaned across the wall, legs crossed at the ankles. He recrossed his legs and then decided to sit down. Moving toward the chair placed next to the door, he thought he heard a scream. He listened carefully, and heard the sound of a metal object landing on the hard hospital floor and breaking. He frowned, wondering what his charge was up to. When a low guttural growl penetrated through the door, the officer decided to investigate. He straightened and turned the door handle, calling out as he opened it.

"Is everything okay in here?"

For a moment, he froze in place when he saw Dr. Whyte leaning over Will and applying pressure. He could also see Will trying to push the doctor away.

The officer spoke loudly and in his most uncompromising voice. "Step away from the patient now. I said 'Now!'"

The physician turned toward the officer and then refocused his attention, encircling Will's neck with his hands. The officer clubbed Dr. Whyte with a baton, sending him flying across the room. Next, he called hospital security to request their assistance. Finally, he dialed Henry's personal cell. He blurted out Henry's name. Just as Henry answered, the officer felt something sharp enter the flesh below his ankle. He screamed in pain and fell down.

Dr. Whyte straightened up and pressed the call button. "We need help in here," he thundered.

The nurse ran in and looked from Dr. Whyte to her patient. "What is going on?"

The doctor gestured at Will. "The patient will be okay. I heard a scream and opened the door. A man impersonating a police officer tried to strangle the patient. I was able to pull him off and he accidentally injected himself." He pointed to the police officer lying on the floor.

"Thank you, doctor. Lucky for us that you were nearby." She pulled out her cell and called Security.

Dr. Whyte smiled at her and left the room. He nonchalantly walked out of the surgical unit and into the elevator.

Henry missed him by minutes. When the officer's call ended

abruptly, Henry accelerated, siren on and lights flashing. He parked in the striped 'no-stopping' area next to the emergency doors. He raced out of the car and ran toward the elevator, pushing the button leading to the surgical unit.

He ran to the patient's room, to be blocked by a burly hospital security guard. "Prove to me who you are," said the guard.

"I'm the detective who assigned an officer to protect the patient. Where is my officer?"

The guard frowned as he scanned Henry's ID. "You can go in, but the patient is in no condition to speak to anyone."

As Henry entered the room, the nurse met his eyes. "Detective, a man impersonating an officer tried to kill the patient. One of our physicians heard the commotion and bravely intervened, preventing what would almost certainly have been a tragic outcome. In the altercation, the person impersonating an officer inadvertently injected himself with a substance intended for the patient. He's being treated in the ER as we speak."

Henry looked worriedly at Will. "Was he hurt?"

"There are bruise marks on his collarbone and around his neck. His heart rate and blood pressure spiked to unhealthy levels. He was traumatized. We had to sedate him so that his mind can rest and his body can heal."

Instead of waiting for the elevator, Henry took the stairs. He flashed his badge to get the triage nurse's attention. "I need to see the officer who is being treated. It's extremely important."

The nurse was accustomed to members of the public imploring her to give them priority. But when she saw the badge, she rose from her seat, came out from behind the partition, and told Henry to follow her.

"I registered him myself. I'll take you to him."

She opened up a curtain in the patient treatment bay, and was surprised to find a vacant bed. "Perhaps they took him for an X-ray." When she tapped the attending physician's shoulder, he shook his head. Henry could see her expression of shock, but not make out what either was saying.

"In nursing school, they told us to treat every patient equally. They taught us to suspend our personal judgment, not to let personal bias influence how we provide treatment. Even though this man impersonated a police officer and tried to kill a patient, I did everything I could to ensure he had the best care possible."

"How do you know he impersonated a police officer?" asked Henry.

"He was wearing a uniform, and one of our physicians bravely prevented him from strangling the patient."

"Can I see him?"

"They were unable to resuscitate him. His corpse has been sent to the morgue. You'll have to ask them."

Henry's eyes widened in horror. "I don't understand. He called me on his radio to say the patient had been attacked."

Now that there was no longer an urgent life-and-death situation, the nurse's naturally starchy manner reasserted itself. "You can find your man in the morgue. Now get out of the ER. We have live patients who need our help."

Henry walked slowly to the morgue. He rang the buzzer at the entrance and identified himself. "I understand that a police officer – or a man dressed in a police uniform – was brought to the morgue from the ER. I need to see him."

Henry heard a whir as the door to the morgue slowly opened. He stepped into a room that was considerably cooler than the outside corridor. The smell of antiseptic permeated the air. The morgue attendant walked over to a bank of drawers, looked at a list on his iPad, and opened a drawer. He slid the body forward.

Henry placed his hand against his mouth. His face crumpled and he swayed on his feet, placing his hand against the cabinet to steady himself. "It can't be," he said.

The attendant watched without commenting.

"This is the officer who was assigned to protect the patient. He radioed me to say the patient had been attacked. I don't know what happened in that room, but I'm going to find out."

Henry's lips clamped together and he exited the morgue.

He returned to the surgical unit and approached the head nurse. "Can I speak to Will Davis?"

"Absolutely not. He was almost killed and has to rest."

"Can you tell me anything about the doctor who interrupted the attack?"

"Certainly. He's a neurosurgeon and his name is Dr. Whyte. If you see him, tell him the nurses on Surgical say 'Thank you' for saving their patient."

Next, Henry walked to the Neurosurgery Unit and asked for the head nurse. "I'm looking for Dr. Whyte. Is he on the unit?"

The head nurse looked at Henry strangely. She paused, at a loss for words. "Dr. Whyte, you say?"

"Yes, he apparently saved a surgical patient from certain death earlier today."

"Detective, Dr. Whyte does not work in neurosurgery. We have no one with that name. I have worked for twenty-seven years in this unit and I know all of the neurosurgeons who have ever worked here. There has never been a Dr. Whyte. We do not have any interns or residents by that name, either. Now if you don't mind, I have work to do."

She abruptly turned in the opposite direction and walked away from him.

When Henry returned to the surgical unit, he could feel every nurse staring at him. He approached the head nurse once again. "You said that Dr. Whyte prevented Will Davis's attacker from finishing him off?"

"Yes, Dr. Whyte the neurosurgeon."

"Well, that's interesting because when I spoke to Neurosurgery, I was told there is no Dr. Whyte on staff at this hospital. They didn't know who he was."

The nurse was momentarily at a loss for words. "Perhaps he's a resident?"

"No."

"I don't understand. He stopped a man impersonating a police officer from strangling my patient."

"Are you sure? Can you tell me what you saw when you entered the room?"

"The patient was lying in bed. There were red marks on his clavicle and around his neck. He couldn't talk. His breathing was ragged. I put an oxygen mask on him and reassured him that everything would be okay. I told Dr. Whyte I'd like to give the patient a sedative and the doctor agreed. I injected the sedative directly into the IV and it took effect immediately."

"Did the patient say anything about the attack?"

"No, but his eyes had a look of fear, like a wild animal being cornered."

"Did Dr. Whyte say anything else?"

"Just that he'd heard a commotion while walking by. When he entered the room, he saw a man in a uniform hunched over the patient."

"Did you see the man in the uniform attacking the patient?"

"No, I came after the call button was pressed."

Henry came to a startling conclusion. "What does Dr. Whyte look like?"

She shrugged. "Like any other doctor here. He has blonde hair and wears it slicked back. He was wearing a jacket with his name monogrammed on it. He had hospital ID on a lanyard around his neck."

"Was he short or tall?"

"On the shorter side, I think."

"Young or old?"

"Definitely younger."

Now it was her turn to ask questions. "Do you think he was there to harm my patient?"

"That's possible," said Henry.

"My God, that means he harmed the police officer."

Henry nodded glumly.

"Do you think he's going to make another attempt to kill Will?"

"I don't know."

The nurse implored Henry. "You've got to find this man and stop him before he hurts anyone else. He's a discredit to his profession."

Day Ten

Chapter 41

Dr. Beatrix Bach was accustomed to getting her way. The surgeons in the British Columbian health authority had long ago learned that not following her wishes meant they would lose precious operating room time and, with that, a significant loss in income. As a result, Dr. Bach was apoplectic when she called Jeannie, commanded her to return to British Columbia at once, and the young woman refused.

"Johal, I've given it some thought. It is not safe for you to remain in Greenville. You need to get out of North Carolina as soon as possible. My assistant has procured an airline ticket for you to return home on Monday."

Jeannie's response was unexpected. "You think I would be safer returning home? Do you mean my home in Mumbai, where I almost died when my clinic was bombed? Or do you mean Vancouver, where my husband tried to throw acid in my face?" asked Jeannie dryly.

The sharp tone and heightened volume of Dr. Bach's voice indicated her disapproval. "Don't give me attitude."

"I am being precise."

Dr. Bach's tone softened and she called Jeannie by her first name. "On the same day that you started working in Greenville, someone poisoned my good friend. The murderer is still at large. You were poisoned and it's fortunate I was there to help. Subsequently, the administrative assistant was murdered. That's not a coincidence. Someone is picking off members of the research team.

"Jeannie, I don't know who and I don't know why. I do know that

I would never forgive myself if you came to harm while doing a favor for me."

Dr. Bach's plea did not deter Jeannie. "I don't think that whoever placed poison on the door handle of my hotel room intended to kill me because I'd be dead if that were the case. I appreciate your concern, but I'm just beginning to understand why the results of some participants in the study have slowed or stalled."

"You're not sleuthing on your own, are you?"

"No, but I did rebuild the database. Once the obvious errors were corrected, I began creating pivot tables to generate charts showing results over time."

"What did you find?"

"Well, we check for AIC levels every three months and we check glucose levels every week. The women with the highest weight relative to height are the ones whose weight losses have plateaued, even though they receive the highest dose of semaglutide, and their dosing has remained constant since the study began. They say they are continuing to exercise regularly and to eat carefully, but they are barely losing weight. Since they have the most weight to lose, it stands to reason that their weight loss would be the highest."

"What do you think is happening?"

"Dr. Bach, you know I'm a data person. I love data because it doesn't lie. I looked at what we weren't measuring, and that may be the missing clue."

"What do you mean?"

"We monitor for results. What we haven't been checking is semaglutide dosage because we assumed it was fixed, based on the manufacturer's statements."

"Could someone have tampered with the dose?"

As Jeannie's voice rose, her accent became more pronounced. "We examined five vials from each box. There was no proof of any kind to suggest tampering took place. The boxes were intact and the plastic around each vial was sealed."

"So, no tampering?"

"No, not as far as we can see."

"Well, what are you finding?"

"What if the contents of the vials were contaminated before they were shipped here? What if the vials that were labeled as containing higher doses were diluted? That could explain why the heavier participants are losing less weight than previously, if no other factors have changed."

Dr. Bach was doubtful. "Pharmacists take their work very seriously. It would be illegal and unethical to do what you're suggesting."

Jeannie's retort was fast. "I am not suggesting a pharmacist would give a patient the wrong drug or the wrong dose intentionally. But what if the shipment we received has been diluted?"

"It's an interesting theory, but unlikely. WellStar Pharmaceuticals, the company sponsoring the study, stands to gain billions of dollars a year in sales if the research project demonstrates without a doubt that these drugs can help very obese patients lose significant amounts of weight. There is no reason for them to sabotage their own study."

"I agree with you, Dr. Bach. I don't know the answer to that question, but I think it's an avenue worth pursuing."

"Well, you should leave that to the project manager. It's not your problem."

"The project manager is an engineer. He won't understand the medical aspects."

"If you investigate the possibility of sabotage, you could be getting too close to the killer. I can't have you stay there. I want you back here before the end of the week. That's an order."

"I think I can manage that," said Jeannie.

Dr. Bach sat forward in her chair, fingertips touching each other as she pondered the researcher's unexpected capitulation. Jeannie's willingness to return to Canada by the end of the week could only mean one thing. Jeannie was confident she would identify Dr. Dunn's killer, as well as the reason for a lack of results among some of the study participants.

She dialed a second number. A deep male voice answered.

"Jaspreet Singh. Who is calling?"

"Beatrix Bach, Jeannie Johal's boss."

She could hear a deep intake of breath. "Why are you calling me?"

"Look, I don't know what happened between you and my girl...."

"She dropped me like a scalding samosa after she went to tea with my mother. She said our relationship would not work and she refused to elaborate.

"When I asked my mother what happened during the tea, she said there was nothing out of the ordinary. She said she told Jeannie she understood why her son had fallen head over heels and she said she would give her blessing to the marriage. She told me she was very happy that I'd found the woman of my dreams and she was sure Jeannie would make a wonderful mother."

"Did you and Jeannie discuss getting married?"

"Well, no, we both have careers and wanted to take things slowly."

"Did you tell your mother this?"

"No. I told her how happy Jeannie made me."

Bach's sigh was prolonged and loud.

"Is something wrong?" asked Jaspreet.

"Is it possible your mother scared Jeannie off with talk of marriage and children?"

"Jeannie is the strongest person I know. I can't imagine anything scaring her off."

"Well, I think it might have been a mistake for Jeannie to have met your mother on her own, without you as a buffer."

Jaspreet became defensive. "My mother is a very gracious lady. She would never try to make Jeannie feel uncomfortable."

"In any case, Jeannie is in Eastern North Carolina and she's in danger."

"What's she doing in Eastern North Carolina?"

"I sent her there to work on a research project."

"What kind of danger?"

"The project lead, my very dear friend, was poisoned on Jeannie's first day of work. Jeannie herself was targeted after the funeral. And now the administrative assistant has been murdered."

"Gracious! What's going on there?"

"I've given Jeannie an ultimatum. I told her she has to be back in British Columbia before the end of the week. Strangely, she didn't argue with me. Now that I think back on the conversation, I am worried that she's going to go full-out investigator and try to get to the bottom of what's going on before she leaves."

"That sounds like her."

"I want you to go to Greenville and protect her."

"You know I have a job. I can't just leave."

Dr. Bach was firm. "You can. And you must. You two belong together and you can sort out your relationship once you're in Greenville."

He was speechless. "We haven't exchanged a word in several months. What's to say she would even talk to me?"

"You don't have to get all chummy with her. Just protect her. Make sure she doesn't get shot by a lunatic extremist wielding an AK-47."

"What!"

"Well, any gun-toting person in Greenville."

"Dr. Bach, you forget who you're dealing with. Jeannie is well able to protect herself."

"She's strong, I'll grant you that. But this may be beyond her abilities."

He was hesitant. "Even if I could get the time off, I'm not sure she would welcome my showing up as her protector. She's very independent."

"I don't care whether she wants you there or not. Now go!"

Chapter 42

Henry couldn't shake off the feeling of doom that engulfed him. In the back of his mind, a little voice was whispering to him, but he couldn't decipher what it was saying, so he did what the son of any God-fearing farmer in Eastern North Carolina would do.

He opened the sliding doors to his backyard. His eyes went to the giant Thujas growing in the park across the road, marveling how they formed a colorful canopy. He strolled over to a raised garden bed in the far corner of his yard. It was brimming with potato plants, carrots, okra, and zucchini. He inhaled deeply, smelling the fresh, fertile black soil. He thanked God for his health and for the food he was growing. Then he heaved a great sigh, got in his car, and went to pick his partner up.

They both began speaking at the same time.

Henry said. "We need to find out more about Will Davis."

Harmony talked over her partner. "We need to speak to Nathan, er, Johnson Johnson."

Always the gentleman, Henry agreed they would see Johnson first. They were met with silence when they signed in and asked to speak with Johnson. The guard made a call after they repeated their request. The deputy sheriff shuffled to their side a few minutes later.

"And how are you on this fine, sunny day," he asked. "Did you come to have a chinwag with me?"

Harmony looked warily at him, while Henry took his words at face value. "It is a beautiful day. Days like this make me remember what a privilege it is to live in the Tarheel State. It's always a pleasure to see you, sir, and we wanted to follow up on the tip you gave us following Dr. Dunn's funeral service."

The deputy sheriff's eyes narrowed. "It seems I may have been presumptuous and altogether wrong in terms of what I told you."

"What do you mean?" asked Harmony.

"Well, a little birdie provided that information to me. Later, I found out that the information was a crock."

"How did you find that out?"

"Earl told me."

"Earl?"

"You know, the prisoner. He's short, but mean. He came to me to tell me that Johnson Johnson had failed the fealty test, and there would be consequences."

Henry looked puzzled. "The fealty test? What's that?"

"Johnson told Earl you asked him to snitch for you. He asked for information he could share. Earl told him some stuff and waited to see what Johnson did with it. Instead of contacting you, he came to me and boasted that he had Earl's ear. Earl was not pleased."

"Johnson told me about a guy who drives a souped-up Thunderbird and delivers packages all over Eastern North Carolina for a pharmacy company that manufactures a new version of 'mother's little helpers' as a sideline."

Harmony was incredulous. 'Mother's little helpers?' What do you mean?"

Henry understood the reference. "You're too young to know, Harmony. Do you even know who Mick Jagger is?"

"The British musician who's a million years old."

Henry grimaced. "His band released a song in 1966 about an anti-anxiety drug prescribed to millions of women around the world."

"I wasn't even born then," she retorted. "What's the new version?"

"Fentanyl in a blister pack. In this instance, it's packaged to resemble cold and flu medicine."

"If it's a sideline, what other drugs does the manufacturer produce?"

"I asked Johnson, but he didn't know. When I asked Earl, he told me to stop asking questions or there'd be consequences."

Henry's expression turned serious. "What happened?"

"When my guard went to check the prisoners last night, he found Johnson quivering on the floor of his cell, surrounded by a pool of blood."

"My God! Is he all right?" said Harmony.

"He took some hard kicks. He has a few cracked ribs and a fractured tibia. Oh, and his jaw is wired shut. He lost a few teeth. He's in the infirmary."

"Did you question Earl?"

"He said he knows nothing about it. The prisoners are in lockdown for 24 hours. They've had their privileges suspended. Anything more and there'll be a riot."

"We'd like to see Johnson now," said Henry firmly.

"You're welcome to see him, but I doubt he'll tell you anything. In fact, I know he can't tell you anything because he is physically unable to open his mouth. Still want to see him?"

Harmony nodded.

Her eyes filled with tears when she saw Johnson lying in the bed, one foot elevated. She marched toward the bed, angrily wiping her tears away. "Are you stupid! We told you to talk to us and no one else. Did you think you could confide in the deputy sheriff without Earl finding out?"

Johnson lifted a hand as if to defend himself against the torrent of words she hurled at him.

She turned to Henry. "This man was the best basketball player I knew. And he was kind. He had so much going for him."

They could hear a whistling sound coming from Johnson's throat as he tried to speak.

She continued to tear into him. "You were my protector, Johnson Nathaniel Johnson from across the street. You didn't let anyone bully me. And you were the best basketball player in the school. You had a dream and I was sure you wouldn't let anything stop you from reaching it. What happened to you?" Nathan's hand beckoned for Harmony.

She slowly advanced toward him. She felt his hand stroke her arm. He couldn't talk, but he smiled at her. "Nathan, I'll do everything I can to help you."

Henry shook his head. "This isn't right." He made a snap decision. He pulled out his cell and moved as far as possible away from his partner and the deputy sheriff. He called his captain. Johnson's eyes followed Henry as the detective spoke on his phone.

The deputy sheriff beckoned to Henry. "You know that Earl can get to him just as easily in a hospital room as in the prison infirmary."

"Not if I have any say."

"Well, it appears you have a lot of say. My boss has ordered me to call an ambulance and have Johnson transferred to the hospital."

"Detective Harris and I will wait with the prisoner until the paramedics arrive," said Henry.

"Very well. He's your burden now."

Henry approached Johnson's bedside. "They'll kill you if you remain here. We're not gonna let that happen."

Chapter 43

It was with a heavy heart that Frank Wright drove into the parking lot. Jeannie and Tanisha pulled up behind him in Jeannie's red Mustang.

Now that they'd been cleared to enter the building, Frank was able to unlock the door and turn on the light switch. Out of habit, he went to pour himself a cup of freshly brewed coffee and remembered that La Donna was not there and would never again be there to make coffee and greet everyone.

"I'll make the coffee," Jeannie offered.

After the coffee was ready, Frank gestured to Jeannie and Tanisha to walk ahead of him. "We need to talk. Let's use the conference table in Dr. Dunn's office."

They moved to Dr. Dunn's office, each being careful to avoid walking on the stains in the wooden floor.

Frank was the first to speak. "If it seems quiet here today, it's because La Donna isn't here. I'm afraid to say I took her presence for granted. The lights were on when I came into the building and she always had a freshly brewed pot of coffee ready. I don't know how to say this."

He paused.

Tanisha broke the silence. "Has something happened to La Donna?"

Jeannie asked, "Why would you say that, Tanisha?"

The younger woman's explanation was short. "Because she's not here."

They both looked at Frank, whose hand trembled as he put down his coffee cup. "La Donna was killed in her home."

"What!"

He nodded. "Initially, they thought that her boyfriend was the culprit."

"That's not surprising," said Jeannie.

Frank was appalled by Jeannie's matter-of-factness. "How could you say that? You've never even met him," said Frank.

"It's what the data say. It's usually the person's spouse or partner, or if not them, then someone they know."

"I see."

An uncomfortable silence ensued. Jeannie was the first to break it. "I also have something to say. My boss in Canada called me. She told me about La Donna's murder, and says she wants me back before the end of the week. She and I discussed the steps Tanisha and I have been taking to clean the data. We may have an explanation for why the women who have the most to lose are no longer losing significant amounts of weight."

"What's that?"

"When it comes to severely obese women, society judges them and assumes they eat too much, eat junk food, are too lazy to exercise, you know, all these cruel stereotypes. But the women report they haven't changed their routines. They are still, for the most part, eating healthily and exercising regularly. If it's not the women's actions, then what is it? Well, it could be the medication itself. We didn't see any signs of drug tampering, but what if the vials themselves were altered during the production process?"

Frank's initial response was to deny. "I don't see how that's possible. The pharmaceutical company providing us with semaglutides is one of the largest international suppliers of the drug. Why would they risk harming their reputation by altering their top-selling product?"

"I don't have the answer to that," said Jeannie.

"Wait, I think I know why," said Tanisha.

Both Jeannie and Frank stared at the younger woman, wondering how she could possibly know what happened.

She explained, "No, I don't know how they altered the product at the source, but think about it. If they can dilute their product, it will go further and they will have more sales."

"That's unethical. No certified pharmacist would ever condone watering down the efficacy of a drug."

"Jeannie, I wish I had your ideals. Don't you know that greed is a strong motivator?"

Jeannie looked sharply at Tanisha. "I still don't think a pharmacist would tamper with the dosage."

"Well, I betcha someone did."

Frank had been silent up to this point. Now he joined the conversation. "Tanisha's got a point. And so do you, Jeannie. We need to consider who supplies us with the product. Yes, it's the pharmaceutical company, but who handles the packages before they arrive?"

He turned to the younger woman. "Tanisha, would you give us a moment?"

Jeannie's body involuntarily tensed. "What do you want to tell me?"

He sighed and shook his head. "This is not a conversation I want to have, but I need to tell you. You met with my wife and her friends for lunch."

"I did. They were very welcoming."

He cleared his throat. He drew out a word. "We-ell. Did they tell you they are the leaders of the local chapter of Moms for Liberty?"

"No. Who are they?"

"They're mostly housewives who worry that the traditional family is disappearing, that their kids are being exposed to dangerous ideas by people who are different from them."

"What do you mean by 'different?' "

"You have to understand that we used to be a state where tobacco farming was king. So many farmers lost their livelihoods when the market fell through. It's become common for their kids to have to leave Pitt County if they want a better job or a chance at a better life. There's not a lot for them here."

Jeannie was losing patience with the project manager. "What are you not saying?"

"Well, you arrived here without my knowledge. It was an arrangement between Dr. Dunn and her foreign friend. I didn't know anything about you and I may have mentioned to my wife that you're darker-skinned and speak with an accent."

"What about my skills? Did you tell her I am a qualified surgeon and epidemiologist?"

He spoke defensively. "I never questioned your skills. The concern was that you were seen as a foreigner taking work away from a North Carolinian."

"I understand what you're saying, but what does this have to do with your wife and her friends?"

"The younger woman works in a nursery watering plants. Under other circumstances, she might have gone to university. But she couldn't afford tuition after her father walked out on the family. My wife told me that Lexi has written a lexicon of poisonous plants in North Carolina. She was going to drip something over the door handle of your hotel room to scare you."

"What! She barely knows me. Why would she do that?"

He bowed his head. "I'm sorry, I didn't know my wife would ever encourage that kind of behavior."

"She did put something on the handle. My hand was on fire. Fortunately, Dr. Bach was with me and she was able to help me."

"I'm sorry. That sounds inadequate, but I don't know what else to say."

"What did she use?"

"*Colocasia esculenta.*"

"Elephant Ears? Those are very large plants. We grew some in our yard in Mumbai."

"Yes, the very same. Lexi discovered that the sap inside the stem contains calcium oxalate and can cause burning and swelling if it makes contact with the skin."

"Dr. Bach insisted I keep my hand away from my face. Thank God I didn't get it into my eyes. I could have been blinded!"

He gulped. "I told Darla that we'll have to contact the police and report what Lexi did. Darla wasn't happy with me, but she understands that you can't go around injuring people."

Jeannie eyed Frank with compassion. "I understand how difficult a conversation this has been, and I appreciate you telling me what happened."

"Darla's been in a tailspin since our daughter passed. I thought she was doing better, but I guess I just wanted to believe that."

Jeannie nodded sympathetically. "When I worked as a surgeon, I saw everything in black and white. Right and wrong. Good and bad. In the past year and a half, I've discovered that there are many shades of what I think of as 'inbetweenness.' I don't agree with your wife's beliefs, but I can understand why she believes what she does. I will ask the police chief to go easy on her."

Frank was incredulous. "You know the police chief?"

She smiled. "I met him when Dr. Dunn died. The governor called him."

"Whoa! The governor! You know him, too?"

"Well, I tended to his son on the flight to Raleigh. The governor learned about it and was appreciative."

Frank looked at Jeannie with wide eyes. "A gifted researcher, a physician who handles emergencies. And compassionate, too. You really are the full package! I'm lucky to know you."

Jeannie dismissed the praise. "I'm not going anywhere yet, Frank, until I know why the participants in our study stopped losing weight. Let's find the missing piece to this puzzle. Let's get this study back on track."

Chapter 44

When they walked into the hospital room, Henry was surprised to see Will dressed and sitting in a straight-backed chair across from the bed.

"Wow. You look a sight different from the last time I saw you," he said.

Will nodded. "My body is healing quickly."

The detective leaned against the edge of the hospital bed. "The last time I was here, I asked if you could think of anyone who wanted to hurt your girlfriend. You were quite emphatic in saying you couldn't think of a single person. Now I want you to think hard about anyone who might want to hurt you?"

Will shrugged. "I'm just a driver. I earn twelve dollars an hour and mileage for delivering packages around the county. From what I hear, migrant laborers earn twice that working on pig farms."

Now it was the detective's turn to shrug. "I grew up on a farm and I would have given anything to be able to earn twelve dollars an hour working on my pa's property. I really need you to concentrate. Someone wrote your name in red, practically accusing you of murdering your girlfriend. A woman rammed your precious Thunderbird and didn't stick around or call for help. Worse, she sideswiped you when fleeing the scene. We still don't know who she is or why she did this. Then we come to the hospital, where a man impersonating a neurosurgeon tried to kill you. Someone wants you dead and we need to find out who it is before the next attempt on your life is successful."

The effort to concentrate made Will's eyes water. "On the night that

La Donna was killed, she and I got into it. I had a late delivery and she came with me. I was dropping off a package next to a bar in Kinston. I told her to wait in the car but instead she went into the bar and had a couple of drinks."

Now that Will had started talking, there was no stopping him. "Oh, wait! Archer and I also had an argument. It got quite heated."

"Who's Archer?"

"Anderson Archer. He's the regional sales representative for the pharmaceutical company I work for. He asked me to drop off a package at an address in Kinston. I did, but he accused me of shorting him. He even threatened me."

"Did La Donna witness this?"

"Yes and no. La Donna was in the bar when she heard shouting. She heard me scream. She also heard Archer's voice. She walked through the bar to the adjoining building. She saw Archer kick me. She told him to let me go. I could tell he wasn't very happy to see her. She and I left immediately after. I told her she should have stayed in the car. We argued. I dropped her at her house. After I got home, I decided to go back to her place because I didn't want to leave things bad between us. But when I got there, she didn't answer. I waited and waited. Then I noticed the door was unlocked. I went in and found her. It was awful! There was nothing I could do." His voice broke and he stared at his hands.

Harmony asked a pointed question. "Is Archer your boss?"

"Yes, you could say that. He tells me where to pick up and drop off packages."

"What does he look like?"

"He wears fancy suits all the time. He has long blonde hair that he combs back from his forehead."

She exchanged a glance with her partner, who nodded faintly.

"Anything else?"

"He has a funny accent. I think he's from the North."

Henry patted his shoulder. "Tell us about the lab."

"Wait," said Will, his eyes opening wide. "Do you think Archer killed my girl? He barely knew her."

"We have to explore every possibility," said Henry.

After leaving Will's room, Harmony ducked into the other room where an officer was posted outside. She bent close to Nathan's head and stroked his cheek. "Nathan, I don't know if you can hear me, but I'm here. You're going to be okay. Just get better."

Henry marveled over the tenderness of the gesture. "The fingerprints in Will's room did not show up in the criminal database. We need to get a sample from Archer so that we can confirm our suspicions."

"Didn't Dr. Johal say the research project in Greenville was funded by a pharmaceutical company?"

"She said it was funded by the county, the NIH, and a grant from a pharmaceutical company."

Harmony asked her partner a question. "Do you believe in coincidences?" She held out her hand and began to count: "1) Will picks up and delivers packages for a large pharmaceutical company. 2) Will's boss is angry over a missing package and threatens him with violence. 3) La Donna witnesses the threat. She's killed. 4) Will is attacked."

Henry's voice was somber when he responded. "Too many coincidences. I think we've found the missing link. Now we just need to locate Archer. We know he killed La Donna and tried to kill Will. He's a madman on the loose. He needs to be stopped before he kills again."

When they called their chief to brief him, he urged them to get some rest while he coordinated the offensive.

Chapter 45

The sky was a perfect Carolina blue, but the air was hot and humid. As he slid open the patio doors, Henry remembered his mother saying 'it's hotter'n a blister bug in a pepper patch.' He smiled, enjoying the sound of the words and wondering how his mother had come up with the phrase.

He curtailed his customary morning walk around the garden when he started to sweat after being outside for only a few minutes. He didn't want Harmony complaining while in the car with him.

He let out a laugh when she climbed into the car and complained, "I'm glistening."

"Are you saying you're sweating?"

Harmony held her head high and affected a haughty demeanor. She laughed at herself. "Southern women don't sweat. We glisten. Lord knows, it's like a steam bath out here."

Her mien and tone changed as they neared the precinct. "Do you remember reaming me out in the church balcony when you thought I was sending texts on my phone?" asked Harmony with a mischievous glint in her eye.

"Well, you were."

"Yes, but I was also observing those attending the service."

"That's true," he conceded.

"There was a man with blonde hair slicked back. He stood out because he was wearing a suit jacket and matching trousers, as well as a tie."

"What are you thinking?"

"Do you suppose Anderson Archer would have the balls to come to the funeral of someone he murdered?"

Henry winced over his partner's indelicate choice of words. "Well, they say that criminals often return to the scene of their crime."

"He's good for it, isn't he?"

Harmony waited for Henry to confirm her suspicions.

"We always presume someone is innocent until convicted guilty, but it sure is pointing in his direction. We need to pin down his whereabouts, talk to him, and get a sample of his fingerprints," said Henry.

After roll call, the detectives returned to their desks. Harmony ran a Google search and smiled triumphantly over the results. "Here's his photo. It matches the description. It says that Anderson Archer is a licensed pharmacist who was born in Stamford, Connecticut." She continued to skim through the article. "He got his MBA and decided to pursue opportunities in the New South."

"That could be Atlanta or Raleigh," said Henry.

"Or Charlotte, or any number of other cities. What it also says is that he is a licensed pharmacist. Who else do we know who has an interest in pharmaceuticals?"

"Are you thinking back to the funeral?"

"And Dr. Dunn's poisoning."

"We need to find him."

They traveled to the hospital to find out if Will could provide any more answers.

"He never mentioned Dr. Dunn by name, but several times complained about a bossy woman who ignored his suggestions. It could have been her," said Will.

On their way out, Harmony stuck her head in the doorway leading to Nathan Johnson's bed. He was sitting up against a pile of pillows and holding an iPad.

"What do you have there?" said Harmony brightly to her childhood friend.

He wrote a note on the pad and held it up for Harmony to read. "I know that you got this for me. Thank you."

She smiled. "You're welcome."

"Can I ask you a question?"

She nodded.

"Earl has followers everywhere in North Carolina. What's going to happen to me when I get out of here?"

Harmony looked over at her partner.

"Johnson, here's what I can tell you," said Henry.

The patient gestured wildly and wrote one word on his iPad, adding exclamation marks to emphasize it. "Nathan."

"My boss has spoken to the District Attorney, who's trying to take down the prison gangs. I can't give you a guarantee, but there are two possibilities. Nathan, if you tell him everything you know, charges against you may be dismissed and you'll be free to go wherever you want. You could also be placed in the Witness Protection program."

Instead of expressing relief, Nathan looked as if a heavy weight had settled on his shoulders. "I will say everything I know. I can't risk putting family at risk by sticking around."

"Let's talk about this after you've recovered," she said.

He shook his head vigorously. "Too late. D.A. now."

Henry attempted to interpret. "Are you saying you'd like to talk to the District Attorney now?"

"Yes."

"Okay, I will let him know."

Henry turned to his partner, whose eyes were glinting with unshed tears. "It's what he wants. We need to honor his wishes."

She sounded agitated. "But if Nathan goes into Witness Protection, I'll never see him again."

"They'll make sure he's safe. He'll have an income and he won't have to keep moving around in search of work. It'll be a while before they finalize the arrangements. In the meantime, we have a criminal to catch. Let's go." He moved toward the door.

The weather had taken a turn for the worse. Thunderous gray clouds hovered overhead. In the distance, they could see that the sky was turning yellow.

"Oh, oh, danger, danger," cried Harmony. "We're in for a storm."

Henry gave his partner a curious glance. "Pa always warned me to take shelter when I saw a yellow sky. It means a tornado may be forming."

"It's in the distance. We have time to go to the public-health offices before the storm gets really bad."

He started to say something and stopped. "Let's go."

During the short drive, they observed the wind picking up, sending white grocery bags and plastic drink cups swirling into the air. The temperature began to drop and Harmony shivered, regretting her decision that morning to wear a sleeveless Vee-neck shirt.

They pulled into the parking lot and Henry ran toward the building, Harmony breathing hard to catch up. The wind was so strong that they could see large recycling bins hurling through the air.

"It's gonna be a bad one. I'm glad we're heading indoors."

Henry grabbed the outer door. Even though the yellow caution tape had been removed, he couldn't open it. Something other than the wind was holding it closed.

He called Jeannie's cell. "Dr. Johal, are you in the office? My partner and I are outside. Can you let us in? The door is locked."

Jeannie approached. They could see her looking left and right. She unlocked the door and beckoned them in. "What do you want? We're in a staff meeting."

"We have a few questions. We won't be long."

They entered the building to find the project manager and data-entry clerk in Dr. Dunn's office, tied to chairs around the conference table.

A man with long blonde hair had his handgun pressed against Frank's temple.

"Anderson Archer?" said Henry.

"The one and only. I can see you've tracked me down."

Anderson gestured for Jeannie and Harmony to sit down. He issued instructions to Henry. "Tie the women up. Don't get any ideas, I've already killed two members of this research team. One or two more won't make a difference. I'll shoot this man if you try anything."

Then Anderson tied Henry to the chair.

"Ask away. What do you want to know?" said Anderson.

"Why did you kill Dr. Dunn?"

"That wannabe man! She tried to boss me around. She had no business leading this study. She was incompetent and she began asking too many questions. It was only a matter of time before she'd find out I was diluting the product. It was time for her to go. I slipped a teaspoon of nicotine into her herbal tea. Did you know that you can purchase liquid nicotine online? You can make your own vaping e-juice. You don't need a license. All you need is a credit card or Venmo, and access to an iPhone or computer."

Jeannie asked another question. "As a licensed pharmacist, weren't you worried about harming the patients?"

"No, what I did was blameless. They were still getting the drug and losing weight as a result. By diluting the doses given to the largest patients, I was able to provide more treatments."

Harmony was curious. "Why didn't you use a gun to shoot Dr. Dunn?"

Anderson explained. "As a pharmacist, I work with chemical compounds, transforming them into medication. It's much more refined than using a gun."

"Why choose liquid nicotine?" asked Henry.

"Because it has no color and no odor. It's also cheap and easily available over the Internet. I could have gathered up and refined nicotine from nightshade plants in the Arboretum and around town, but that would have required more effort. Don't you think what's happened is a case of natural justice? After all, it's the public-health offices, with their unfettered power, that pressured government to put tobacco farmers out of business."

"La Donna was just an administrative assistant. Why did you have to kill her?"

"She's a heavy drinker and a discredit to the fair sex. I was hoping to make it appear that she drank herself to death, and if that didn't work, to implicate her boyfriend. She burst into the lab next to the bar. I couldn't risk her telling anyone what she saw."

"What did Will do to you?"

"He isn't the brightest bulb in the room. For two months, he picked up packages intended for the public-health unit and brought them to me instead. All I had to do was ask. But the last package was short, and I thought he was stiffing me. When I asked him what he was up to, he pretended not to know what I was talking about. I couldn't take the chance that he'd double-cross me."

"Are you going to say he knew too much, too?" asked Harmony.

"Well, he did. He just didn't realize it."

The next question came from Henry. "Who was the woman who rammed her car into Will's?"

Archer shrugged. "That I don't know. Just some bimbo who was drinking and texting while driving. I saw the whole thing. I couldn't believe my eyes when she pulled out to pass him and sideswiped his door. It just goes to show that drinking, driving, and texting is not a good combination."

He took a few steps backward, waving his gun at his hostages. "It was profitable while it lasted, but I'm afraid the gig is up. The Caribbean is calling my name. I will kill anyone who follows me or calls for help."

Henry's reply was calm. "It started as a tropical storm and now we're under an active tornado watch. First responders are not going to risk their own lives when everyone has been told to shelter in place. You're signing your own death sentence by walking out that door. Wait until the hurricane has passed."

"I will not."

Anderson Archer walked out and drove directly into the eye of the tornado.

Day Eleven

Chapter 46

It was her final evening in North Carolina. She packed the scarlet Mustang and sped down the highway towards Raleigh. Two vehicles followed her, a compact Kia and a spacious Escalade. Jeannie and the other drivers slowed down after pulling up to a black iron gate framed by the American flag and the state flag of North Carolina. Jeannie provided her name and the gates opened.

The driveway led to a 37,000 square foot mansion, a magnificent structure built in the 1880s for the Governor of North Carolina. The exterior of the Queen Anne-style building was made from materials native to that state – the bricks from Wake County clay, sandstone trim from Anson County, marble from Cherokee County, and oak and heart pine from across the state.

Governor Murrell himself opened the door to the mansion. "On behalf of the citizens of North Carolina, welcome to my home and the peoples' home," he said.

He introduced his wife, who asked if they would like a tour.

"A short one would be very welcome," said Jeannie. Her response had Darla raising her eyebrows.

"Of course," said the governor. "I understand you're catching a flight back to Canada in three hours."

Following the tour, Mrs. Murrell handed the baton back to her husband. After ensuring his guests were seated and enjoying North Carolina-themed appetizers, he leaned in and gave a broad smile that transformed his face. "Thank you all for coming. When I invited Dr. Johal, she explained that she was part of a team that brought this phase of the research project to a successful closure. She asked me to include her colleagues. While she won't be continuing with the project, the team will remain active. Dr. Carey, a top endocrine-disorders research-er at East Carolina University, will become the Primary Investigator, taking Dr. Dunn's place at the helm. WellStar Pharmaceuticals claims that Anderson Archer was a rogue actor, and they've already designated a replacement. Frank will continue to serve as project manager, and Tanisha will continue to provide data-entry services."

He turned to Tanisha. "Young lady, becoming a full-time employee of the university means that you will be able to study for free. I encour-age you to take advantage of this opportunity."

"Governor, thank you. I will."

He addressed Jeannie. "Dr. Johal, thank you for bringing your for-midable skills to our neck of the woods. You saved my son when he had an allergic reaction at 35,000 feet in the air. You braved multiple attempts on your life and those around you to get to the truth. You prevented a serial killer from destroying the research project. Your zeal and commitment are second to none. I would be remiss, though, if I didn't mention the human qualities you demonstrated. You gave a disadvantaged young woman hope by hiring her and allowing her to prove herself. You gave Lila-Jean a purpose when she needed one. You helped Frank find an outlet for his grief by refocusing on the research. And you said that although you disagreed with the actions of Moms for Liberty, you could understand how concerned they are for good jobs for North Carolinians."

He grinned. "As for the young girl who tried to harm you, well, there are no words to express my admiration for your actions. You asked for mercy for her, and you called me asking if I could find a scholarship for her to enroll in NC State to study botany. When I gave you my phone number, I never expected you to call me. I'm pleased to announce the girl has been awarded a full work-study scholarship to pursue her dream after she completes 100 hours of community work. I hear the Arboretum has accepted her offer to volunteer. She may never say 'thank you' to you for your selfless actions on her behalf, but I will."

Darla's eyes filled with tears as she nodded vigorously. "I'll make sure Lexi knows. I was wrong about you. Not only did you not take work away from us, but you gave us hope and showed us that, sometimes strangers are just different looking and different sounding versions of ourselves. Thank you."

Lila-Jean smiled and placed her arm around Tanisha before addressing Jeannie. "I knew you were going to rock Greenville when I saw you in that red Mustang. Stay passionate, girl. Reach for the stars and don't let anyone tell you that you can't get there."

Jeannie smiled and looked at those gathered around her. "I came here because my boss didn't give me a choice. I wasn't keen to stay and work in what I saw as a rural backwater, a city cobbled together from small villages lined with tobacco farms. What I found is that the people here are just like people elsewhere. They care about their daughters and sons, they work multiple jobs so that their children will have a better life. And they are kind and decent people. Lila-Jean warmly welcomed me to Greenville and gave me my first helping of Southern hospitality. Governor, never in my wildest dreams would I have imagined being invited to the Governor's Mansion. The people of Eastern North Carolina will forever hold a warm place in my heart."

She held out her hand to shake his before leaving the mansion. To her surprise, the governor gave her a gentle hug. "You'll always be welcome here," he said.

Epilogue

In Vancouver, Canada, Jaspreet Singh paced up and down the aisles of Vancouver International Airport, champing at the bit. It had taken him two days of pleading and cajoling with his boss just to get a few days off. Now, he was experiencing more delays as the result of unexpected storm fronts in North Carolina. His flight had already been delayed three times. He groaned when he saw the cancellation posted. When he approached the reservation counter, he was told to go home and return the following morning.

He arrived at the airport early the next morning and was informed that the early flights were already full. It was all he could do to restrain himself from lashing out at the hapless attendant. Instead, he paced the length of the airport, walking back and forth from the departure gates to the arrival areas.

He was stretching his shoulders when he caught a glimpse of a petite woman dressed from head to toe in bright red. She was wheeling a large red suitcase that was large enough to double as her bed. He ran towards her and stopped abruptly.

"Jeannie!" He stammered her name.

She looked up at him. "Jaspreet, what are you doing here?"

He broke down and his voice cracked. "I-I heard you were in North Carolina. Dr. Bach told me she sent you there on a special assignment. She said there was a serial murderer on the loose. I know you're strong but I was so worried! I've missed you every day that we've been apart. Thank God you're safe."

At that moment, an on-air announcement advised that more flights were available to North Carolina.

Jaspreet grimaced, while Jeannie grinned. "Where's your luggage?"

She joked, "You weren't coming to rescue a damsel in distress, were you?"

"Never. But I was looking forward to walking up the slope in Kitty Hawk, where the Wright brothers had their first flight."

"And I was looking forward to climbing the Cape Hatteras lighthouse and looking out over the ocean. We didn't get to plan a vacation together. When your mother told me she looked forward to our marriage and grandchildren, I panicked. Let's start over," she suggested.

They walked hand in hand toward the exit.

Book Club Questions

1) Why is this novel called *Bless Your Heart*? What are the mixed meanings inherent in that phrase?

2) Do you prefer living in a small city or a large metropolis?

3) What is the role of data in making medical decisions?

4) What are some of the factors that contribute to obesity in adults?

5) What is the purpose of the chapter that takes place at the OK Corral?

6) Is La Donna an innocent victim or an entitled opportunist?

7) Why do you think Henry and Harmony make good partners?

Liked this novel?

Go to www.susanncamus.com for free vignettes
and an excerpt from the first Jeannie Johal thriller, *See Me*.